WULF'S TRACKS

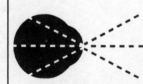

This Large Print Book carries the
Seal of Approval of N.A.V.H.

WULF'S TRACKS

DUSTY RICHARDS

THORNDIKE PRESS
A part of Gale, Cengage Learning

GALE
CENGAGE Learning

Detroit • New York • San Francisco • New Haven, Conn • Waterville, Maine • London

GALE
CENGAGE Learning

LIBRARY OF CONGRESS CATALOGING-IN-PUBLICATION DATA

Richards, Dusty.
    Wulf's tracks / by Dusty Richards. — Large print ed.
    p. cm. — (Thorndike Press large print western)
    "A Herschel Baker novel."
    ISBN-13: 978-1-4104-3222-3
    ISBN-10: 1-4104-3222-X
    1. Baker, Herschel (Fictitious character)—Fiction. 2.
Sheriffs—Montana—Fiction. 3. Montana—Fiction. 4. Large type
books. I. Title.
PS3568.I31523.W85 2010
813'.54—dc22   2010036518

Published in 2010 by arrangement with The Berkley Publishing Group, a member of Penguin Group (USA) Inc.

Printed in the United States of America
1 2 3 4 5 6 7 14 13 12 11 10

I want to dedicate this book to some great guys who I called my friends and who have gone on to make camp on that big ranch in the sky. They'll be there waiting with the coffeepot on and enough split wood for three roundups. PRCA rodeo announcer and Oklahoma politician Clem McSpadden — words won't describe his melodious voice and all he did for cowboys starting with the National Finals Rodeo; Ben Glover, a rancher, adviser, and dear friend; John Cleary, a New *Yawk* lawyer, trout fisherman, and with his New England accent a dandy to have in camp — he'd remind us of Teddy Roosevelt. And Guy Terry, another cattleman, who, calmer than any person on earth, could put the huge Rodeo of the Ozarks parades in the street every July 1 and 4 as well as keep things organized. Amigos, we're sure going to miss each one of you.

Dusty Richards
www.dustyrichards.com

PROLOGUE

Andy Carter busied himself repairing a weld on the Number Seven Oliver turning plow. The coal smoke from his forge made a thin fog in his blacksmith shop. But he ignored it as he hammered on the heated steel. Jacob Heldebrande would be back in half an hour or less, demanding his repaired farm implement be ready.

Andy looked up in time to see Wulf Baker ride past aboard his paint stallion with his stock dog Ranger seated on the saddle right behind him. Wulf was a real hard worker and a heckuva animal trainer. The real shame of the whole business was that his widowed mother, Jenny Baker, had gone and married Kent Hughes. No way that Hughes and Wulf Baker would ever get along on that place of hers. It wasn't big enough.

Andy considered Hughes a windy braggart, and a bully when he wanted to be.

Especially with someone lesser than him. There — Andy stepped back from his work. That weld looked good enough to hold for that old kraut-head anyway. He set the walking plow on the floor, and went out the open front doors of his shop to get a breath of fresh air.

It was a nice warm early March morning, and he nodded to a passing farmer in a wagon. They could use some rain, but when did it ever rain enough in the hill country of Texas? A young boy, out of breath, ran up and asked him if he could tack up a bill on his door.

"Sure. Here let me read it." He took a copy and scanned the artwork and words. Colonel Stacy Armstrong, the world's greatest animal trainer, would be in Mason, Texas, Saturday March 10. For a ten dollar-entry fee, he would match one of his world-famous Border collies against anyone's best stock dog. Any local entry that could beat one of his dogs in the show ring competition would be awarded fifty dollars. Admission twenty-five cents, families one dollar, at the Mason, Texas, city ballpark.

Where had Wulf gone? Why, his Ranger dog could do wonders gathering stock, cattle, pigs, sheep, or goats. Those two needed to be entered in that competition.

Andy hung up his apron on the door and turned around the wooden sign that read, "I will be right back."

Then he headed up the crowded Main Street, filled with buggies, wagons, and people, to find Wulf. It was Saturday, and everyone was in town shopping or gossiping. Halfway down the block, he heard a woman screaming. Alarmed by her shouts, he began to run left and right through the boardwalk traffic to get close enough to see what was happening.

"Mad dog! Mad dog!" someone shouted.

He searched around for a weapon as he hurried on in case he needed to put a stop to such a beast. Around the corner, he caught sight of a frightened mother holding a baby and backing away from the advancing brindle cur. Raging mad, the cur showed all the symptoms of hydrophobia. His open mouth was running with saliva foaming off his teeth, tongue, and lips. He was stalking the woman stiff legged — ready to lunge at her any second.

"Here," someone said. "Give me your gun."

Blocked by the retreating people himself, Andy watched Wulf coming on the run through the onlookers, jerking a revolver out of a man's holster as he raced through the seemingly helpless crowd. Wulf walked boldly past the mother. The cur made a stiff-legged lunge for him, but the six-gun in Wulf's fist roared smoke and fire. In lightning fashion, Wulf put three quick bullets in the cur's diseased brain. Down on his side, the dog was still churning his legs in the dirt, and he was issuing guttural sounds from his throat as he died.

"Don't touch him," the marshal ordered when he arrived out of breath.

"Ain't no one that dumb," Wulf said, emptying the spent shells out of the man's weapon into his palm.

"Thanks for the use of it." He handed the handgun and the empty casings back to the owner with a nod.

"You saved my wife and baby's life," a flush-faced young man in a business suit said, joining him out of breath. "How can I repay you?"

Wulf shrugged the notion off. "Hell, anyone here would have done the same thing."

"No. They didn't. They were all too shocked. No one moved to save her but you."

"Mister, I'm glad she and her baby are fine. That's enough."

"Wulf, the man wants to pay you," Marshal Volker said.

"He don't owe me nothing." He turned to the woman. "What's that baby's name?"

"Christian. He's two months old."

"Mighty fine-looking baby. Well, you two are all right now. I better tend to some business I came after."

"If I can ever do anything for you, my name is Fiest. Robert Fiest. I'm going to practice law here. My wife's name is Effie."

"Well, Mr. Fiest, I'm sorry about this happening. We usually treat folks better than this when they first get to town."

"May we buy you lunch?"

"No, thank you. I see my good friend Andy Carter over there. I better go speak to him. He's the blacksmith here and can fix anything broken if you ever need help in that line."

"Thanks again," they both said.

Wulf waved good-bye with his small felt hat to the three of them. Then he hurried over to where Andy stood at the edge of the street.

"First excitement we've had in Mason in a month," Andy teased him, folding his muscled arms over his chest and appraising his friend. The boy was close to six feet tall.

"You doing all right?" Wulf asked, looking

around and acknowledging some people going by.

"I'm fine. How is it going for you out at the ranch?"

Wulf shrugged, and then he slapped on his hat. "Aw, Andy, I'm going to have to leave there pretty soon. There's no way that I'm ever going to get along with him."

"You know you can always come stay with Myrna and me."

"No, Andy. If I leave out there, I'd have to get clear out of the country to avoid him." Wearily, he dropped his chin, took off his hat, and beat his leg with it.

"I'm sorry it's turned out so bad. Hey, before you leave, did you see those posters they're putting up today?"

"That world-famous dog trainer?"

"Yeah. Why, Ranger could win that hands down."

"No way. They've got sheep that they've trained to work for their dogs. They'll panic when another dog comes in that ring."

"What if we challenge them to a wild goat-herding contest?"

"Why, Andy, I ain't got any money to bet on anything."

"Let me handle that. Would you try to beat them if I had it set up?"

"Sure."

12

"Good. Don't leave home yet."

Andy watched the smile on Wulf's face as the barefoot boy in his wash-faded overalls and a short-sleeved shirt bounded up on the well-muscled stud Calico. The horse's hide looked like it was painted on in three colors, a mostly red roan pattern. The animal came from Comanche breeding and showed all the blood.

Wulf gave a sharp whistle, and his yellow and white collie Ranger leaped up and took his place seated behind his master. Andy shook his head in amazement. Why, that boy was as good at training animals as anyone he knew. Then Andy headed back to work. Lots of good horses were killed by the army in the subduing of the Plains Indians. But the most wasteful was the slaughter of the Comanche horse bloodlines. Those red devils might have done lots of bad things, but their horse breeding programs were head and shoulders above any white man's efforts. Andy felt certain that Calico came from those bloodlines.

Better forget about horses and get back to his forge. Besides, he still needed to round up some betting money for this stock dog competition. That conceited Colonel might just meet his Waterloo right here in the hick town of Mason. He smiled to himself. Win or lose, it would be fun challenging that so-called world-renowned dude, and even better to beat him at his own game.

Hell's bells, there was that crotchety old Heldebrande out in front of his shop wearing out the dirt walking back and forth.

ONE

The sunset bled all over the hills. Spring was ready to start. Wulf had even seen a few peach blossoms while coming back from Mason. Riding up Cherry Creek, he'd passed several oat fields with the short blades waving in the wind. His father would have said the oats had broken their winter dormancy. Up the lane he trotted, the powerful stallion between his knees and Ranger at his back.

Dread balled up in his stomach at what lay ahead. He wasn't going home. He was riding into a newfound hell, now the domain of his stepfather, Kent Hughes. The Three Crosses Ranch was no longer the Baker ranch. Not since his mother had married Kent Hughes six months ago. The ranch that spread out before him had became his stepfather's property — lock, stock, and bank account.

What confrontation would they have next,

him and Hughes? The way the red-faced braggart was taking over everything stuck like a sand bur in Wulf's craw. But a seventeen-year-old had no rights. No say-so about anything. Hughes had told him so, and it seemed true.

At the corral, Ranger bailed off and Wulf slipped from his horse's back. Calico gave a deep snort and Wulf patted him on the neck. "Easy, buddy, there's hay waiting."

His horse turned into the pen, and Wulf closed the gate, watching him roll in the dust.

"When do you plan to have that damn pinto castrated?" Hughes asked, swaggering over to join him.

Taken aback by his stepfather's words, he blinked at the man in disbelief. Hughes stood with his Stetson cocked on the back of head. "I don't want that gawdamn Injun nag breeding any of my mares."

"Then leave them over on the H Bar S."

Hughes's eyes narrowed and that ugly look swept over his face. "I don't like your mouth, boy."

"That goes two ways. Calico is my horse. He's — hell, I'm not explaining it all over again. You lay one hand on him and you'll answer to me."

"Listen, as long as you put your bare feet

16

under my table, you'll take orders from me."

"Stay, Ranger," Wulf ordered before he ducked under Hughes's swing. Wulf moved fast enough to snatch up a singletree and raise it up to meet his stepfather's head-on charge at him. "Now things are a little more even. Come on. We'll see who whips who tonight."

"Stop! Stop!" his mother screamed, running down from the house. "Can't you two even get along for ten minutes without fighting?"

"Stay out of this," Hughes said sharply as the two men circled each other. "Your son needs a lesson in manners toward his elders."

"Your husband needs some sense beat into his head," said Wulf.

Hughes made a charge, and Wulf used the singletree as a club, battering the arm Hughes stuck up in defense. The blow dropped Hughes to his knees, and Wulf struck him again with both of his hands on the singletree. This time, he hit him hard across the shoulder.

With a sharp cry of pain, Hughes went facedown, spilling his fancy hat in the dust.

"Stop it! Stop it!" his mother protested before Wulf could hit Hughes again.

"Oh, for God's sake, you'll kill him, Wulf."

She pushed him away with both hands, looking at the downed Hughes with concern.

"You hear me, Hughes?" Wulf gripped the singletree in both his hands like a bat and tried to see past her. No way he wanted to hurt her, but that same restraint did not apply to her husband. "You hear me, Hughes? I ain't taking another beating. I'm not taking a whipping from you ever again."

"Gawdamn you, boy." Hughes was on his feet at last. He jerked Wulf's mother aside and came for Wulf again. "I'll ki—"

The word never got out of his mouth. The whack of the singletree upside Hughes's head and the ring of the hooks filled the air. Hughes went down like a poled steer, and only his mother's panicked intervention stopped Wulf from clubbing Hughes again.

"Stop! Stop! He's my husband, Wulf!"

"That night he beat me with those bridle reins, you never made him stop. The night he used that quirt on me, you didn't say one word. I'm through taking his mouth and his beatings. How I lost this ranch I'll never know. Dad promised it to me."

"You're still a boy. You couldn't run it. You have to be —"

"I ran it those two years Dad was dying. We paid off the bank. We had things. Now

18

this son of a bitch you married has it all. Why, Mother? Why did that happen?"

She dropped to her knees and cried in her hands. "You don't understand. You don't understand."

"Was it to have someone to lay in bed with?"

"You can't talk to me like that —" Tears shut off her protests, and Hughes moaned as he tried to get up.

"Lay right there facedown," Wulf ordered. "Or I'll hit you again. Now listen. I'm going to the house. Get my things and Dad's. Either of you try to stop me, I'll shoot him. I shot a rabid dog today in town. I consider him no better."

"You can't —" Hughes protested.

"No, you aren't telling me anything. The only reason I didn't kill you tonight was for Mother's sake. Don't risk what I'll do if you push me."

In the dimming light, Wulf could see the dark blood and Hughes's mangled left ear, which his mother blotted with a kerchief. Maybe Hughes wouldn't be so cocky pretty from here on.

"Go take anything you want!" she cried out, waving Wulf away. "Just leave us alone!"

"If that's the way you want it, fine. I'm going, and he'll hear from my lawyer. Dad left this place to me. That worthless son of a bitch isn't cheating me out of my inheritance."

His breath raging through his nose, he stormed into the house, took his father's gun and holster off the hook on the wall, and strapped it on. If she wanted to live with Hughes, fine. *He* didn't have to. Maybe this new lawyer in town, Fiest, could help him.

He heard someone coming into the house. He could tell by the sobbing it was his mother.

"What do you need?" he asked, sharper than he intended.

"My shawl. I'm taking Kent to the doctor to have his ear stitched. I don't know if you know it or not, but you could have killed him."

"Mother. Mother. Listen to me. The man's a bully. He'll beat you next. Don't stay with him."

"Stand aside. I never thought the boy I raised would turn into such a vicious outlaw."

He let her go by. She'd never listen to him anyway. Why was she so stuck on Hughes? There were much better men who had seriously courted her before him.

Wulf found his father's spurs, good boots, and felt hat. That and his saddle in the barn would be enough. Though Hughes seldom used any of those things — Wulf wanted them. He wanted them so Hughes didn't get his hands on them.

When he went outside in the night, his mother and Hughes whizzed past him in the buggy, and the horse, at breakneck speed, raced out to the lane with her precious cargo. Maybe Hughes'd bleed to death on the way to town. No way. Wulf wasn't that lucky. He took his father's heavy hat off. That Stetson would take some getting used to. Then he settled it back down on his head. How could his life be falling apart like this?

Dad, wherever you are up there, help me.

In the barn, which was really a tall, open-sided shed, he saddled Calico in the dark under the starlight. All the things he'd planned and dreamed about were going up in smoke. The knot in his throat made it hard to swallow. He could go to Andy's. Much as he hated to bother them, he needed a place till he got his thinking straight. Chewing on his lower lip, he felt at a loss about what he should do next.

Had he really expected his mother to leave Hughes over their confrontation? In his heart, yes. They'd been through so much together over the past three years. But he should have known better. Recently, Hughes had managed to drive a steel wedge between them.

Why did she always believe Hughes instead of him? Hughes had talked her into selling the yearlings. There was no good market for them. Buyers wanted two-year-old steers. Hughes had put the money into his own bank account. Nor would he replace the two roan Durham bulls they'd lost. He'd said *thoroughbred* stuff was too expensive, and sent Wulf over to his outfit to get two half-longhorn bulls to replace them. They'd sure get some good calves.

In disgust, Wulf slapped down the stirrup. If he lived to be a hundred, he was going to keep on trying to get this ranch back. With the expensive purple silk scarf, boots, and spurs in a gunnysack tied on the horn, he swung in the saddle and went back by the house. He took his father's vest and suspenders to add to his things. He also found his father's long-tail canvas coat in the back hall, and took two blankets and a ground cloth he considered his own. On the kitchen floor, he rolled them up and bound them with rawhide lacing.

When he went out the front door, his heart stopped. He was leaving his home. The only one he'd ever known. His gear tied on his saddle, he headed Calico for Mason under the stars.

At the edge of town, he waited for daylight before he rode up to Andy's place in town. Sitting cross-legged on the ground in the cool night gave him lots of time to think. There was no way he could stay around Mason. Shifting sand from hand to hand with Ranger's head in his lap, he wondered how to handle it all. He had no money. Should of thought of that before he'd beaten the hell out of Hughes. They owed him, but he had no way to collect that.

If he had not promised Andy to stay till the following Saturday for those dog trials, he'd already be a long ways from there. There was no justice and no God in his life. When the sun peeked over the eastern horizon, he rose, shoved the big hat on the back of his head, brushed his butt off, and vaulted into the saddle. Maybe Andy would have some answers.

"That you, Wulf?" Andy's wife, Myrna, called out from inside the kitchen when he knocked on the door facing.

"Yes, ma'am."

"Well, come in and wash up. You had any breakfast?"

No, he had not ate in twenty-four hours. "No, ma'am."

"Put that hat on the rack there and come inside."

"Morning, Wulf, what brings you to town so early on Sunday morning?" Andy asked.

"I had all I could take last night, Andy. All I could take." Wulf dried his hands on the towel. "He started in about cutting my horse. Next thing, he took a swing at me, and so I used a singletree on him."

Andy's eyes narrowed. "Is he still alive?"

Wulf nodded sharply. "But I guess if my mother hadn't stopped me — he might not of survived."

"Sounds serious. Sit down. Myrna, get him some coffee. This might be big trouble."

"How is that?"

"Hughes will make a formidable enemy. You being a minor and all. How old are you?"

"Seventeen."

"When will you be eighteen?"

"Next December. How does that work?"

"I'm not certain. But we need to see your new friend, that lawyer Fiest, first thing Monday morning."

"Can he help us?"

"Best shot that we've got."

"I don't understand."

Andy put his large hands on the tabletop and folded them. "Being a minor means you can't do lots of things, and till next December you're a minor."

"What'll happen?" Myrna asked, pouring the steaming coffee in their cups.

Andy sat back in the kitchen chair and let his arms drop. "I ain't sure."

What was eating his guts out, besides hunger, while he was sitting at the table in the bright little house Andy and Myra lived in? Fear of the unknown? There were lots of things he had no answers for. Maybe he simply should have run? But he'd promised Andy —

Kent Hughes was the sumbitch causing it all.

Two

Billings, Montana, was hosting a bitter March snowstorm that same Sunday morning. Looking out the second-story window from his office at the blinding flakes, the wind tearing at the eaves in a high-pitched whistle, Sheriff Herschel Baker dreaded hiking the three blocks back to his house. His wife, Marsha, and his three stepdaughters usually attended church on the Sabbath. This looked like a day they'd miss services. He doubted many others would make it either.

He said good-bye to his new night jailer, Billy Short, and satisfied all was well there, he buttoned up his heavy coat and started for home. Storms like these made him wish he'd taken up the offer of his father, Thurman, to help ramrod his new south Texas spread — maybe his blood was too thin. His head turned sideways, the wool Scotch cap bound down by a scarf as he bent into the wind and rock-hard bits of ice pecked his face.

Men got lost and died in storms like this, and cattle roamed off their home range, walking over fences buried under the white stuff. Grateful his cattle down on Horse Creek had hay to keep them in place, and that the valley was somewhat sheltered by the hills, he went step by step into the biting wind, headed for his house.

At last, he burst into the warm interior of his living room with a grateful feeling of relief. Stomping his snowy boots on the rug set there for that purpose, he nodded to the girls seated in a ring before the fireplace.

"We aren't going to church today," five-year-old Sarah announced.

He stood on the carpet and agreed. Marsha came out of the kitchen with a smile. "I'm certain the Lord will forgive us." She helped him take off his heavy coat and cap and hung them in the hall.

"This storm is a fright," she said, pulling the scarf off his neck and kissing him.

He gave her a quick hug, then shed his outer layer of pants. "I can tell you one thing. It isn't ever this cold and bad in south Texas."

"You thinking about your father?" she asked.

"I'm thinking about a place to get warm." He went to the fireplace to hold out his hands and warm himself. "Aw, every place on earth, I guess, has its drawbacks when it comes to weather. Montana winters are our tough times."

"What's bad in Texas?"

"Heat and drought."

Marsha brought him a steaming cup of coffee and he winked at her. "Thanks."

The morning passed with the girls singing hymns and the oldest, Kate, playing the used piano he'd bought at an auction. Marsha said she thought that would suffice for their church for that week. He read the latest newspaper from Minneapolis.

After dinner, there came a knock on the door. Herschel frowned and went to answer it. The snowy man he let in was his chief deputy, Art Spencer. He was short, broad, and built like a bull. Today, even Art's large handlebar mustache was coated in snow.

Herschel had a feeling something was bad wrong the moment he looked at him. "What's happened?"

"Three men robbed and half killed old Buffalo Malone."

"When?"

"I guess yesterday or the day before. That old breed works for Malone, Happy Jack, is

28

frostbit and nearly froze to death over at Doc's office. He said his horse died coming in and he walked the rest of the way."

"He say how much they got?"

"You can't half understand that old man, but he said thousands of dollars. I can hardly believe that old buck-skinner had that much money."

"You know, he might have. He spends very little, and heaven knows what he had to start with. He always paid cash for what he got." But Herschel could hardly imagine the squaw man having that big a fortune.

"You're right about that. What're we going to do about it?"

"Good question. It's impossible to get up there today. We'll have to hope for a break in the weather. Did Malone's man say who did it?"

"No, he said he didn't know them." Art, out of his heavy coat, acknowledged the girls and thanked Marsha for taking the coat.

"Have you had dinner, Art?" Marsha asked. "We have plenty left over. I can fix you a plate."

He grinned at Marsha's offer. "That would be wonderful and sure worth the hike up here."

"I don't know about that," she said, and hurried off to fix him a plate of food.

Art sat across from Herschel at the dining table and began to fill him in. "Happy Jack said they rode up and asked Malone if would he sell them a meal. He told them to get down and he'd have his squaws fix them a meal for twenty-five cents apiece.

"They ate the meal that Malone's wives fixed for them, and then they drew their guns on the old man. They demanded he tell them where he kept his money, and he said he had none. They never believed it, and began to torture him, burned his soles with hot irons. Then they half hung him — he said nothing. But when they started to torture his youngest Sioux woman, he told them where it was.

"It took three packhorses to haul off the money. Happy Jack said most of it was coins. Buffalo didn't believe in paper money or banks. They even stole three of his best horses to haul it away."

"White men?"

"Yes. One was older. Happy Jack thought that they might be father and sons."

"But he'd never seen them before?" Herschel touched his forehead with his fingertips. This crime sounded more bizarre by the minute.

Art paused in his eating and held the fork near his plate. "You know, Happy Jack gets

30

drunk whenever he comes to town. I doubt he knows many of us even."

"That's right. Did he think Malone knew or recognized them?"

"No. Happy Jack said neither Buffalo nor the women has ever seen these men before."

"How would they simply ride up to his place and know that old man had any money?" Herschel shook his head. Malone's place looked like a Sioux buffalo hunting camp, not a bank to make a large withdrawal out of.

"I can't tell you a thing more than that."

"Oh, you did good, Art, getting all that out of that half-frozen half-breed." Herschel rose and looked out the window at the thousands of white moths streaming past. The high pitch of the wind outside whistled at him. Somewhere out there, three tough men with heavily loaded packhorses were getting away with the loot.

Damn, and he was locked in until this blessed storm broke.

THREE

Early Monday morning, Wulf and Andy found Robert Fiest in his new office over Shipley's Store. Surrounded by the boxes of law books and papers strewn all over the room, the young man looked up at them.

"Good morning, how are you fellows?"

"Fine," Wulf said. "I have a problem, it seems, and you told me —"

"Hey, anything I can do for you. I'm in your debt."

"Well, it's a long story."

"Let's clear some things away and we can all sit down. This is a legal matter, I take it?"

"Oh, yes, and Mr. Fiest, this is Andy Carter, my friend."

They each emptied a chair and carried it over, and met in the center of the room, where they set the chairs up. The morning sun slanted in the bay window, and at Fiest's request, Wulf started at the beginning.

"My father was dying from cancer for two years. I ran the ranch on his instructions until his last six months, when I had to do it all by myself. Mr. Jacobs at the First State Bank will tell you I paid off the debt we owed. Fifteen hundred dollars.

"Kent Hughes came courting my mother six months after Dad finally died. She married him, I thought too quickly, but I ain't judging, 'cept him and I don't get along.

"Then he sold the yearlings. Heifers and steers last fall. Give them away and he put the money in his own account."

"Did your father leave a will?"

"Yes."

"Do you have a copy of it?"

"No. It's in the bank."

"Can you get a copy of it?"

"I don't think so. Hughes had me taken off the account." Wulf grew more upset the further he went into his story.

"Was the will filed?"

"Yes, but somehow Hughes got my mother to sign everything over to him."

Fiest nodded. "I can do some research and learn all I can. Then we can decide what to do."

"One more thing," Wulf said. Then he sucked on his lower lip for a moment. "Hughes tried to whip me Saturday night. I stopped him with a singletree."

Fiest looked startled. "Is he dead?"

"No, but he's got a mangled left ear and a bad headache, I'd say."

"Had he whipped you before?"

"At least twice severely. Once with bridle reins and another time with a damn quirt. I took them beatings. I wasn't taking any more."

"I may have to ask for a change in your guardianship."

"Do what you have to."

"I'll be the guardian," Andy said. "If he needs one."

"Good. As a businessman, you'd have a strong reputation. Wulf, you stay with Andy. I'll check at the courthouse and see if any charges have been filed against you. We can go from there."

"Charges?"

"Yes, he may have filed assault charges against you."

Wulf dropped his chin. This became more complicated by the hour. Shame he didn't just kill Hughes and they could try him for murder.

"We'll be at the shop or my house on Westmoreland Street," Andy said.

"Good, I'll go to the courthouse and see what I can learn and check back with you in a few hours."

They left the office and went back to open Andy's smithy. A man stopped by and wanted a shoe reset on his horse. Wulf took the job. Wearing a leather apron, he held the right front hoof in his lap and began to pry the loose shoe off with nippers.

"How do you do this work barefooted?" the man in the business suit who owned the horse asked, looking amazed.

"Damn careful," Wulf said. "I just feel freer being barefooted when it's not too cold."

The man shrugged. "I'd have stickers in my feet in no time."

With the horseshoe about off, Wulf grinned. "They'd get calloused enough in time."

Turning the plate over, he noted the wear. "I can put it back on, but you're close to needing a new shoe."

"Thanks. Just tack it on. It was loose and I need to go over to Fredericksburg today."

"Whatever," Wulf said, and nipped off the excess rim of the horse's hoof, before rasping the hoof down. Then, with a horseshoer's knife, he trimmed the frog. The hoof, now freshly cut down, was white with streaks of gray. Checking the old plate, he stepped over and bent it some on the anvil.

Then he picked up the hoof again. He felt pleased when he saw it would work all right. Sweat stung his eyes and blurred his eyesight until he blinked twice. He couldn't get his problems out of his thoughts.

With a mouth full of nails and a short-handled hammer, he drove the first nail in and then bent it over the front side so it didn't stick the horse in his leg. He worked around with each one until the plate was in place. Then he put the hoof on a stand, clipped each nail, and bent them down. With a rasp, he rounded the shoe and hoof, then took it off the stand to see how the horse set it down.

It was the flash of a badge that caught Wulf's eye and made him notice someone standing there. "I'll be right with you."

Wulf turned to the man who owned the horse. "Look all right to you, sir?"

"I'm impressed. You did good. I wish now you'd reshod them all, but I need to get over to Fredericksburg."

"That's fine. Pay Andy," Wulf said with a head toss toward Andy, who was working on repairing a wagon wheel.

"Yes?" he said to Deputy Sheriff Armand Shultz. The short man, armed with a huge Walker Colt on his hip, was standing there before him.

"Wulf Baker?"

"You know my name."

"Wulf Baker, you are under arrest for the attempted murder of Kent Hughes. Put out your hands, I am going to handcuff you. Make no move to escape or I'll have to shoot you."

Andy rushed up from the back of the shop. "Shultz, what the hell are you doing here? You've known Wulf all your life. Put those gawdamn handcuffs away."

Wulf raised his hand to stop Andy. "Don't—"

Shultz staggered back and fought the huge six-gun out of his holster. He must have cocked it while drawing it for it fired in the air. The ear-shattering report caused a stampede of spooked horses in the street. Three horses hitched in front of the Adobe Walls Saloon next door jerked back in head-slinging fashion and tore down the hitch rail. When they went flying backward across the street, they spooked Mike McCarty's big team of shires. They jumped over the rack and tore down Austin Street with the wagon scattering green-cut boards out the back in their wake like playing cards.

In Andy's shop, he was shouting at Shultz to put up that gawdamn gun before Andy stuck the barrel in his ass. Three cowboys yelling their lungs out came busting out of the saloon mad as hell about who was shooting around their horses. At the same moment, Mrs. Sherry's terrified buggy horse came charging with one side of narrow wheels on the boardwalk and the other side on the ground. He came flying on the inside of the hitch rail and mowed the three punchers down. Andy snatched Wulf back in time against the open front door of the shop so it could pass them, but the high-stepping horse knocked Shultz on his backside out into the street, which in turn caused him to fire another round in the sky.

Andy ran over and jerked the .45 out of his hand. "You can't use it right, don't pack the damn thing."

Marshal Volker arrived about that time. "Who in the hell's doing all the shooting down here? My gawd, this is a mess. That cowboy all right?" He motioned to an unconscious man on the ground.

"Hell, no, he ain't all right," the taller, bareheaded cowboy said, with his shirt sleeve shredded and him bleeding somewhere up where his hair quit on his balding head. "That damn runaway buggy horse ran right over him."

"Take him up to Doc's office." Volker turned to Shultz, who was sitting on the ground in the street rubbing his leg. "What's wrong with you?"

"Damn horse broke my leg."

"What in the hell were you shooting at?"

"Wulf Baker, for resisting arrest."

"Why gawdamn, man, he's standing right here."

"Well, I've got a felony warrant for his arrest."

Volker shook his head in disgust. He looked over at the onlookers and said, "Couple of you fellas as take Shultz up to the doc's. Where is that warrant?"

Shultz pointed to the folded paper on the ground that had been run over by the buggy tire. The marshal bent over and picked it up. "Says John Doe!" he shouted to no avail after Shultz, who two big Swedes, one on each side, were hauling off to Doc's.

"Wulf, go turn yourself in up at the courthouse," Volker said. "I'm sure this is something that can be worked out."

"Volker, we ain't so sure of that," Andy said, handing the Walker over to the lawman.

"I'll tell 'em how he shot that rabid dog yesterday and saved that woman and her child," Volker said.

"That might not be enough," Andy said. "He's had words and a fight with his stepfather. We think this is a charge he made against Wulf."

"It's better to get it straight than mess around. The law's fair."

"All right," Wulf agreed. "Andy, I'll put up Ranger and I'll go up there. You tell the attorney where I am if I don't come back."

With a big lump in his throat, Wulf took a rope and tied up Ranger. "Stay here, fella. Andy will feed you. Stay."

Ranger dropped down. Not because he wanted to, but because his master told him to. Wulf knew how badly Ranger had wanted a piece of his stepfather the night before, but the dog also knew Wulf's commands to stay out of those things when he ordered him to. He didn't want Hughes taking anything out against his dog, who would have loved to have come to his aid.

"I'll see you," Wulf said, and went with Volker.

Despite the words and efforts of the town marshal, Wulf soon found himself in a cold cell with bars. Hughes finally had him out of the way. What he'd wanted all the time.

Where was his lawyer?

FOUR

Twenty-four hours later, a Chinook came down the face of the Rockies, and Herschel woke to the ping of water dripping off the eaves. Things were thawing outside. He sat up in bed. Thank God. The weather was letting up.

"What is it?" his sleepy-sounding wife asked, rooting her face in the pillow for more sleep.

"A Chinook rolled in last night."

"Oh, my, how wonderful." She threw her feet over the side of the bed and found her carpet slippers with her feet, then took the robe off the bedpost and quickly belted it. "I better get busy and get some food cooked. A Chinook means my husband wants to leave and go find those robbers."

He reached over and hugged her shoulder. "That's my job."

"And we fought hard to get it, too."

"Took them all on and won because I had

41

you to help me."

Buttoning up his wool shirt, he recalled the big rancher-small rancher war he'd had to solve upon taking office. That same conflict still smoldered, but he'd kept it in check since taking office and he treated each side equally. This robbery of Buffalo Malone needed to be solved and the criminals responsible rounded up. No telling what that would entail.

"I know you want to see Buffalo Malone and find out all you can, but do you think it's thawed enough to get through the drifts?" Marsha asked.

"Cob and I'll make it." He kissed her on the cheek and she left to fix breakfast. Monday morning, and he was off to find the robbers. This snug two-story house was a long ways from the log cabin he'd had on his small ranch before he married Marsha and those bastards had burned it down to get to him.

Being sheriff was a busy job, and also a job that called on him to solve crimes. Many weren't cut-and-dried — this Malone robbery might have more repercussions and twists in it than tying a knot in a cat's tail. Dressed, he went downstairs into the lighted living room and stoked up the large fireplace with fresh wood. That done, he went into the kitchen, where smells filled the air, like her sourdough liquor as she worked on the dough atop her dry sink.

"There will be more snow. It sure isn't spring yet," she said.

"Oh, I know that dear, but —"

"Yes, I know. Snow or no snow, you need to get those three men. But where did Malone get so much money that it required three packhorses to haul off?"

"I have no idea, but I expect to find out."

She nodded, busy cutting out biscuits from the flattened dough. "You amaze me at times."

"How is that?"

"You went from horse breaking and trading to law work like you were born to do it."

He nodded. "First, law needs to be fair and the same for everyone."

"I know, but you are just doing a swell job as sheriff. You still thinking any more about your father's offer to help him run his large ranch down in south Texas?"

"Some, but not enough to give up all this."

"I know you'd be happier ranching."

"Maybe."

"It would mean a lot less worrying about you for me."

"Marsha, I'll be fine."

"I still worry when you go off to track down killers and robbers. Especially alone."

"Coffee water's boiling," he said to change the conversation.

After breakfast, Herschel found his horse, Cob, was ready. After several days in his stall, the now-saddled Cob came out of the barn full of life. Mounting him, Herschel checked him up several times, and at last, in a shaky truce between the two of them, he rode him to the office in the slush.

Things were going fine in the office and jail, so he left the operation to his men and headed west. Art told him Happy Jack had disappeared from the doctor's office and no telling where he'd gone. Probably to get drunk.

Since there was no one to interrogate, Herschel headed for Malone's place. On the road, he found teamsters digging out snow-buried freight outfits, getting them ready to move again while they were able. With an hour of warming sunshine, the snow was fast turning to slush running off. It could cause flooding. There was frozen ground beneath it, and that meant no place to soak in. All it could do was run off. He reached the valley where Buffalo Malone lived, or more accurately, camped. There were three colorfully painted tepees and several hide-covered lodges. Plenty of barking black cur Indian dogs and a dozen winter-weary-looking horses in the pole pens.

A tall straight-backed Indian woman in a beaded leather dress came out of a flap and waited for him to draw closer.

"Hello, I am the sheriff." He reined Cob and made him stand.

"I am Running Water. He said you would come. You must come into his lodge. He cannot walk on his burned feet."

"Thanks —" Herschel looked around for a place to tie his horse.

She shouted something in Sioux, and from one of the lodges a wide-eyed boy in his early teens came on the run.

"Hold his horse," she said to him.

The boy nodded, and grinned when Herschel thanked him. To enter the tepee, Herschel had to crawl, making his pants knees wet. Inside, he handed Running Water his hat. In the dim light, he could see the bulk of Buffalo Malone lying on his back, propped up on a pillow with his feet wrapped in dirty bandages.

"I see that dumb Happy Jack made it to town. Did he die?" Malone asked in a rusty voice. "I'd sure as hell get up and shake your hand, Baker, but I'm not walking good right now."

Herschel shook his hand and then squatted on his boot heels. "Happy Jack lost a horse and had a bad case of frostbite yesterday when he got to Billings. But he left Doc's office last night and they don't know where he went."

"To get drunk, I suppose. That's all he's good for. Sit down, man. I've got a whole earful to tell you."

Herschel nodded and remained squatted on his heels. Malone started his story with three riders coming to his camp asking to buy some supper. His women (Herschel didn't know how many wives the man kept) fed them and then the ungrateful three, as Malone called them, drew guns on them and demanded his gold.

"When I wouldn't tell them where it was, they tied me up and went to burning my soles with hot irons from the fire. That didn't work." Malone went to flailing around to sit up, and two of his women helped prop him up. Then, in the half-light, he showed Herschel the purple bruises and scabs around his neck. "That's from where they hung me until I turned blue. I never told them anything. Then they caught Little Deer and said they would cut off her breasts. I knew they would have done it, too. Mean sumbitches. I could not let them do such

46

foul things to an innocent girl. Could you?"

"No."

"So I showed them my money. They took all of it and then stole three of my best horses to carry it away on." Behind his bushy beard, Malone looked and sounded very troubled or pained.

"How much money did they get?" Herschel shifted his weight to the right boot.

"I don't know. I can't count that high."

"What form is it in?"

"I'll get you some." Malone spoke to Running Water in Sioux, and she went for it.

The coin she put in Herschel's hand when she returned was five-sided and heavy enough in his hand for him to recognize where it came from. It was certainly old Spanish treasure. How did this buffalo hunter ever find that much of it?

Malone raised up and looked at the coin. "Lots of them were round, too."

Herschel shook his head in disbelief. "Where did you get them?"

"Ten years ago or so, I was down in western Kansas hunting buffalo and I found some bleached human skulls in some blow sand. Things were tight then in that country. Cheyenne didn't like hunters, and I was too close to them and too damn far away from Fort Dodge for the army to save my ass."

With a nod, Herschel gave up and sat down on his butt.

"Well, besides the human skulls, I also saw a metal-bound edge of a chest sticking out of the sand. It was creepy down there. Any moment I expect some pissed-off buck to come riding over the hill with murder on his mind and me wondering what I'd found."

Herschel laughed. "I bet that was fun."

"Fun, hell, I sure wasn't constipated either at that time. I finally dug out that trunk. Hell, I couldn't lift it and I sure wasn't going for no help. You know, most of those buff hunters were outlaws. Why, hell, they'd've cut my throat for a small sack of them gold coins. When I finally managed to open that first trunk and I found it was full of them doubloons — that's what they call 'em — my heart stopped. It was so bad, I had to sit on my butt for thirty minutes, unable to even breathe." Malone looked still in awe.

"What happened next?"

"Well, I reburied that trunk and tried to cover up things. Buried them skulls over it. Injuns don't like dead things very well. I figure if they did some digging where I'd been and found them, they'd quit. I left that outfit of roughnecks I was hunting with and went back to Fort Dodge. Bought me two spans of mules and a wagon with them coins. There was lots of that Spanish-Mex money around those trading posts at the time, so it didn't draw too much suspicion. I found me two big stout squaws that had been whoring around them black soldiers — they came easy.

"I got four Spencer repeating rifles, too. Fifty-caliber, and lots of ammo. Trying to keep all this business quiet and all them hang-around fellas asking me where I was going hunting next with my new outfit.

"I just acted like I didn't need any skinners or help — 'cause I really didn't trust a one of them not to cut my throat for even a small sack of that gold. Besides, those two squaws were big enough to handle the job of skinning."

Herschel laughed. "You were in a tough spot. Buying equipment, supplies, and weapons. I imagine they did watch you close."

"Oh, hell, yeah. I got all set with supplies, shovels, and we left in the middle of the night. That squaw I called Timber could damn sure drive mules, and her sister, Hoss, could swing a whip. I rode one horse and led two more ponies. We made thirty miles the first night and day, which was fast on those rough roads leading south.

"Along the way, we shot a few buffalo and the women stretched out the hides. I didn't want anyone that followed us to think we wasn't any more than hiders. It was working. We drove over there one night, dug it up, and loaded that first trunk and came back to our camp before sunup."

"Were you excited?" Herschel asked.

"About pissed in my britches I was so excited. Then I got to thinking where there was one, there could be more. And there was. We went back and dug them up. Six trunks in all. They were still on the pack train animals' backs. You'd find a skeleton of a horse, and there would be two trunks still on the packsaddles. There were arrows in the horses and trunks, but I think they'd got away from the Injuns and then died of their wounds and the blow sand covered them."

"So all these years, you've had all this treasure and no one knew about it?"

Malone nodded. "It's been a burden, keeping it a secret. A mule kicked Timber in the head near Fort Douglas, Wyoming. I hated that she died. Syphilis took her sister, Hoss. The doc said there was nothing he could do for her." Malone dropped his chin and shook his head. "They was damn good women. And by gawd, I done all I could for 'em."

"I know you did. How do you think these three men knew you had it?"

Malone shrugged. "Word got out somewhere that I'd spent a little of it. Someone said that old squaw man's got some Spanish gold. I could tell they were shocked half to death when they found that much. I used to keep them trunks separate. I got lazy. It was all in one lodge. But they could have left me one trunk."

"You could have lived the rest of your life on that," Herschel said.

"Hell, yes. Now I may never walk again. My feet hurt so bad. I was foolish not to give it to them at first, but I thought I was still a tough old man."

"I'm sorry, and I intend to find them."

"Why would you do that for an old buff like me? You're a busy man. I'm a squaw man with more women than Brigham Young. I don't even vote."

Herschel looked over at Malone. "I catch them, you better vote for me next election."

Malone laughed out loud. "If I have to crawl there on my hands and knees, I'll vote for you."

"Good." *Now where did those three go with Malone's gold?*

51

FIVE

"Your Honor, my client is not any danger to this community, nor is he going to flee," the young attorney told the judge as Wulf and Fiest stood before the bench.

The judge looked serious. "They took several stitches in the plaintiff's head."

"Turn around and raise your shirt," Fiest said to Wulf. "Show him your back. See these scars? They are the result of Kent Hughes flailing him with a quirt."

The judge had risen to look over the bench at Wulf's scars. When he settled in his chair, he looked more upset. "Your client must promise to refrain from fighting with Mr. Hughes any more and remain in this county until his trial is over."

"I'll see to that, sir."

"I hope you realize that using a singletree on a man is felony assault?"

Fiest quickly looked over at Wulf, and he understood from his lawyer's expression that he did not want him to contest the judge's statement. "Yes, sir."

"Very well. I'll release him until his trial in two weeks."

"Thank you, Your Honor," Fiest said, and Wulf nodded. They left the courtroom and once outside, Fiest put his hand on Wulf's shoulder. "I am filing a lawsuit against Hughes for violating the probate of your father's estate. It will work. His sale of those cattle and not placing the money in the estate's account will be rectified in court."

"I sure don't know about all this legal business, but I'm hoping something will work."

"It will, Wulf. What are you going to do now?"

"Andy is setting up a wild goat-penning contest with this famous Colonel Armstrong who's coming to town. Andy thinks my dog Ranger can beat any dog the Colonel's got."

"Can he?"

"I think so. He's a great dog."

"When will that take place?" Fiest led them into the Blue Mill Café. "I'm buying you a real meal. That jail food isn't very good."

"You're right about their food. The competition will probably be Sunday or Monday, since the public show is Saturday."

They took a center table. An attractive girl in her late teens with a Dutch accent waited on them. In a starched blue and white uniform, she looked fresh as a Texas bluebonnet.

"What do you want to eat?" Fiest asked from behind his menu.

Wulf had removed his big hat and she asked for it. What did she want his hat for?

"I'll put it on the rack," she said, and he handed it over.

Whew, she was pretty, and he was half-cocked anyway. Just to be out of that pissy, smelly jail, being before the judge, all Fiest had told him about the probate business, and to walk into this restaurant and see her — it all got to him like a Texas dust devil.

"What're you having?" he whispered at Fiest while she was hanging his hat on the peg.

"I'll order for both of us. You drink coffee?"

"Yes."

"Miss, I don't know your name," Fiest said, and Wulf listened like a hawk for her reply.

"Dulchy Hiestman."

"Dulchy," Fiest began. "We both want scrambled eggs, fried ham, German fried potatoes, biscuits and gravy, as well as coffee."

"Tank you." She made a small curtsy and disappeared into the back.

"I saw those signs —" Fiest stopped, and Wulf realized he was talking to him. Why didn't he know this Dulchy? Man, she was sure pretty.

"Oh, the Colonel, huh?" He tried to get back on track with Fiest. "I don't know him. But my father told me all about all those people. They train their dogs and they train their sheep, so when a strange dog comes around, those sheep go wild. Dad said you couldn't beat them, though there will be lots of folks with good dogs that will try on Saturday."

"You won't enter that competition?"

"No, but we're hoping that this Colonel is so proud of his dogs that he thinks he can beat Ranger or any other dog in the world."

"Does he have good dogs?"

"Yeah, he wouldn't come and make such offers like that unless he really had well-trained ones. 'Cause he's got to have plenty of the competitions or lose money."

Dulchy brought them coffee, and he had a lump in his throat he couldn't swallow. He finally managed a weak "Thanks."

Maybe the hot steaming coffee would help him.

"Back to business," Fiest said. "Is this Kent Hughes rich?"

"You asking me or him?"

The lawyer chuckled. "What do you mean?"

"He's got an outfit. One Mexican named Sanchez runs it for him. How big can that be?"

"You ever been over there? Seen it?"

"I went over one time to pick up two half-longhorn bulls he was putting in with our cows since we lost two good Durham bulls. He sent me over there and I knew he figured there was no way I could get those two bulls and drive them through ten miles of open range back to our place by myself."

"You did it, of course?"

"Ranger, Calico, and I did it in four hours. You should have seen his face when I drove the bulls down the lane. I mean, he like to lost his jaw it sagged so far."

"What about his place?"

"Some jacales. Some pens made out of poles, some fighting chickens scratching at horse apples, and a few straight-tail shoats running around. Old Sanchez wasn't doing nothing the day I got there. Said he'd hired six vaqueros to gather those two bulls, and it took them a week to get them up there in the corrals. Hughes told me earlier that he left them bulls 'cause they were such outstanding animals. I think they just got away as calves. He wasn't fooling me. Their brands were real fresh and they were three years old. They won't get calves like a good Scottish shorthorn bull will get. They were just cheap."

"You and that dog of yours have trouble with them?"

Wulf laughed. "Ranger chewed on their ears and heels a little and they soon learned my rules of the road."

Dulchy delivered their heaping platters of food. Wulf's eyes about bugged out when she said, "I'll get the biscuits and gravy next. Either of you need hot sauce?"

He looked straight into her sky blue eyes. "I sure do, ma'am."

A smile turned her mouth up. "I'll bring it back, too."

They ate breakfast, laughing and talking about his dog and the trial ahead.

"We may have to show your back to the jury, I know Judge Arnold was shocked today when he saw it."

"What did you say the legal term was for what I did?" Wulf blew on his second cup of coffee.

"Self-defense. Under the law, if a man is coming to kill you, you have the right of self-defense. Taking whatever measure is required to stop him."

Wulf nodded. It sure felt better to be in the café with other free men than that jail cell he'd slept in for two days and nights. Whew. The rich food drew the saliva into his mouth — and this Dulchy blew his mind away. Why didn't he know her?

"You'll have to dress up for your court appearance. We need you in a suit and tie."

"I'll get a shirt and pants. I have my dad's neckerchief, suspenders, vest, and boots."

"Come as a cowboy. That will work in Texas. I will probably see you at the big show then?"

"Yes. I want to see the Colonel's dogs in action."

"How can I get in on this other bet?"

"You need to talk to Andy. He's doing that. Thanks for the meal."

"You're welcome. You stay out of trouble."

Wulf then left the Blue Mill Café and went to Mr. Farnsworth's Dry Goods. The short man with the square glasses on the end of his nose greeted him when the bell tinkled overhead.

"My, my, Mr. Baker, what may I do for you?"

"I need a pair of pants, not overalls, and a long-sleeve shirt and some socks."

Farnsworth measured his waist. "We need the pants big enough so when they shrink, they'll still fit you."

Wulf agreed. His mother always bought his pants. He knew nothing about buying them. Farnsworth told him wool was the best material, and he went and got a pair of black wool pants and presented them to Wulf for him to try on. They were way too long, and Wulf had to hold them up for they'd fit a fatter man — *but they'd shrink.* The little man, on his knees, soon had the hem pinned, and Wulf went back to put on his overalls. This dressing up for the court looked like it would be a pain.

The black and white pinstripe shirt was a pull-over with three buttons. The material was heavy, and the little man promised it would be long lasting. It, too, was plenty large. The socks were wool as well. Farnsworth said the pants would be hemmed in two hours, and that Wulf owed him three dollars.

"I'll be back in two hours and have the money."

"Oh, you can charge it on your mother's account."

He considered that for a moment. "No,

I'll have the money when I come back."

Maybe he was bragging. Where would he get three dollars? He'd try Andy first. Dang, he had no money of his own. Before, he'd never needed anything he couldn't simply charge. His life had taken another twist. To survive in this world, he'd need a job.

Who'd hire him? What could he do for money? How could he impress that girl back at the café? Dulchy. A barefoot kid wouldn't ever do that. Maybe it was time for him to grow up. He'd talk to Andy about a loan.

He walked into the blacksmith shop, and Andy smiled at him, sweaty-faced while pounding on some iron strap at the anvil. He put his things down and shed his gloves. Meanwhile, Wulf untied Ranger and tousled his ears. Grateful to see him, the collie sat perfectly still as he'd been taught until Wulf told him to go make a run. Then, he bounded away like someone grateful to be free.

"Good to see you. Bob said he'd get you out today."

"It wasn't too soon. Say, I need a loan."

"How much?"

"Three dollars. I bought some clothes down at Farnsworth's to wear for the trial."

"I can pay you three, but you can earn it

sheing Joseph Simons's mule team."

"How come so much?"

"They aren't easy to handle. We may have to lay them down to shoe them." Andy laughed. "But I figured an animal trainer like you can figure them out. They're hitched up out back."

Wulf considered what he needed for mules. "You have a twitch to put on them?"

"Sure."

"Then I'll need someone to hold it."

"No problem. We can get one of the town loafers to do that for two beers. That's twenty cents."

"I can shoe them. They really must be wild."

"They aren't kittens."

"Find me the man to hold them and I'll get on those mules."

When Wulf came around the corner behind the shop, the right mule caught sight of him. He laid back his ears and prepared to kick him, braying like a wild ass at the top of his lungs. Before the mule could kick, Wulf had him by the tail and pulled himself up so he was standing on the mule's back knee with one foot, using the mule's tail for his balance and kicking him in the soft part of his belly with the other foot.

The mule stopped braying and went to

screaming. Wulf knew every time he buried his big toe in that mule's underside, he hurt him. It was only minutes before Wulf moved up and stood by the mule's dropped head. Trembling all over, the mule looked ready to collapse. Speaking very softly to him, he untied the heavy lead rope. When the mule did not respond, he slapped him in the soft underbelly with the lead rope and woke him up.

He led the mule inside the barn, where a scruffy-looking man stood holding the twitch in his hand. Wulf tied the mule up short to a ring on the post.

"Just stand there. He may not be any trouble today."

The man nodded as Wulf put on the leather apron. He'd drawn a crowd of onlookers at the open front doors to watch how he did it. He heard someone say, *That's one of Joe Simons's mules —*

He carefully lifted the left front hoof, and the mule murmured to him. All the time, he was speaking to the mule. The hoof in his lap, he pried off the worn shoe. When he dropped the hoof, there was a sigh from the crowd.

"Hell, that ain't one of Joe's mules. He's got a ringer in there."

"Go look. His mate's out back. That's

damn sure his mule."

Andy helped, punching holes in the shoe blank for the nails. Wulf heated and made them the right size to fit the freshly shaped hoof. Soon, the mule was shod on all four hooves, and the crowd stepped back when he started for the second mule. At a safe distance, the small mob of onlookers moved in a wave around after him to see this operation.

When Wulf came around the corner and walked under the live oak tree, the second mule went to kicking and braying. Wulf reached over and took the twitch from Charlie. "I don't have time for him. Besides, my toe is sore from kicking that other devil."

The mule flashed his yellow teeth and snapped them like a bear trap at Wulf. Avoiding the bite and using his right hand, Wulf reached up, grasped his long ear, and bit down hard. The mule's cries went from anger to pain and Wulf, with a full bite on him, put the twitch on his upper lip unscathed. Wrapping the loop of chain on the mule's lip, he twisted the chain on the stick until the mule froze with his top lip pulled away from his teeth.

"Now, Jack," Wulf said to the mule. "I don't have all day for this training. So you better act nice." And he led the distressed mule around and inside the shop. Andy tied the mule's lead. Wulf gave Charlie the twitch handle to hold, and out in the street the onlookers clapped their hands.

In record time, the second mule was shod, and then the two were led out and retied in back. Joe Simons came along and shouted at Andy, "When're you getting to my mules?"

"Why, Wulf shod them an hour ago."

"That boy shod them? They kick or bite you?" Joe looked shocked.

"The left one kicked at me, but I kicked him right back and I bet he don't kick no more." Wulf put down the horse's hoof he was working on and straightened his back.

"Well, I'll have to see it. What do I owe you, Andy?"

"Five bucks."

"Kinda high, ain'tcha?"

Andy put his hands on his hips, looking peeved. "No one else would touch those crazy mules. I figured I'd have to lay them down to shoe them. I'd say five dollars was cheap on those mules."

"All right, all right, but I doubt I'll be back." Joe went to digging the money out of his pocket. After paying Andy, he left.

"I thought he knew the charge." Wulf shook his head in dismay at the man's complaint as Andy handed him the three dollars.

"He knew what it was going to be. He just conveniently forgot what I told him about those mules. Don't worry, ain't no one else in Mason going to shoe his wild mules. They know them."

After completing the job he was on, Wulf ran down to Farnsworth's, picked up his new clothing, and paid the man.

"You have any trouble or need more clothing, you just call on me," Farnsworth said.

"I will, sir. Thanks again." If Robert Fiest didn't do something, his next suit would be prison stripes and he wouldn't need a tailor.

At Andy's house, Myrna hung the clothes up with the vest, suspenders, and the silk kerchief. "That outfit will look real nice. Your daddy would have been proud of you."

He sure hoped so. He thought about wearing his outfit to the dog trials on Saturday, but Andy changed his mind, saying, "A barefoot boy in overalls would be someone I'd figured I could beat easy at a wild goat-herding."

That sure made sense. But he wondered if Dulchy would be there at the ballpark, or if she might have to work. There would be a big crowd in town for the event. Mason's social schedule was normally not crowded,

65

so this was a big thing and there would be lots of folks from far and near cheering on their relative or neighbor in the ring competing against the Colonel's dogs.

The stands were packed by one o'clock. The short wooden panels like those used at shearing time were set up on the baseball field to fence in the event, and the folks standing around made a larger crowd. There was a peanut-roaster stand doing land-office business and hot-popcorn merchant selling small bags of it for a nickel.

The Colonel's troupe came in three large red-and-gold-trimmed wagons with painted signs of him and his dogs at work. Wulf slipped around down there, hoping to look over the black and white Border collies lolling their tongues out in the sun's warm heat. Six good-looking dogs, slick coats and very alert looking.

"You like dogs, boy?" a deep voice asked from behind.

"Yes, sir," he told the tall man in tan pants, white shirt, and black tie with an expensive white Boss of the Plains Stetson hat on his head.

"Those you are looking at are the dogs of the kings in Scotland. Cost five hundred dollars apiece over there — untrained. Of course, I wanted them trained by my methods."

Wulf agreed.

"Well, things are about to get under way. I hope you get your money's worth this afternoon — what is it, Norton?" the Colonel asked one of his men who'd ran up.

"There are some men here that want to challenge you to a wild goat-herding contest."

"Oh, they do, huh?"

"They want to bet that a local dog can beat one of your dogs at herding three goats into a trap."

"How much are they willing to bet?"

"Five hundred dollars."

"That would be a tidy sum to win. You learn all you can. Find out about the dog, too. Their dog may be up against one of our dogs that competes here today."

The man smiled, looking confident. "I'd say it was a good bet."

"Learn all you can. We could sure use their five hundred." The man hurried off, and the Colonel turned back to Wulf. "The show is about to begin. We'll have to see about that wild goat-herding."

Wulf nodded. Have to see? Sounded like the great Colonel Armstrong was about to take the bait.

The announcer used a bull horn to get the crowd's attention. Wulf saw the handler take the first collie on a leash. This dog had one white ear.

The first competitor's entry was a brown cur. One White Ear took his place on the ground beside the Colonel, who was now wearing a pith helmet and a Sam Brown belt with a holster containing a silver-plated Smith and Wesson pistol with a pearl handle. At six feet tall, the Colonel did look very formidable compared to the five-seven German farmer with the wool pancake cap and cheap overalls.

They drew for position, and the Colonel won the first try. The five sheep acted high-headed, but the Colonel's soft commands to the dog and the dog's attention to the Colonel were what Wulf watched. White Ear never paid any mind to the crowd. His focus was on the sheep and his master. The dog was well trained, and the Colonel really had command of his every move. It was as if the dog was an extension of his arm.

The dog dropped flat with a hand signal from the Colonel. Then slowly crept around the flock, acting like he was a snake on the ground. When in place, he rose and the sheep moved to his right. This could not look too easy, so when the sheep headed for the pen at a trot, the colonel moved his dog around to settle them down again. When they were bunched again, the dog, at his master's command, moved the sheep slowly along the fence so the entire crowd could see him work. If a sheep acted ready to bolt, the dog was ready to face him off and turn him back.

When at last the dog "herded" them in the smaller pen, the crowd went wild and applauded.

The sheep were brought back and the Colonel took his seat in a high canvas folding chair under an umbrella for shade. The sun felt too good on Wulf's back as he watched the German farmer drag his dog in on a rope leash.

First of all, Wulf could see the dog was obviously shocked by the crowd. A dog that would work good in the cedars and live oak was going to be awed by the smell alone of all those people. It was a wreck. The sheep went wild over the cur like Wulf had expected, and the man lost his ten bucks.

The Colonel politely shook his hand. White Ear was used three times. Then a new collie with a black ring around his eyes won the fourth contest. Wulf wasn't certain his dog Ranger could win against these dogs. But a small smile crept in the corners of his mouth — wild goats were not well-trained sheep. The Colonel's collies were good, but an eager young one slipped up and the Colonel lost ten bucks against a good local dog owned by a Mexican man named Hidalgo.

They took a short break in the program. Wulf saw Andy and Bob talking to the Colonel and his man. They waved him over.

"So you are the dog man challenging me," the Colonel said, as if he'd made a discovery.

"Yes, sir."

"Well, where is this dog?' he asked, looking around.

"Have your announcer tell them to let Calico come through."

"George, tell them to let the dog in."

The announcer shouted for them to make way for the boy's dog. The crowd snickered. Wulf put two fingers in his mouth and made a shrill whistle.

They made quite an entrance. His dog Ranger was sitting aboard his horse Calico, who came trotting up through the aisle made for them. Then, with no effort, Calico leaped the low fence to come up the arena and put his head against Wulf's one-strap overalls. The crowd went wild, and Wulf saw the dollar signs spinning in the Colonel's blue eyes.

As Ranger continued to sit on the horse's back, Wulf nodded at the Colonel. "Yes, that's my dog. Ranger."

"Well, this shall be interesting. I'll collect a ten-cents admission wherever you will have this event to cover my expenses. The five hundred from each party will be entrusted with a man of high respect."

"How about Judge Arnold?" Bob Fiest asked.

"He a local judge?" Armstrong asked.

"Yes."

"Send for him. What else can this horse do?" The Colonel turned to Wulf.

"Count, bow, rear up and walk on his hind feet."

"And come when you whistle. How long did it take you to teach that dog to ride?"

"A while. Back then, he'd much rather've been down here than up there. Now he don't care."

"I think I'm being led into a trap. Your training certainly impresses me, young man. Where are we having this event?"

"Two P.M. tomorrow at Blair's ranch," Bob announced. "Wulf has never been on that place and those goats have never seen his dog, Ranger, or yours."

"What are the rules?" the Colonel asked.

"We'll draw position like here," Bob said. "Paint three goats with red stripes and move them from one pen to the next."

"Why the paint?"

"So we know the goats in the pen are the right ones."

"Use six goats, paint three red, three blue. So we both start with fresh goats. How's that?" Armstrong asked.

"Fine," Wulf agreed.

So competition was set for Sunday. The public was invited. Admission was going to be ten cents, which the Colonel would collect. Texas-style wild goat-penning by two good dogs. White Ear and Ranger.

Wulf noticed his stepfather, with his head all bandaged, and his mother in the crowd as they were leaving. It was the only thing that ruined a good day for him.

SIX

"He had so much money he couldn't count it?" Art Spencer asked in disbelief.

"I believed him. Ten years ago, Buffalo discovered a Spanish gold train in some blow sand down in Kansas. No telling what it was, but there were six trunks of gold coins on the skeletons of dead horses. Oh, he's got some left, but they got most of it. It's why they stole three of his horses to haul it. Malone thinks, and I agree, the amount of all that gold shocked them. They thought he only had a small sack of the stuff."

Art was turning over the five-sided coin in his fingers. "I never saw one like this before."

"It's real gold and real old. He thinks Indians attacked the guards. The horses were full of Cheyenne arrows. The guards got away and then they later died. He found two human skulls there as well. Couldn't trust any men up there, so he got two tall

73

Indian women who'd been bedding them black soldiers and used them. He hunted some buffalo to cover his recovery operation since they had to dig up lots of sand to get all of the trunks.

"Malone said he did some business cashing some coins with the First Bank of Montana, and I checked with Phillip Hinds over there. The coins are real. Five sides and all."

"Where do we start?"

"We send telegrams to every sheriff in Montana, Wyoming, Dakota, and Nebraska. Ask them to investigate anyone who uses old Spanish coins for money. Tell them that we have had a major robbery and want to speak to anyone who knows anything about such coins."

"You don't think the robbers are anyone local?"

"I can't rule it out. But I suspect those men heard way off somewhere that Buffalo had spent a few gold coins and must have a sackful somewhere. So we start with telegrams."

"I can do that. It sure made a big heist."

"Yes. He said he hoped they would leave him some, but in the end they stole his best horses to pack it all off.

"I'm going to make a circle south today.

Check some stores and outposts. See if anyone saw them leaving the county. I may be gone a few days. Is the new police chief working out?" Herschel asked.

Art made a sour face. "I know we'll need him this spring and more. That railroad will push in here or be close enough, we'll be the biggest boomtown in Montana, but he's not my kinda law."

Herschel knew what he meant. He and his men took troublemakers aside and made them promise no more trouble. This new chief and his three men used billy clubs any time they got a chance.

The afternoon sun was bright. The snow was relegated to the shade and north slopes when he rode up to Killian's Store on the northern edge of the Crow land. Several wagons and teams as well as hipshot horses were parked about, no doubt from Crows doing their shopping.

He found Major Rhine, the store operator, in his office at the back of the large operation.

"Well, the high sheriff is here," Rhine said, glancing up from his paperwork. The heavy-jowled man with thick sideburns rose and shook his hand. "Who are you looking for?"

"Three men spending old Spanish doubloons."

Rhine opened his desk and tossed five coins out on the desktop. "My head clerk gave them a hundred dollars for them. Are they real?"

"Real as they can be. May I talk to your man?"

"Sure you can. Who in the hell did they steal them from? I couldn't believe they were real. How old are they?" Rhine held a five-sided coin up between his fingers.

"I have no idea. A buffalo hunter discovered them ten years ago down in Kansas. These men robbed him of them five days ago."

"I was worried they were a hoax, but we get some Mexican coins up here. Texas cattlemen carried some with them on the herd drives. But I knew these were either old as hell or fakes."

"They're real."

"Let me get Tim Blaine, my head clerk." Rhine went to the door and called out to Blaine.

"Something wrong?" the balding man in his thirties asked. He wore a green celluloid visor.

"It's about these doubloons," Herschel said, indicating the ones on the desk. "And the men cashed them in."

"They are real, aren't they?"

76

"Yes," Rhine said, getting back in his chair and indicating Herschel and Blaine should each take a chair, too. "They were stolen."

"Oh, my, I had no way to know that."

"I know" said Herschel. "Can you describe the men brought them in?"

"One man. He was tall. Your height, but barrel-chested. Needed a shave or needed to grow a beard. It was gray-flecked. Large nose, hard brown eyes. His hair was brown and long. I guessed he was forty plus. Had a raised scar on his — left cheek. Ran from the corner of his left eye to beside his mouth." Blaine drew the line with his finger on his own face. "Called himself Tom Downing. I figured that wasn't his name."

"And the others?"

"If there were others, they never came in. I never saw them. They must have stayed with the horses, huh?"

"What did he buy with that much money?"

"Foodstuff mainly. Flour, baking soda, beef jerky, candy, sugar, raisins, bacon, dry beans, and rice."

"Any ammunition?" Herschel asked.

"He must have a .50-caliber Sharp rifle. He bought ammo for it anyway."

"That's not good for you," Rhine said with

a frown at Herschel. "He's got a long-range gun."

"Some .45 ammo, too," Blaine said.

"Sounds like they're well armed and ready to hide out," Herschel said, and dropped his chin. "Any chance that any of the other store workers saw any other men?"

"Billy Gates loaded it out. I'll go ask him."

"Bring him in here," Rhine said. "Baker wants these men. He's rode all the way down here, he's serious."

"Yes, sir." Blaine hurried off to find the worker.

"I can get us some coffee or whiskey," Rhine said.

"Coffee will be fine."

"I'll get us two cups while he's finding Billy."

"I'd be obliged."

Rhine left him to study the ten-point elk head mounted on the wall, the mule deer horns, and the ram horns of a mountain sheep with a three-quarter curl. The former army officer had collected some great trophies. If he'd ever shot anything, it was for meat, so he could eat it and never worry about how fancy it would look on the wall.

"Billy, this is Sheriff Baker. Tell him what the men looked like bought those supplies I mentioned." Blaine indicated for the boy to speak.

The pimple-faced youth nodded and shook Herschel's hand. "All three were dressed pretty much for the cold. All bundled up so I couldn't see much. I'd say they were in their early twenties. One called the other Grayson and they called the fella ordered the stuff the Old Man. They had the five packhorses loaded when they left."

"They had five packhorses?" Herschel asked.

"Yeah, three were stout enough paint horses they must have bought off Indians, but the other two were half draft horse and big — ah, red roan color. Their saddle horses were all brown or bays. I wondered about them paints. Most of those kind of fellas ride and lead horses kind of match the land — I mean, don't stick out. You could see them paints a mile or more away."

"Were the paint horses bearing trunks?"

"Yeah, that's all. One on each side, but I could tell they had all that they could haul. I could tell they were heavy loads by the way those horses left tracks."

"Them trunks full of these coins?" Rhine asked, setting down the two coffees.

Herschel thanked Billy, and when the youth left, he told Rhine that they were full.

"Holy shit. That means they have thousands of dollars in gold?"

Yes, and they had a week's jump on him.

Seven

Clouds were gathering from off the Texas
coast. The wind had a sting to it, but Wulf
knew that after church, the threat would
not diminish the crowd headed out the
Buckhorn Road for Buck Blair's place. Buggies, buckboards, wagons, horses, and even
riding burros, the one-lane road choked
with folks coming out there for the competition. Dust would be boiling up higher than
the trees.

Folks around Mason, like most frontier
towns, were starved for entertainment. And
good stock dogs were a part of their life in
the hill country. Such gatherings combined
business and pleasure as well as a chance
for the women to gossip.

Wulf sat chewing on a stem of grass on
the sunny side of the slope, with Ranger lying close by and Calico chomping off the
dried bunchgrass. Considering all that had
happened in his life over the past few

months, he felt down at the heels. Living off his friends Andy and Myrna, facing a court trial for attempted murder, and that damn Hughes in charge of his ranch. He closed his eyes and prayed for something good to happen to him.

It did. She came with a small picnic basket on one arm and a tablecloth as well. In a fresh-looking dress, Dulchy came up the cow path and smiled at him. "I brought you some lunch. They said you were up here."

He struggled to his feet and brushed off the seat of his old overalls. "Why — why —"

Her hand on his chest, she pushed him down. "Sit. We are going to eat before you win today."

"You know?"

"Everyone in this county knows about you and your stock dog."

He smiled. He sure liked how she said *joo* instead of *you*. Her accent made her even more precious.

"Spread out the cloth," she said, handing it to him. "I looked all over down there for you."

"If I'd known you were coming — I'd've met you."

"I know that you have lots on your mind. But I also know that you have to eat as well."

He reached over and caught her wrist. "Why are you doing this for me? I am a criminal in some people's eyes. I'm nobody. There are a dozen rich German farm boys who would sweep you up in a snap of my fingers."

She wet her lips. "Maybe I don't want a rich German farm boy."

"Look how I'm dressed. No shoes. A suspender button gone. Dulchy, does your mother know you're feeding me?" He looked around, but they were far enough from the ranch headquarters that no one was looking at them.

"My mother and father are dead."

"Oh, I'm sorry."

"But my Aunt Frieda said she thought it would be all right."

"She your guardian?"

"I am nineteen."

"Oh —" He swiped his hat off and then combed his fingers through his too long hair. Could he possibly say or do anything else to chase her away? "I'm sorry. I'm upset today."

"This competition you entered in makes you nervous?"

"No. My stepfather has taken over a ranch that my father left to me. Twice he beat me, once with reins and then with a quirt. I was not taking another of those beatings. The other night he started for me, and I beat him with a singletree to stop him. He has me up for attempted murder. I stand trial next week. So what do you see in me?"

"I see the bravest man in the world. When everyone was frozen in place, you stepped right in and shot that rabid dog. You saved that woman and her child from a horrible death. And I watched you do that."

His felt his face turn bright red and he shook his head. "That was nothing."

"We better eat our lunch. They will start soon. I have potato salad and ham sandwiches on rye. I hope you like rye bread."

"Dulchy, I love rye bread."

She looked a little taken aback by his words, but he sat up and moved closer to her. She handed him the sandwich, and then set a mason jar with something yellow in it beside him. "That's lemonade."

"You're spoiling me real bad." He looked over at her before he took a bite of the sandwich. He was short of breath and every nerve in his body tingled, until he worried he might start shaking.

"Good," she said, dishing out some of the salad on a plate and adding a fork to it.

"Put it down and you eat," he insisted.

"You are the one to eat. I have all day to eat."

"Dulchy, you may be betting on the wrong horse."

She shook her head to dismiss his words. "You only are upset today. When you win, I want to celebrate with you."

"What if I don't? What if Ranger can't manage these goats?"

"I will still be proud of you for trying to beat this famous man."

"What if I have to cut and run from this country?"

"You could send me a letter through your friend the blacksmith, and I would come to meet you wherever you are."

He put down the sandwich and climbed on his knees to hug her. They quickly kissed and he dropped back on his heels. "I hope I didn't shock you, but I had to kiss you."

She looked down and nodded. "Me, too."

"I better eat and get Ranger ready."

"They told me you whistled and the horse came with the dog riding him through that big crowd. Someday you must show me how you teach them."

"Oh, Dulchy, I'd love to do that. I had practiced doing it in town before when it was crowded so I knew they'd come to me. Calico showed off jumping over that low sheep fence."

"People talked about it all afternoon long in the café."

"Today it will be serious."

She moved closer to him. "Eat. I want to see you win today."

He nodded with his mouth full. That she was so close made every nerve in his body feel like a blasting powder cord sizzling away. His breath grew even shorter and his palms were sweaty. No one had ever done this to him before, and he wasn't sure what to call it. They were like two magnets ready to snap together.

Good thing she'd never asked him his age. Lots of good things. Her potato salad. Her blue eyes. Her full lower lip. He was out of time. They were blowing the cow horn to get everyone together.

"I must run."

She rose with him and he hugged her. They kissed harder, and it was even harder for him to let go of her, but at last he whispered, "Good-bye."

Then he leaped on Calico and told Ranger to join him.

"Win today," she told him.

When his dog was in place, he short-loped for the starting line. He looked back and waved once. She waved, too. His stomach felt upset as he left her — not because of her food, but because of their separation.

Kissed his first girl. Damn, things were happening fast. Too fast.

A cheer went up as he loped though the opening the large crowd there made for him and his horse. Colonel Armstrong sat on the rise in a tall canvas folding chair with an umbrella for shade. Wulf halted Calico and bailed off close to the man. Ranger jumped down, and Wulf simply let his horse go off grazing.

"You ride that stallion everywhere without reins?" the Colonel asked.

"My knees guide him. He rides fine with a bridle and saddle, too."

"Why don't you join me? My show, I mean, with your horse and dog?"

"There are several reasons I can't. But thank you anyway."

The Colonel looked over at the crowd. "Are your parents here?"

"My father died. My mother is here with my stepfather, I imagine. I haven't talked to them in over a week."

"I see. Ready to start?"

"Judge," Armstrong said to the well-dressed man that Wulf barely recognized without his robes. "Toss the coin. Young man, you may call it in the air to see who

87

goes first."

"Heads," Wulf called.

"Tails it is." The judge looked at the coin, and then he showed them the results.

"I think I will let you go first. Which pen do you want?" the Colonel asked. Then he began to grin. "Or does it matter to you?"

"No, sir. Goats are goats. Especially wild ones."

"Since you will be first, and the colors of our land are red first, you get the red pen."

"Fine. Come on, Ranger. We've got goats to gather."

When he was thirty feet from the pen, Wulf stopped and Ranger sat down beside him. "Now, my friend, see that pen down there? That's where they go." He pointed to the pen set up at the foot of the hill. People were lined up on both sides of the runway, the lines maybe 150 feet apart. These goats would avoid them unless driven into them by the dog.

"Ready?" the announcer asked, and when Wulf nodded, a .22 shot went off. Three of the toughest-acting big billies came charging out with escape written on their faces. Their curled horns looked like the ones on unicorns, only they each had two.

The goats, seeing the crowd, tried to break back for the pen they had been driven out of, but Ranger was off like a flash. Dodging horns and battering rams, he used his teeth in a series of quick nips to convince them. The fight was short, and the high-headed goats burst for the other side of the line. Wulf shouted to Ranger, "Circle 'em."

Like lightning, Ranger rounded them up in the center. While they slung their heads at him, they warily stayed clustered in the center of the field halfway to the other pen.

"Easy," Wulf said, loud enough that Ranger could hear him, and made down signs with his hands.

The crowd applauded. Then, moving like an animal ready to prey on them, Ranger inched them in a mass down the grade. These wild billies had never been so challenged before, except maybe by a coyote. And a coyote wouldn't bother them unless he was absolutely starving, for he knew they'd taste like the piss dripped off their chins. Foot by foot, Ranger outmaneuvered them. Cutting them off from any possible way to escape, until he finally put them in the end pen and a roar went up when the official closed the gate.

Wulf used two fingers to whistle. Calico threw his head up and came galloping off the hill. Wulf vaulted on his back, caught Ranger to ride behind him. Then, he nodded to the cheering crowd and rode back up the hill to join the Colonel.

Armstrong took off his hat and bowed to Wulf. "I am conceding this contest to you, sir. My dogs are sheep herders and I could not risk injuring them with these wild beasts. They are far too valuable for me to chance their being killed or injured."

Wulf slipped off Calico and walked over to shake the man's hand.

"And furthermore," the Colonel announced loudly, "I wish to inform all of you that I have purchased this dog and horse from this boy's guardian for three thousand dollars."

Wulf whirled and saw the smug look on Kent Hughes's face as he stepped over and took the money from Armstrong. "They're all yours, Colonel. Let's go home, son."

Home — son? His knees threatened to buckle. His breath left him. No way.

EIGHT

The weather stayed clear the next day, and when Herschel reached the trading post at Hardin near where Custer had made his last stand, he found and spoke with a half-breed named No Horse. The man described the three men and their paint packhorses to him.

"The big man, he tell 'em what to do. They were not boys, but they did as he said, and stayed to guard the horses with rifles while he went in the trading post. Everyone see them say, my, they must have valuable load on them horses to guard them so well."

"You get a good look at those two?" Herschel asked, squatting with the man wearing the unblocked black hat in the late afternoon sun.

"No. Their collars were turned up and they looked so mean, no one got close. One Indian woman went to offer her services to them. She talked to them." No Horse shook his head, amused. "But they did not want her."

"What else?"

"That big man has a scar on his face. His eyes are gray and so is his hair. I thought I knew him, but so many white people look alike. Under his coat, he wears two guns and carries many knives One in his boot, one on his back — I saw it. He could reach up and have it. I bet he could toss it and sink it in a man's heart."

"Do you think this woman got a good look at those two?"

"Judy White Goat is her name. She doesn't speak English. Oh, a little, but you'd never understand more than what her trade is about."

"I'll hire you to find her and pay you to translate what she saw."

"I can do that."

"What does she charge?" Herschel stopped when his man broke into a grin. "No, I mean, what does she charge her customers? I can pay her that for helping me."

"Two bits, huh?"

"You a dollar. Her fifty cents, if she knows anything constructive to me."

"I will find her."

Herschel raised his gaze to the log trading

post on the hillside above them. "I'm going to put up my horse in the wagon yard. Then I'll eat some supper. You find her while I am there. I will feed you and her, too."

No Horse nodded his head in agreement. "I can find her and we be there to eat with you."

Herschel rose and watched the breed jog away. Fastest he had probably moved in years.

Maybe this woman had noticed something about the robbers. No one else got closer before they rode on. The better the description he could get, the easier it would be to find them. With his horse, Cob, eating grain and hay, he went in to the outpost office and wired the sheriff in Sheridan to be on the lookout for three men with five packhorses. Three of the horses were loud paints. The men were armed and dangerous.

When he came out of the telegraph office, No Horse and a tall Indian woman wearing soiled beaded buckskins stood waiting for him. Her long thick hair was in her face, but cleaned up, she might be handsome. Then she burped, and followed that with a giggle. No Horse scowled at her, squeezed her arm, and she tried to square her shoulders.

At the outpost restaurant, the waiter put

them in a booth. Roast beef, potatoes, gravy, and corn was the menu. Herschel ordered them all coffee.

"This Judy White Goat," No Horse said in hardly more than a whisper.

"You ask her about the men?"

No Horse nodded. "One had a mustache. She thought the third one was a boy."

She said something that came out fast in Crow.

No Horse translated. "She says she knew that one was a virgin."

That was no help. "What color were his eyes?"

When her answer came back, No Horse said, "They both had blue eyes."

"Any scars or noticeable things?"

No Horse translated her answer. "She says they both wore heavy gold crosses on chains around their necks. Their coats were unbuttoned and she saw them."

Those items probably came from the treasure in those trunks. Blue eyes, and maybe the young one was hardly more than a boy. Their food came and Judy White Goat gathered her hair and tied it in back, then sitting very straight, began to cut up her food.

"Where did she go to school at?" Herschel asked, pointing his fork at her. This woman had been schooled in how to eat at a white man's table.

"A mission school, I think. They say she got with child there. They were going to give her baby away. She ran away from there to keep it. The baby died at birth. She had it alone with the coyotes. Disgraced by her own people, she came here. That is why she does what she does and drinks firewater to forget the good days."

"Judy White Goat," Herschel said to get her attention. "These men I'm after burned an old man's feet so he can't walk to get this treasure. He has a young Sioux wife, and they threatened to cut off her breasts, so he told them where his money was at. If you know one thing more about them, tell me, please."

She put down her fork. "The young one has only three fingers." She showed Herschel how the last two were missing on his right hand by grasping them in her hand.

No Horse shook his head in disgust, and before he went back to eating, said, "She never talks in English. Never have I heard her say a word in English."

She smiled privately at Herschel. "There are not many worth talking to in English."

The next morning, Herschel rode south. It was a long two days' ride to Sheridan, and he felt certain by this time that the robbers weren't going to try the outlaw trail that was buried in snow on top of the Bighorns. But where would they go next? They'd left Hardin headed south three days earlier after buying a gallon of white lightning from a character called Louisville Shorty. The stable man Ira told him about Shorty's sale to the older man before they rode on. Paid Shorty two gold *Mexican* coins for it.

Ira had seen the older man, who, he said, bought grain for their horses, but he said the boys stayed back like they needed to be with the pack animals. He'd never caught the man's name, but said he acted gruff and short.

Ira dug out and held up a five-sided coin for Herschel to see. "He paid me this for the grain. It any good, Marshal?"

"Worth over twenty-five dollars, they tell me." Herschel never bothered to correct him. Marshal — sheriff, what was the difference? He always carried his deputy U.S. marshal badge with him, just in case.

"Holy cow, I hope he comes back."

"If he does, wire the sheriff's office in Billings. There is a big reward out for him."

"I will. I sure will."

Late afternoon, Herschel stopped at the

Dare Stage Stop near the halfway mark to Sheridan. It was a log-adobe low-roofed building that made him duck to enter. Inside, the candle lamps threw quaky shadows on the wall and the shake ceiling.

"Aye, sir, ya just passing through?" a plump, red-faced, Irish-sounding gal asked, drying her hands from washing dishes in a tub.

"I'd like to spend the night and take a meal here."

"Aye, and to rest your weary butt. No doubt ya rode a lengthy way to get here. I'll stir up the stable boy, Erin, and he can grain and put up your horse for twenty cents. Beds are a quarter and meals the same." She turned and shouted for the stable boy. "Erin!"

"Coming. Coming. What ya need?" the sleepy-eyed boy asked, coming from the side wing.

"We got a customer. Put up his horse and grain him well."

"Aye, I can do that, sir." And Erin hurried off.

Herschel removed his thick gloves and then unbuttoned his coat at her invitation. She helped him out of it, hanging it with his Scotch cap and scarf on the wall pegs.

"And where you be from, sir?"

97

"Billings. I'm the sheriff up there. My name's Herschel Baker."

"Mine's Birdie. And you must be through here on business," she said, pouring him some steaming coffee in a tin cup. After putting the coffee in front of him, she took a seat on the bench opposite him and pushed up her sleeves. "I don't get many folks to talk with here. They get off the stage, poop in me outhouse, complain about the food they eat, and then get back on the stage."

Herschel chuckled at her words. "I'm looking for three men that committed a major robbery in my county in Montana."

Her clear blue eyes met his gaze. "And they had a five-horse pack train."

"Yes. Did they stop here?"

"Two days ago." He could tell by the grim set to her once-open face that something bad had happened.

"There was trouble here?"

She hunched her shoulders and dropped her chin. "There was, sir."

"Were you assaulted by them?" He waited for her answer, seeing that she was pained to speak about the matter.

"Yes, Calvin and Grayson McCafferty both." Her eyes flooded with water, and she dug out a rag to sniff into.

"Two of them?" He reached over to

squeeze her arms. "Where was the third one?"

"Watching the damn horses. He wouldn't come inside." She stopped and blew her nose. "They tied up Erin and made him watch."

"What happened next?"

"They rode on — thank God."

"So you and the boy were the only ones that saw them?"

"I can't hardly talk about it." She cried some more, and finally said, "Yes."

"And their last name is McCafferty?"

"Yes. Calvin is the father. He's the meanest one. Grayson imitates him, but he's not that tough. The young one's name guarded the horses is August. They call him Auggie."

"He a son of this Calvin, too?"

"By another woman, they said. That was why he didn't come in."

"How long were they here?"

"Maybe an hour or so. That boy grained their horses, and after those two bastards were through with me, they rode on." She shook her head in despair. "It was a horrible experience."

"I imagine so." He'd never heard of Calvin or Grayson McCafferty, nor did he recall ever seeing any posters bearing their names.

But there would soon be wanted posters out on them. He'd wire Art from Sheridan and get him on that.

"Sorry I am so slow on their trail, Birdie, but I intend to bring them to justice."

"God bless ya. I had a shotgun up there by me door. I started to shoot at 'em as they were leaving, but Erin, he stopped me saying I shot one, the others'd be back and kill us both."

"He gave you good advice."

"I won't ever feel safe here again. I loved this place before. They ruined me Garden of Eden, huh?"

"You probably won't ever have another bad incident like this happen in your whole life here."

"Thanks, Sheriff Baker. I'll pray over it."

Before daylight, she made him a big breakfast. He thanked her, then left to saddle his horse. Mounted, he started to head for Sheridan. She rushed out in the frosty cold to stop his steam-blowing horse and give Herschel a cross and a chain of black beads.

"May the Virgin Mary protect you," she said, and clapped his stomping horse on the shoulder. "Get them devils, Sheriff Baker, before they hurt another woman."

"I will. I'll get them. Thanks." He pocketed
the cross and beads and rode on.

NINE

Andy and Bob held Wulf by the arms and herded him away. He knew both men were fiercely upset but had a good reason for getting him out of there. Good thing he didn't have a gun.

"Hold your temper. Hughes has dropped the charges. Said the entire matter of the will and probate didn't need a lawyer. You would get your equitable portion. That your mother had agreed that the sale of the horse and the dog was better for both you and Hughes to get along."

Shock hit his heart like a sledgehammer blow. "I don't even have anything to say about this?"

"No. Not here. Hughes has the judge convinced it was all a misunderstanding. Family matter, and he's going to heal it."

"He can sell my horse and dog?"

"Your mother can. She signed the bill of sale."

Blinking tears in his eyes, he was forcibly guided away from the Colonel and the rest to the side of the crowd by the two men.

"You two working for him?" Wulf's pain turned to bewilderment.

"No, listen. Bob can fight this in court. You can't win out here in this field," Andy said in his ear, not letting go of the vise-like grip on his arm.

"I can't win in court either."

"Yes, yes, you can," Bob said in his other ear. "But you can't do any good causing a fuss right now."

"They are taking away the only two things that really matter to me. Ranger and Calico." Off in the distance, the stallion screamed in protest. Wulf shook his head. They could never handle him. How could his mother have signed that bill of sale? Hughes had her under his power. A family fuss — *my ass.*

"Go on. Let me be alone. I'll not start anything here. I need to think."

"You are coming back to Mason?" Andy asked. "Sorry, but when we heard Armstrong was going to buy them, we knew you'd go crazy. We had to be the ones to stop you from doing any more damage."

They agreed to let him go think, and he promised to be back at Andy's house later on that evening.

"But you won't have a way to get home," Andy said.

"I can walk. Give me more time to think."

Parting with them, he went back to the hillside where he'd shared lunch with Dulchy. She must have had to go home with her own people. He'd never even gotten to talk to her after Ranger won. Aw, hell, his life got worse and worse by the damn day.

Finally, full of self-pity, he set out walking the dusty road back to town. It would be long past sundown before he reached Mason. His world felt so empty without Ranger at his side and without the great horse that he could ride without saddle or bridle.

Could he ever get another horse and dog? Not yet. He wasn't over the loss of Ranger and Calico. That would take a long time to get over. Worse yet was thinking about what the Colonel's handlers were doing with them. They would miss him. Damn, his mixed-breed yellow and white collie and his horse from the nearly extinct Comanche bloodlines, along with all his hours of training, were gone forever.

He threw stones at cottonwood trees and skipped them over water in the creeks he crossed while stepping on the dry rocks. The day grew shorter. He still had no plans to recover his animals and get away. Maybe the money they'd promised him from the bet would outfit him with another horse to ride and enough money to escape the Colonel's clutches with his own animals in tow.

Long past dark, he came up Andy's back stairs. Weary, tired, and defeated, he put his hand on the facing.

"That you?" Myrna asked, sitting in the dark at the kitchen table.

"Yes, ma'am."

"We were worried you'd do something crazy."

"Like kill Kent Hughes?"

"Oh, Wulf —" She rushed over and hugged him. "Andy and I never had a boy of our own. You are our boy and if you ever did something like that, it would break my heart."

"But he needs it."

"No, no, he's one of God's children, too."

He held her. "God wouldn't have him. Today Dulchy brought me lunch. But I fear that in all that trouble I've lost her, too."

"If she really is worth having, she won't leave you."

"Is that how you tell?"

Myrna raised her face up in the dim light of the kitchen and looked at him. "That is the God's truth."

He closed his eyes. *Maybe she would be back?*

"I have some food in the oven."

"Where's Andy?"

"Gone to bed. He was so upset about today and worked up, I told him to go get some sleep." With a gopher match, she lighted the candle lamp on the table.

He looked at her, feeling consumed by guilt. "I'm sorry, this is all because of me."

She put the plate before him. "No, Andy has been your friend and he hates what happened today, but he worried more that you would only bring on bigger problems. He said the judge liked the case against you being dropped and you making up with your parents."

"But that was all a lie. I'm never going home and be with them. You know my mother signed that bill of sale?"

"Oh, Wulf, I am so sorry."

"I'm getting me a horse and getting the hell out of this country."

"Where will you go?"

"Montana. My cousin Herschel Baker is a sheriff up there in Billings. I spoke to his sister, Susie, a few weeks ago. Says Herschel's doing real well. Did you know their daddy who walked away from them when they were kids?"

"No."

"I didn't either. Well, after the war he came home and became a cattle buyer, and one day he simply rode off, they said. No one knew where Thurman went for years. Herschel and the others grew up. Went on cattle drives. His brother, Tom, got killed on one, but Herschel is doing good. It turns out that Thurman has a big ranch down in south Texas — but the way things have turned out, I want to see that other end of the world."

"What will you do in Montana?" she asked, seated across from him.

"I ain't sure. But no one will steal my dog and horse from me up there."

"Talk to Bob and Andy both before you run off half-cocked. Bob thinks he can win your case against Hughes. Maybe you should give him a chance. And Andy loves your help at the shop and you know you always have a place here."

"If I stay here, I may kill Hughes. I came within inches of that with the singletree."

"That won't solve your problems. Now eat. In the morning, things will look better."

In the morning, Wulf sipped coffee in the lighted kitchen and talked with Andy. During the night, rain had moved in and the drip off the eaves made a song.

"Myrna said you wanted to go up to Montana and see your cousin Herschel. He's a sheriff up there?"

"That's what his sister, Susie, said. I saw her a few weeks ago when she was in town. She didn't even know my dad had died. I guess the Bakers all kind of broke up way back then. I was too young to know that Thurman rode off after the war and no one knew where he went. He showed up recently and has a big ranch down in south Texas. Has a young Indian wife and a baby."

"I never knew Thurman. I knew Herschel and Tom. They made tough cowboys. Worked hard to keep up that place for their mother. If you have to leave, I understand. I know your losses can't be easily forgotten. But be sure to fill out all the papers for Bob before you leave. He's going to court and fight for you."

"Fight for what?"

"He's a smart lawyer. Give him a chance. Oh, yes, your part of the prize money was one hundred dollars." Andy put five twenty-dollar gold pieces on the table. "What now?"

"I need to find a tough saddle horse if I'm going that far."

"Ule Matters has a Kentucky-bred horse. No one can handle him. Tough, fast, and very green, broke in all the wrong ways. I bet one of them gold pieces will buy him today."

"A big black gelding?"

"You've seen those boys leading him between two horses and him bucking the whole time. That's the horse. I ain't meddling, but what about the girl that brought you lunch?"

Wulf swallowed hard. The damn knot in his throat about gagged him. "I'll go by to see her."

"Good," Andy said as if relieved. "Drop us a letter. Let us know you're all right."

"Oh, I will." What would he do about Dulchy? Nothing for the time being but go by and talk to her. "I better go see Matters about that horse."

"See Bob first at his office."

"Yes, sir. I'll be by to help you as soon as I can."

"Take care of your business first."

After breakfast, he went to find Bob in his office. Things were looking much more organized, and the rain was sheeting on the panes of the bay window panes when he hung his sodden hat and canvas duster on the coat rack.

"Come in. Come in." Bob stood up behind the desk and shook his hand. "I didn't hardly sleep a wink last night over that shady deal Hughes pulled on you yesterday."

"That's behind me. I'm going to go see a cousin in Montana. No way I can stay here this close to Hughes."

"Then give me your power of attorney. That's so I can fight this in court and you won't have to be here."

"Sure. Will it work?"

"No problem. I'll go for the heart of this and make Hughes put all the money he spent and didn't deposit in the probate account."

"Include the money he got yesterday."

"Oh, I will." Bob sat back in his chair. "It will take maybe a year, but I'll have it all back and you in charge by the time you're old enough to take over the ranch."

"Tell Effie hi for me. And the baby," Wulf said. "I'll send you my address when I get up there."

Matters lived on the edge of town in a two-story brick home. He kept all his Angora billies and rams in a small fenced-in paddock, feeding them hay in the winter. The smell of wet goat and sheep was strong on the rainy wind. The rest of his herds were out on several ranches he owned west of town.

"Good day, Wulf," Matters said, answering the door with a newspaper in his hand. "My, you and Ranger did a great job yesterday. Come in. I couldn't see you selling them after the big win, but that was lots of money."

"My stepfather Kent Hughes sold them. I would never have agreed to selling them. I got no part of that money."

"You know — have a seat — that man is a scoundrel. That must have been pure hell."

"Mr. Matters, I'm leaving Mason and going to see a cousin in Montana until I can look at things better around here. Andy said you might sell me the black Kentucky horse."

"Sell him to you?"

"Yes, sir."

"No, Wulf, I'll give him to you. That horse is the biggest disappointment in my entire life. He's bred to run. But he's a crazy fool." Matters pointed the folded-up newspaper at Wulf from the other morris chair. "I'm sorry I never thought of you as a trainer. Why, you rode a stallion all over without a bridle. Jenny, come in here. I'm giving Nightmare to Wulf Baker."

A gray-headed woman came to the kitchen door in an apron. "Well, thank God. Oh, I hope he doesn't hurt you," she said to Wulf.

"He won't," Wulf said to reassure her.

111

"Then I have some hot apple pie dished up, fresh cheddar cheese melting on it, and a new pot of coffee in my kitchen for both of you."

"Sounds all right. Let's go, Wulf, before she changes her mind."

That saved him twenty bucks. But there was no way to simply get on Nightmare and ride off to Montana.

His goal was to have the gelding ready to go in five days. Lots more to do. Next, he needed to get the backbone to go see Dulchy and tell her his plans. He'd do that after he looked in on the cranky black that Matters told him was in a plank-walled box stall. To show his impatience, the horse kicked the thick timber on the side of his box stall when Wulf came in to the barn to look at him.

Taming him would not be a Sunday school picnic — the black horse was not going to be a pushover. Wulf stood in the alleyway listening to the rain patter on the barn roof shingles. Nightmare was his old name — he'd call him Kentucky instead.

You got that, Kentucky?

TEN

Herschel left Cob at the livery and headed for the Palace Hotel. Three days hunched in the saddle and the cold weather had him stiff as a board. The short day's red sundown glistened in bloody light on the shoveled snow piles. He'd be glad when winter lost its grip on the north country. In March in Texas, spring would be busting out all over. Wild plums and peaches first, oat shoots growing a couple inches a day.

After he took a room, he went around the corner to a barbershop and bathhouse. He got a shave and bathed as well. It was dark when he set out for the café where he usually ate when in Sheridan. The wind whistled around every building, and he was grateful at last to be inside the busy eatery. Earlier at the livery, the hustler said no one with paint packhorses had stopped there in the past week.

Feeling fresher, in the café he went over

the other things he needed to do. Wire Art the outlaws' names for posters. Come daylight, he'd check on all of the other stables and the two wagon yards. No reason for the McCaffertys not to have come through Sheridan. Which way they went from there was the next question. Either south to Cheyenne or east to Deadwood. Somewhere where the lights were bright, by his calculations, and they could spend money. With that much treasure, they must be itching to blow it on raising hell someplace.

The hot meal was tasty, and he went by the police station afterward. The night man recognized him.

"You're the law from Billings," the desk man said and laughed. "We got any more killers here in town that ya looking for?"

Herschel shook his hand. "No, I'm looking for three men did a robbery in my county."

"Must have been a big one to bring you clear down here."

"It was. Three men, a father and two sons named McCafferty, tortured and robbed an old man a week ago. They headed south. They raped a woman running a stage stop at Dare on their way south."

"Real nice fellas."

"Yes, real nice. The old man they tortured may not walk again."

"So how may I help?"

"The only money they have to spend are gold Spanish coins. Rare, since they're old coins. If your policemen will ask around if any was spent, I might get a lead on where they went."

"Heavens, Sheriff, they leave here, they could go anywhere."

"Call me Herschel. They're rich enough. They'll either go to Deadwood or Cheyenne, maybe on to Denver after that."

"Ya don't know where they come from?"

"No. I only learned their names a day ago."

"My name's Taylor. If they're such high rollers, maybe I could let you have Patrolman Hines take you around to see the finer ladies. They might have stopped and paid their respects in one of our parlors."

"If he has the time."

"No problem, Herschel. Hines always got time for that. Checking them out."

So when the patrolman came by, he showed Herschel to the better parlors. The first one they entered reeked of perfume and another odor that must have been from human bodies, though Herschel couldn't be sure.

Madam Blue came down to speak to them. She was covered with caked makeup and rouge, had too many rings and pieces of jewelry, and wore a silk dress that rustled when she walked.

"Oh, Officer Hines, what brings you out?"

"We're looking for three men who may have passed through here with a pocketful of gold coins."

She threw a scarf around her neck and gave them a haughty look. "I should be so lucky. No men that I did not know have been in here in a week, and none who were here had gold in their pockets."

He tipped his hat to her and they left. The next stop was Madam DeGray's establishment, and the girls all acted anxious to accommodate either or both of them. They moaned when Hines said they were there only on official business.

The madam was younger than the last, with black hair and the dark eyes of a wolf, Herschel decided. She spoke in a smoky-sounding voice when Hines asked her about the men.

"Nooo. They did not stop here, or I'd've had a necklace made of the coins and be wearing it. What about you, tall and silent? You can have any or all of them." She indicated the half-dozen women seated on the couches. "Business is slow these days."

"We're busy," Hines said, and they left.

"Helluva looker, that DeGray, ain't she?" Hines asked when they were back out in the cold night air.

"Yes, she was," Herschel said, making small talk. Damn, he was lucky to have Marsha and his life up there in Montana. Maybe he'd get lucky and find those three soon and get to go back home to her and their warm bed. None of these women appealed to him even for a minute.

Two more houses of ill repute and they learned nothing. Back outside the last one, Hines shook his head. "I don't think they were in any of them."

"I think you're right. I appreciate your assistance. They had to come through here. They just didn't stop for long, I guess."

"One more place they might have stopped is out on Goose Creek. Kate Devero's."

"Who's she?" Herschel asked.

"Whore. Bootlegger. Horse thief. You name it. If they knew her or knew about her, they might have stopped out there and she put them up. Wouldn't be the first or the last outlaws she's hid out."

"I'll go see this Kate in the morning."

"I warn you, Herschel, they ain't nice folks. Go armed and with your pistol cocked."

"Thanks."

"Better yet, take some off-duty men with you. They won't charge you much and then you'd have your backside covered."

"If you think I'm in for it, I'll do that."

"She's tough, and so are the hard cases hanging around out there."

At nine the next morning, the desk man, Taylor, and another patrolman named Fogarty were on horseback and packing double-barrel shot guns as they met him at the livery as arranged. Cob acted spooky the first quarter mile, breathing great vapor clouds out his nostrils, but never bucked.

Kate's place was a large low-walled cabin, with weather-darkened sheds and some corrals. There were no paint horses in the pens when they rode by them.

Someone shouted, "Oh, gawdamn!"

Everyone in his small posse turned in time to see a bareheaded man in boots and red underwear with the flap down take off running for the snowy Bighorns.

"That's Mike Powell!" Taylor said, standing up in the stirrups. "Get him."

Fogarty charged his horse after Powell to cut him off before he reached the box elder brush. The race was short and the police-man came back herding the fugitive, who

118

was holding his hands on top of his head.

"Well, we've got all kinds of law out here today," a female voice called out. "Button up your flap, Powell, before you freeze it all off." Then the woman laughed and tossed her thick curly hair back as she stood in the doorway. Dressed in men's pants and yellow suspenders, she wore men's red underwear for a top that was unbuttoned enough to show her deep cleavage. A real attractive woman who stood close to five-ten. It was her tough voice that jarred Herschel after looking at her. He assumed this was Kate Devero.

"Come on in. There's just Powell and me here."

"Where in the hell did they come from?" Powell asked with a toss of his head, going past her.

"How should I know?" She looked peeved at him.

They all came inside and unbuttoned their coats to stand around her potbellied stove.

"Well, this ain't a Powell visit. What do you want?" she asked, standing shoulder to shoulder with them while Powell mumbled about his bad luck over being caught and got dressed.

"The McCafferty clan," Herschel said.

"When were they here and where did they go?"

She nodded like she'd expected his question. "I told that old bastard they'd track him down."

"Calvin?"

"Yeah, they called him Tally, but his real name was Calvin."

"Who called him Tally?"

"When he rode with the Whitten brothers down in Nebraska. I hadn't seen him in years. Figured he'd gone straight." She held out her long hands and rubbed them together in the radiant heat.

"How much did he make in the robbery that you are after him for?" Her brown eyes were hard as she looked for an answer under the longest dark lashes.

"Thirty thousand is a low estimate."

She stomped her foot and grimaced. "That lying sack of shit. He told me maybe two thousand."

Herschel had her talking and he didn't want her to quit. "Who told him about the gold?"

"He said he'd heard rumors for years how that old squaw man had a big sack full of gold Spanish coins. Finally ran him down up there. But he told me he'd only got that one buckskin sack. That no-good sumbitch

120

showed me how full it was. He poured about half out on that table over there."

"He show you the six trunks that those paint horses carried?"

"Hell, no." She looked peeved. "I know now that's why he made the youngest boy of his sleep with 'em at night."

"Where are they going next?"

"Why, Deadwood, of course. Why not? Hell, now I know why. He could buy the whole gawdamn place out — lock, stock, and barrel."

"He say where his place was in Nebraska?"

"How did you know about Nebraska?" She gave him a dark suspicious frown. "Oh, I told you about him riding with them Whitten brothers. It's somewhere south of the White River Reservation is all I know."

The stove's heat had begun to sting his face. Somewhere south of the White River Reservation. Somewhere north of Ogallala. That was a vast country.

He better get back to Sheridan and wire Art. He was still on their trail thanks to a tall brunette with the sharp tongue of a mule skinner and maybe — no, she *was* as tough as any man.

They called him Tally when he rode with those highwaymen down there.

ELEVEN

Wulf waited in the alley outside the café's rear exit. Dulchy had told him earlier she would be off work at four. Dark clouds rolled overhead, dimming the daylight and turning everything to shades of gray.

"How are you doing? Dey all said he sold your dog and horse to get even with you."

"He sure lied to everyone. Make up and forgive me, he said, too. Dulchy, I have to leave. I stay here, I'll kill him."

"Where will you go?"

"I have a cousin in Montana who's a sheriff. I am going up there to see him."

She glanced over at him with a concerned look. "Montana. That is very far away."

"I know — I won't hold you to coming up there."

Her back straightened and he saw the reaction coming. Hell, he'd said the wrong thing again.

"I said if you would have me, I would

come to join you."

"Dulchy. Dulchy, slow down. I would need to work for someone for years —"

She looked over at him. "I can work, too."

Man, was she ever hardheaded.

"Mr. Matters has given me his Kentucky-bred black horse. I'm going to need to break him in a week. Then I'll leave for up there."

"That horse is an outlaw, isn't he?"

"So am I."

With a disapproving shake of her head, she reached over and squeezed his arm for a second. "No, you aren't."

"May I come walk you home every day that I can get away from the horse?"

"No."

He wet his lips. What was wrong now?

"I will walk out there after work and watch you for a while. You will need all the time you have for him."

"Thanks, Dulchy. We better hurry. It's beginning to rain again."

At last on her aunt's front porch, they sat in the swing and held hands. Her gray-haired aunt stuck her head out the front door as if testing the air. "You two come inside. It's cold and wet out here. I have tea and pastry made."

His sodden hat in hand, he nodded.

"This is Wulf Baker, Aunt Frieda," Dulchy

said, introducing him.

"I am pleased to meet you, ma'am."

"So am I. You can call me Frieda, too." The woman's bright smile warmed him to the core.

After the tea and rich pastry, he swung by to see Matters, who answered the door. "Wulf, you're back?"

"Yes, sir. I have a request. Don't feed or water the black horse anymore, and may I use your round pen to train him?"

"Use anything I have here, son. Anything. We sure won't feed or water him another drop."

"Thanks. I won't hurt him, but I want him to know where his food and water come from."

"I thoroughly understand. Come inside. That wind's turning colder."

"No, sir, I have to get back to Andy's. I'll try not to bother you with my training."

"I'm going to love to watch."

"Some days might not be nice. Good night."

After supper, Wulf made some forked-stick bean flips. It was like a slingshot, except at close range much more accurate. He made several, while Myrna sewed him a pouch like a nail apron.

"And all this is going to do what?" Andy asked.

"Teach him to come to me."

Andy, seated across the table, examined one of the shooters. "Might make some girl in school jump if you hit her hard enough in the rump."

"Andy." His wife gave him a disapproving frown.

"You've seen that black horse, Myrna. He's a handful and tough."

"But didn't David slay the giant with a slingshot in the Bible?" Wulf asked.

"Killed him."

"I won't kill him, but he'll learn when I say, 'Here,' to put his head on my chest."

Andy sat back. "Wulf, I am not doubting this process. I just have to see it."

"Come by tomorrow in the afternoon. Mr. Matters has let me use his round pen to train him in."

"Well, bronc buster, don't get hurt is all I can say. You about through sewing, Myrna?"

"Yes, I have it made. There's your pouch." She put it on the table and smiled at Wulf. "I may come along, too, Andy."

Chewing on his lower lip, Wulf wondered if he had overloaded himself. It might take days to teach this crazy horse anything, or even longer. He blew out the light and went to bed.

Dawn was creeping through the clouds when he walked inside Matters's stable. The black horse was circling in the stall. Blowing fire out of his nostrils and snorting at Wulf's smell and presence. Wulf spoke softly to him and went to set the gates so his new horse could escape to the round pen with its high wall. Anytime a horse like this one thinks he can escape you, he will take that open route.

When everything was set, Wulf opened the reinforced stall door. Kentucky leaped out in to the aisle and saw the daylight. He tore out for the round pen. When he was galloping in circles inside the ring, Wulf managed to close the high gate and get to the center of the pen armed with a buggy whip.

A horse would run all day in a circle pen because he thinks that by running, he is getting away from a person. Wulf knew this from Sam Bellows, who showed him many things about breaking a horse. Lots of cowboy bronc busters scoffed at Bellows's ways, but they never owned a horse they'd trained and could ride without a bridle.

Wulf used the crack of the small whip to keep the big horse running. Turning with him, he watched the powerful muscles of this animal as he barely exerted himself. Kentucky had more strength than any horse he'd examined up close. If he could harness this horse's power into a usable form, he'd have one of the fastest horses in the country.

Then he took out the bean flip, drew back, and sent the bean hard into the running Kentucky's tender flank. "Here," he said.

The gelding responded by kicking both hind heels over his back and loping faster. Again and again, Wulf shot his beans at the horse's flank and said, "Here." Kentucky began to flinch at each strike, and found that kicking at his own belly did not help. In a short while, breathing hard, he stopped and started for Wulf. Dancing back and forth on his hind legs and pumping his head, he acted like he wanted to find the source. Then, with a defiant scream, he whirled and resumed his running around the wall.

Good. Wulf smiled. *You aren't stupid. You know I am the source.* "Here." He struck him again with a bean. Kentucky began to weary of the game and punishment, but Wulf made him keep running with the small whip. The horse's side toward Wulf was jerking each time Wulf said, "Here."

Two more stops and takeoffs and then, looking frustrated, he planted all four hooves and came forward cautiously. Wulf slipped him a cube of sugar, all the time talking softly as he put on the halter with care. Watching the horse's ears and eyes for the first sign of rebellion, he rubbed him carefully. All this big horse had to do was have a fit, and Wulf could be crippled for life. But Wulf never let that fear materialize in his mind, and hence his body didn't secrete any smells or signals for his horse to realize. Animals can sense it and they use that to their advantage. With the words of Sam in his ears, he stepped back.

"Now run free."

Shaking his head in the halter, Kentucky trotted off and, coaxed by the action of the whip, began to run again. Armed with his slingshot, Wulf said, "Here." Kentucky, head high and tossing the halter around, never stopped. Wulf reloaded and hit him again.

Stopped dead on his heels, Kentucky whirled and came to put his head on Wulf's chest.

"It's lunchtime, Wulf. My wife wants you to come and eat dinner with us," Matters said from a place high on the wall. "That is unbelievable."

"I'll need to put him back in the stall. I'm coming in a minute."

With the gates set, and using his arms to

herd the horse, Wulf got Kentucky back to his stall, and he closed the gate. At his water pail, Kentucky started pawing as if that would fill it. Wulf smiled to himself. The horse had to learn that, too. He had not earned that reward yet.

While he washed up on the porch, Mrs. Matters came out to greet him. "Ule told me you are doing so well with him."

"Thanks, ma'am. It was a good half day — so far."

"Do be careful. He's hurt people."

Drying his hands, he agreed with her. Most were probably hurt because the horse panicked rather than because of the horse's overall madness. After her wonderful meal of fried chicken, he thanked them both and resumed his lesson in the round pen until at the word "Here," Kentucky came in submission to put his head against Wulf's chest.

At last, when Kentucky was tired enough to stand hipshot, he permitted Wulf to rub him all over. With caution, of course, Wulf worked his hands all around. Watching Kentucky's ears for any sudden change in his disposition, he kept talking softly. By mid-afternoon, he was leading him on the run, and the horse acted like he enjoyed it.

Then Matters's Mexican handyman,

Paulo, set a bucket of water inside the gate for Kentucky. The older man looked over at the two, and before closing the gate, he made the sign of the cross for Wulf.

Wulf only let Kentucky drink half of the pail's contents. Then, with water streaming off his muzzle, Wulf led him away from the pail. Kentucky danced sideways and acted upset on the lead rope, but he was learning that the way to get water, and later feed, was from this new man. Even the hay he would eat had to come from Wulf's hands.

Letting him stand, Wulf took a break. Matters stood above the high wall and asked, "What's tomorrow's lesson?"

"I'll need a large tarp to lay him on. I'll borrow Andy's, and we'll lay him on his side and trim his hooves and make him feel helpless. Then, when I let him up, he'll know I have that much control over him."

"Can you lead him back to the stall?"

"We'll see." Wulf smiled at him.

"Get up here, young lady. I think the show is over for today," Matters said.

Wulf knew who he was talking to — Dulchy. She had come.

"How did it go?" she asked.

"We have a small understanding," he said.

"He's beautiful," she said, sounding impressed.

130

Wulf used his hand to shade his eyes from the sun. "He'll be prettier when I can ride him."

"You'll do that."

"Wait. I'll walk you home. I've done all I can do here today."

"I'll see you tomorrow," Matters said, and left them.

"Stay up there until he's in his stall. I don't trust him."

"Sure."

"Here," Wulf commanded, and Kentucky raised his head and spun around to walk over to him. With soft words, he coaxed the big horse until his head was against Wulf's chest. He rewarded him with a sugar cube. Then he turned and opened the gate. This would be a test. Never look back. That was one of Sam's rules. If Kentucky followed him, he'd won a great battle. If not, he'd have to start over in the morning.

The horse nickered and he knew that he was behind him. In the barn, Kentucky even used his nose to push Wulf faster. Impatient as Wulf knew Kentucky was, that did not shock him, and he kept talking in a low voice. Kentucky went into his stall, and Wulf gave him a bucket of water that he held so the horse would know he was the source. Then he went out and took an armful of hay and put it in the manger, petting Kentucky as he crunched on it and pawed with his front hoof.

"You're impatient, I know," he said, and satisfied they were bonding, he closed the stall door.

"He will make a wonderful horse for you."

Wulf couldn't contain himself a minute longer with Dulchy standing before him in the barn aisle. He gathered her in his arms and kissed her. Then they fell in and walked across town to her aunt's house, making small talk about her day and his.

"How long will it take you to get to Montana?" she asked, going through the yard gate.

"Weeks, maybe months. I've never been there before. I don't know what's up there."

"I will be patient then, though it will be hard."

"I agree — it will be hard. How long have you been in America?" he asked.

"Two years. My parents and I sailed from Ijmuiden, Holland, for New York. They both died at sea."

"Aw, Dulchy, I'm sorry."

She clutched his arm as they went up the porch steps. "We were going to farm here because my father's sister, my aunt, was here. My father had great plans. He was a hard worker."

They went and sat on the porch swing.

Wulf began, "I lost my father a year ago. It was best. He suffered a lot at the end. My mother and I ran the ranch until she married Kent Hughes."

"He is the one —"

"You two come inside," her aunt said from the doorway, and rubbed her sleeves. "I have hot tea and some pastry. It's getting cold out here."

"Coming," Wulf said, not wanting to miss out on her great pastry. "Yes, Dulchy, he's the one sold my horse and dog."

Her aunt was, as always, cheerful and her pastry mouth-watering. He even liked her English tea. After a short while, he excused himself and went back to Andy's.

Myrna had to know how the horse training went before Andy came in. From the look on his face when he entered the kitchen, Wulf knew he was upset.

"Did Matters give you a bill of sale for that horse?"

"No, why?"

"Hughes was boasting today in the Adobe Walls that that horse would now be his horse also since you are a minor."

"I'll go tell Mr. Matters to keep the ownership."

Andy shook his head in disappointment. "For your sake, I think it would be best. Hughes has sold one of your horses already."

"I'll be back, Myrna. You go ahead and eat." Wulf slapped on his hat and his canvas coat and headed for the Matters place in the growing darkness. The wind out of the north had caused the temperature to drop.

Matters's wife answered the door. "Something wrong?"

"I hope not, but I better speak to your husband."

After he explained his plight, Matters nodded. "He's my horse and you're training him for me."

"I'm sorry —"

"No, Hughes is the one that's sorry. Keep on. Ride away on him when you're through."

"Yes, sir."

"The Dutch girl is very pretty," Matters said, showing him to the door.

"Yes, Dulchy is a very nice person."

"She'd make a good partner."

"Maybe it will happen someday."

"It will if it is intended. I'll straighten Hughes out on the horse."

Walking back to Andy's, he thought hard about what Matters had said. *If it is intended.*

Twelve

Herschel and Cob headed south to catch the main road out of Buffalo, Wyoming, that went to Spearfish. He spent the night in a bunk in a Buffalo wagon yard, lying on his side half dressed against the cold room's lack of heat and going over all he'd done. Before he left Sheridan, he'd wired Art the names of the robbers and their possible destinations, and told him to tell Marsha where he was going so she'd understand. Being a sheriff's wife wasn't always the greatest thing in the world — but she would understand. At last, he fell asleep.

In the cold dawn, he dressed, saddled Cob, watered him, and then rode him to the only café with lights on. Inside were several teamsters and men in fur coats who looked like trappers.

"What have you got for breakfast?" Herschel asked the waiter.

"No eggs. They froze. Ham, fried potatoes,

biscuits and butter, and coffee."

"Sounds good." He knew this would be his last meal until night at the Powder River crossing.

"Where you headed, Tex?" A big man sat down uninvited across from him, wearing a buffalo coat and wide-brimmed hat. "I could tell where ya come from. It's that Southern drawl."

Herschel looked hard across the table at the man. "Where I come from, you don't ask a man where he comes and goes. That's his own damn business."

"Kinda tough, ain't you?"

"I ain't kinda. Now get the hell out of here before I gut-shoot you under this table."

The man's blue eyes flew open. He fell over in the chair getting up, and held both his hands out.

Several men around the room laughed as he ran out the front door.

"What did you tell him to make him move like that?" one man asked.

The waitress brought Herschel's coffee. "Good riddance," she said. "He thinks he's some kinda hard case."

When she was gone, Herschel answered the man's question. "I told him to go buy a pine box. He was fixing to need it."

More laughs.

After his big breakfast, the first spears of sunshine came over the eastern sky as he rode out of Buffalo. It was a land of low-growing sagebrush that gained altitude as the road wound eastward. Stark cotton-woods lined a few watercourses. There were plenty of antelope and mule deer and long-eared jackrabbits that went bounding away at his approach. He short-loped Cob, passing a few freight wagons going west, and at last went over the top in late afternoon and came off the mountain to the Powder River crossing. A wooden bridge spanned the sluggish-looking water between mostly frozen banks on each side.

Frazier's Wagon Yard offered food and lodging and stabling. He stopped there since the next stopover was another day's ride east. A stable man took Cob and promised to feed him a double measure of grain. Herschel gave him a dime tip. That would buy a schooner of beer at most places. The food was set up in the style of stage coach stopovers, with benches beside a long table.

A mammoth fat woman came out of the kitchen and looked across the room at him. "Antelope stew and corn bread. You want some?"

"Sure."

"Pick you out a place. I'll bring coffee, too."

"Thanks."

She squeezed back through the doorway into the kitchen like a huge bear going through a juniper thicket. The room was cold, but he removed his gloves and opened his heavy coat. He could see his breath when he talked. Must be a coal shortage. East of there, coal was lying on the ground for picking up.

She brought his food on a tray as she lumbered her way across the room toward him.

He thanked her. She must have wanted to talk or was out of breath. Instead of going back to the kitchen, she plopped down beside him on the bench, looking the other way.

"This is a gawdamn isolated place, mister."

He agreed, warming his fingers by curling them around the tin cup of coffee. The coffee wouldn't be too warm for long.

"When I come out here, they said this was the booming place in Wyoming. If this is booming, I'd hate to see the rest."

"When does the stage come through here?" he asked to make small talk. Her perfume and unwashed body odor filled his nose. She stank.

"Around seven, if he don't get held up or break down. Broke down last week. They had to go get the passengers in a buckboard. Like to froze 'em to death."

"Three men come through here with packhorses a few days ago?"

"Yeah, yeah. A tough fella with his sons. I knew the sumbitch from a place where I once worked north of Ogallala."

A hog ranch, he figured. Probably in her final days as a soiled dove. Ogallala was where all the outcasts of prostitution entertained fort soldiers mostly, black or white. It was the lowest place to work their trade and the best place to catch venereal disease he knew about. What he remembered about those kinds of places was that many of the women had lost their minds from smoking Chinese pipes or from disease.

"Tally McCafferty?"

"Yeah. The vigilantes or Wells Fargo hung them Whitten brothers he rode with over at South Platte."

"Wells Fargo hung them?"

"Listen, I knowed three other fellas who were planning to hold up a Wells Fargo shipment when they could find out when it was going east. They got loose-tongued one night in a saloon, and next day they found 'em facedown in a sand pile along the Platte. All shot in the back of the head."

"I couldn't ever figured why Tally never got the same medicine."

"A woman told me he went straight for a while. When was he here?"

"Oh, two days ago or so. I'd've gone straight, too, if I thought they'd hang me. Why do you want him?"

"He robbed a lot of money in my county in Montana."

"I figured you for a bloodhound. I know men. Well, when you catch him, tell him Dorrie said hi." Then she labored to her feet and shook her many chins. "He's just some old mean sumbitch is all."

"Thanks," Herschel said after her. Her antelope stew was stringy and flat-tasting, with potatoes and turnips as filler. But it did fill him up.

The westbound stage rolled in and five passengers came inside all bundled up. Dorrie began handing out food at the kitchen door. There was lots of small talk. The driver came in the door last with a shotgun guard. Herschel took his coffee cup and cornered the man.

"Excuse me, I'm sheriff in Yellowstone County. My name's Herschel Baker. Coming this way, did you pass three men with three paint packhorses?"

"Around Sundance," the guard said to the driver.

"We seen them close to there. They had five packhorses but, yes, three were paints."

"Thanks."

"What did they do?"

"They robbed a lot of money in my county."

The driver looked over at him. "You're one helluva lawman tracking them this far."

"Oh," Herschel said, "I'm not giving up on them if they ride to hell and back."

THIRTEEN

Andy accompanied Wulf the next morning, and they put a running W hitch on the black horse and gently laid him down on the tarp, which they had spread over the ground. Then, with soft cotton ropes, Wulf four-footed him. Kentucky fought his restraints for a while, tossing his head and acting fierce. But Wulf sat on his rump like it was a seat and patted him, ignoring his fits. He worked over every inch of the horse, sitting on his shoulders and patting him, rubbing everywhere until Kentucky lay there and took it — then Wulf went back over him again. Soon, the black horse surrendered, and then Wulf trimmed his hooves. Before he left Texas, he would shoe him, but that would be left for another day.

His hooves had been long neglected because of his disposition, and needed much shaping. It wasn't until Dulchy came and spoke to Wulf over the high wall that he realized it was time to water the horse and reward him.

Matters and his wife had gone to see a relative, and he'd not noticed lunchtime go by, he was so busy working on his prone horse. When he untied him, Kentucky came to his feet. No longer the crazy stall kicker, the horse was now nickering to Wulf.

"I'll still have to water and feed him," he warned Dulchy.

"Go do it. The Dutch pastries will wait."

Not for long, he hoped, realizing how hungry he was.

"Where are Mr. Matters and his wife today?" Dulchy asked.

"Went to see a relative. They will be back tomorrow."

"I wondered where he was at. He really enjoys watching you work."

"Yes. You hear any threats toward me today?"

"No, why?"

"My stepfather told someone in the saloon yesterday that he was stopping me from leaving on this horse. I came by to talk to Matters. He's now saying I am training it for him."

"Will that stop your stepfather?"

Wulf led the way, and the big horse followed him to the stall. "No, I don't think so, but at least we stopped that attack."

After watering Kentucky and feeding him an armful of hay, Wulf closed the stall door and bolted it. "Now, let's go eat that pastry."

What was wrong? They stood in the dark hallway face-to-face. Oh, he knew — and swept Dulchy up in his arms and kissed her. "Sorry I skipped lunch today."

She laughed and squeezed his arm. "See? You don't take care of yourself."

They left the barn, skipping hand in hand for her aunt's house. After the wonderful pastries, he left for Andy's place, feeling he was doing all he could to fight off Hughes's efforts against him. Wulf went to wondering what would happen next.

The following morning during breakfast at Andy's house, Paulo, the Matters' handyman, came to the back door with his hat in hand. "Señor Wulf. Señor Wulf. I found the horse's stall open this morning. Someone had released him or stolen him, Señor."

"Easy, Paulo," Wulf said, taking him inside the lamplit kitchen.

"How could that happen?" Andy stood up, frowning at them. "Come in, Paulo. Myrna, get him some coffee."

"No, no, I only come to tell you that his stall it is empty when I get to work."

"What did Ule say?" Andy asked.

"He is still not home, Señor. Señor Matters went to see his wife's cousin."

"I see."

Wulf paced the kitchen. "There is only one person I can suspect is behind all this — Kent Hughes."

"What do you mean?" Myrna asked.

"He couldn't claim the horse, so he stole him or had someone else steal him."

"We can't prove that right now," Andy said as Myrna served Paulo a cup of coffee. She also coaxed Wulf to sit down at the table.

"Wulf, sit down," she said. "Eat your breakfast. I believe you'll need all the energy you can find today."

"It'll be daylight in thirty minutes," Andy said, emphasizing his words with his fork. "Wulf, you go up there and look for his tracks. I'll go find Marshal Volker."

"I know I barred the gate last night," Wulf said.

"Señor, it was wide open this morning."

Wulf nodded. His stomach felt like a hard ball. He'd find that black horse or die trying. Damn the thieves anyway.

After breakfast, he hurried over to the Matters house, and in the shadowy early light saw the stall door gaping open. He went outside and studied the ground. There were tracks of other shod horses and Kentucky's freshly cut-down hooves. They went out the driveway and he found their trail. The thieves had led Kentucky out of there and ridden north.

Marshal Volker and Andy joined him. They agreed the horse had been taken and led away.

"What do we do now?" Wulf asked.

"I can send word to other law authorities," the marshal said. "The only deputies the sheriff has couldn't track themselves across an anthill."

"Andy, where can I borrow a horse?" Wulf asked.

"Jerome Kane. He's an old friend of your father and has several. I'm sure he'd loan you one."

"I'm going up there and borrow one. Then I'll go home and put on real clothes and go find whoever took them."

"They could be real hard cases, stealing a man's horse out of his barn," Volker said.

Wulf nodded. He had his father's .45. He'd wear it. He'd have to go by and leave word for Dulchy. Maybe Myrna would do that for him. Wasted minutes meant more miles and more distance between him and those rustlers.

Jerome Kane came to the door tousle-headed and barely awake when Wulf knocked on his door. "What you need, Wulf?"

"To borrow a saddle horse. Someone stole Mr. Matters's black horse last night and I'm going to try to track them down."

"Stole him? Why, lordy, that wild thing may eat them before they're done with him. You been training him?"

"Yes, sir. That's probably why they could steal him."

"Let me pull on my boots. There's a gray horse I call Goose that's long-winded. He'd be the best one. Just don't go getting yourself kilt over this horse. They could be tough rannies that stole him."

When Kane's boots were on, they went to the corral. Wulf saw the gray. A fine long-backed horse.

"What's he worth?" Wulf asked when Jerome opened the gate.

"Thought I was loaning him to you." He took a reata off the fence and shook out a loop.

"You are, but if something happens, I'll pay you for him."

"Son, as much hell as you've had with that worthless Hughes, I'd scratch that debt off my books."

Wulf wasn't going to argue. "Thanks. Someday I'll repay you."

"You can come up here and train horses for me any time."

He threw the loop over the gray's neck. "Get that bridle on the fence, you can use it. I got an old saddle —"

"No, sir. I have Dad's good one."

"Fine. You bring it?"

"No. But I can ride bareback."

"You better grab you a hank of mane. Goose ain't been rode in a spell and he might buck."

"I'll be all right."

Goose did crow-hop several times going away from Jerome's lot. Wulf could hear Jerome's rusty voice. "I warned you. I warned you."

But the pony soon straightened out, and Wulf waved at Jerome as he short-loped for Andy's. Back at the house, he put on the too big pants and shirt. Hooking up the suspenders, he tied on the silk kerchief, then the vest. Seated on the cot, he brushed off his soles one at a time, pulled on socks, and then fought on his father's boots. Standing up in them, he felt tilted forward on the high heels. They'd take some getting used to. Then he strapped on the holster and gun, and picked up the heavy Stetson hat and placed it on his head.

"My, you look very nice," Myrna said

when he went in to the kitchen.

"I need another favor."

"What's that?" She dried her hands on a dish towel.

"Go by and tell Dulchy for me what I had to do."

"Oh, I'm sure she'll understand. I'll change and go do that."

"Thanks. I used to have a mother. I guess you're it now. Thanks, Myrna."

"Oh, your mother will return to her senses in time."

He never answered her about that. "I need to go saddle the horse Jerome loaned me and go now."

"Sorry for the flour sack, but here's some biscuits, some cookies, and some hard-boiled eggs. You be careful."

"I will. And thanks."

Those thieves had a good head start. When Goose was saddled, Wulf tied on his bedroll with his canvas coat inside. At last, he threw his leg over, adjusted the Colt on his hip, and waved to Myrna. When he went by the Matters place to pick up the tracks, he noticed their buggy was not back yet. Matters would be upset when he returned and learned the black had been stolen.

At the first crossroads store that Wulf stopped at, a balding man in an apron was out sweeping the porch. He looked up and smiled at Wulf.

"Morning, mister. I'm looking for two men leading a black horse."

"I seed 'em. Rode by here about sunup. Watered over there at that trough. Looked around like they had an itch and rode off."

"Had an itch?" Wulf frowned at the man.

"I meant, they acted like their necks itched thinking about a hemp rope around them."

"Can you describe them?"

"One was tall and one was short. The short one had a bob haircut like a woman. He weren't no woman. Tall one had a big mustache. Kinda bent over like a lot of tall folks get trying to hear what the rest of us are talking about."

"Know their names?"

"Short one called the tall one Kinney when they was over there. That black horse was upset. He was wet with sweat and you could tell they didn't trust him."

"That's my horse and I was breaking him."

"How old are you anyway?"

"Nineteen," he lied.

"Well, don't go and get yourself killed over a damn horse."

"I am obliged." Wulf led Goose across the

street and watered him at the tank. When the horse was through drinking, he loped him on north. They'd probably make Brady by dark. Best place to sell a stolen horse was Fort Worth. It was a ways on northeast, but they were started in that direction anyhow. This part of the hill country was all new to him.

Next, he stopped a man on the road driving a buggy. He was bearded and somber looking as he sat in the rig.

"Good day, sir. I'm looking for two horse thieves leading my black horse. You pass them on this road?"

"They're up the road a ways. Saw them —" He used his hand to shade his eyes and checked the sun time. "Maybe two or three hours ago."

"Thank you, sir." Wulf tipped his hat to the man.

"No problem. I hope you catch 'em."

"I will, sir."

By late afternoon, he was in Brady. A check of the liveries and wagon yard brought no sign of the two men or of Kentucky. The tracks in the dust had become too hard to follow. He had to rely on visual sightings.

An old man, seated on a porch stoop whittling, looked up when Wulf pushed Goose in closer.

"You ain't seen two fellas leading a black horse through town, have you?"

The old man went back to his whittling. "I seen lots of horses go by today."

"Two men. One's tall. One's short, got long blond hair."

"Real tall?"

"Yes, sir, his name is Kinney."

"No, it ain't, if we're talking 'bout the same worthless sumbitch. His name is McKinney. Oral McKinney, and that other little twist is called the Culpepper Kid." The old man spit in the dust between his run-over boots. Wiped his mouth on the back of his sun-spotted hands. "Now they wouldn't hang around town much, but they might be hid out at Mrs. Clary's place."

"Where's that at?"

"Oh, she's got a place east of here about three miles. It'll be on the left. Two-story house right on the road. You can't miss it." The old man spit again and then looked up. "Don't tell your mom you've been out there." Then he laughed. "I hope you get your horse back."

"He's out there, I'll get him."

At sundown, he located the house of ill repute. If that's what it was. With all the horses standing hipshot at the rack, plus the tinny piano music drifting out the open doors and windows, as well as the women dressed in their underwear flouncing in and out of the house kissing and rubbing on cowboys on the porch — he figured he'd found Mrs. Clary's place.

Riding up easy, he looked over the horses at the hitch rack. Kentucky wasn't there. Then he heard a familiar nicker, and rode past the house up under the tall oaks to the corral. There, going back and forth up and down along the fence, was Kentucky.

He hitched his six-gun around and dismounted. Goose was trained to be ground-tied, so Wulf dropped the reins. Letting himself in the corral, he said, "Here."

The big horse whirled and came to him, laying his head on Wulf's chest. Wulf found a cookie in his vest pocket and fed it to him.

"Interested in that horse, cowboy?" a short man on the outside asked, standing aside in the twilight.

"I could be."

"He's cheap. Fifty bucks, and he's a racing horse."

Wulf left Kentucky and went out the gate. Even if the man had seen him before, he'd never seen him dressed like this. Still, every nerve in his body tingled, and he wondered how fast he could draw down on this fella.

"Yeah, helluva horse. Too much to handle

for the last owner. You look like you get along good."

"We should. He's my horse."

The kid gave out a loud "Huh?" His hand went for his gun.

Wulf went for his own.

FOURTEEN

Two cold days later, Herschel rode into Sundance. Dark ominous clouds were spitting snow, and they looked like they'd only begun. He found that the wagon yard was a complete operation — stables, hotel, and café. It also served as the stage stop. After he stabled Cob, he went and took a bath.

He felt disappointed that the man who handled the stable had not seen the McCafferty clan or anyone with three paint horses in tow. When he finished shaving and was walking down the hall, he looked out the window he went past. In the twilight, the snow was falling in big flakes the size of goose feathers. Had the robbers doubled back or cut south on him?

Times like these, he'd've given a lot to have been home with Marsha and the girls. Popping popcorn in the fireplace, playing his harmonica for them to dance to. Instead, he was going to share a bunkroom with some grunting grizzly bears who could fart as loud as they snored. The girl in her teens took his order for supper. A fresh-cut elk steak, large-size portion, and mashed potatoes and sweet corn. She also promised him bread pudding for dessert.

He was sitting alone when a man in a business suit asked if he could join him. Herschel told him yes, and motioned to the chair opposite him.

"Randolph Cunningham." The man put his bowler hat on the chair beside him. "New York City is where I am from."

"Herschel Baker, Billings, Montana."

"You are a long ways from home, too. But you have a drawl."

"I was born and raised in Texas."

"Ah-ha. My ears have not deceived me. Good to meet you, sir." Cunningham shook out his cloth napkin. Without a look at the menu, he told the girl, "The same thing he's having." Then he turned back to Herschel.

"I could ask why a man from New York is in Sundance, Wyoming," Herschel said.

"Coal. I understand west of here there are vast deposits of fine-burning coal."

"I guess the only thing that keeps it in the ground is that there is not a railroad to pack it out."

"Exactly. But the rails will come. Investing in coal-bearing acreage now, before the iron rails get here, might be a good way to increase my wealth."

Herschel agreed with a smile.

"That answers your question," said Cunningham. "What does a transplanted Texan do in Montana?"

"We have a ranch up there, my wife Marsha and I. I'm also the sheriff of Yellowstone County."

Cunningham leaned back as if to appraise him. "And you are not down here on vacation?"

"No. A man was tortured and robbed of a large fortune by three men. I am on their trail."

"My, my. How far are you from home?"

"Doesn't matter. That old man may never walk again, they burned his feet so badly."

"You take your job very seriously."

Their food arrived. Herschel nodded. Maybe he took it too seriously at times.

"You say it is lots of money they stole."

"Upwards of thirty thousand dollars."

"They did make a big haul. How did some old man in Montana ever acquire that much money?"

"Dug up some Spanish treasure."

"Ah, gold doubloons, huh?"

"Exactly, and lots of them."

"Here we are in this rather unique way station. Me looking for a quarter million dollars in coal land, and you looking for thirty thousand in treasure." He raised a bite of his steak on his fork. "It is rather tasty meat."

"I like good elk."

"How close are you to the felons?"

"Not far."

Cunningham used the napkin to wipe his mouth. Then, looking taken aback, he asked, "They staying here?"

"No, but I think they are in this area."

He swallowed hard and nodded across at Herschel. "Be sure to advise me when they get close. I want to duck and hide."

After his meal, Herschel parted with Cunningham and decided to check out some of the bars and try for more information. Bundled up for the weather, he left the wagon yard. The snow was already at the tops of his boots in the street when he mushed over to O'Malley's Saloon. It was going to be a real snow. Still falling by the inches each hour. He stomped his boots off on the porch of the saloon, and found the doorknob loose when he tried to turn it. At last, it engaged and opened.

"Come in, stranger," the red-faced bartender shouted at him.

"Thanks." He beat his hat against his leg to remove the snow, put it back on before he took off his gloves and unbuttoned his coat.

"What'll it be, sir?"

"Glass of beer."

"Coming up."

Waiting for his beer, he turned, and could see several men in the smoky atmosphere of the place. Card games at some tables, serious drinkers at others, they all paid him little heed. He was looking for a scar-faced man. A big man.

"What brings ya to Sundance, sir?" the Irishman asked, delivering his beer.

"You know Tally McCafferty?"

The bartender looked all around and then lowered his voice. "Aye, I know him. He was in here yesterday, but you'll not get him to help you." The man dropped his voice more. "He hit a rich vein and said he ain't doing no more road-agent work."

"He's gone, huh?"

"Spearfish or Deadwood. Him and his boys going to celebrate a little before they ride home."

Herschel nodded.

"You must a rode with the Whittens, huh?"

Herschel nodded. "Guess he's still on that place south of the reservation."

"Yeah, in Nebraska. Shame you missed him. He left this morning."

With that knowledge, he paid for his beer and went back to the wagon yard. He found Cunningham in the lobby reading a newspaper.

"Any luck?" the man dropped his paper to ask.

"They left this morning."

"You are close. Good luck."

"Same to you."

Herschel turned in for the night. He didn't sleep well, and before dawn he was dressed and out looking the situation over. He'd better wait a day. The sun might evaporate and melt enough of the snow to make it easier on Cob. He went back inside and had breakfast.

If the McCaffertys didn't stop in Deadwood or Spearfish, he'd head home, take public transportation to Ogallala, and ride north from there to find them. That country south of the Black Hills was as desolate as any place he knew.

At dawn the next day after breakfast, he started east. The day dragged by and the sun's progress disappointed him. The stage had trampled out some of the snow and the going wasn't bad, except he had to get off the road for wagons and let them pass. He was a day and a half getting to Spearfish. After lots of inquiring, he decided the robbers hadn't stopped there but had gone on to Deadwood.

He found Deadwood was all slush and mud. Folks went from one side of Main Street to the other crossing on boards. He put Cob up in a livery near the base of the hill. No one there he spoke to had noticed any paint packhorses. He began going to the various saloons and gambling halls that lined Main. In the smoke-hazed interiors lit by candles, and a few by kerosene, it would have been hard to recognize anyone.

But he was looking and listening for any lead he could find. It was behind Mc-Combs's Livery on the back street where he noticed two big horses with packsaddle marks on them. Then he found the paints covered with dried-on mud. No one would have recognized them. Standing on the pole corral to better view them, he twisted around. Where were the robbers? Good question. With the thousands crowding up in that gulch called Main, they could be anywhere.

"Them Tally McCafferty's horse stock?" he asked the man who was supervising the hostlers.

"I got it down as Calvin McCafferty."

"Same gent. Where's he staying? I've got something for him."

"Kate Malloy's. What'cha got?" The man narrowed his eyes suspiciously.

"I can't tell you. It's a surprise for him."

"This whole gawdamn world's full of surprises."

Herschel agreed, thanked him, and headed back for Main Street. Malloy's house of ill repute was on Main over the Texas Saloon.

A buxom woman wearing only a chemise and a short slip blocked the doorway at the head of the stairs. "Can't you read, you dumb son of a bitch? The sign down there said closed for a private party."

"I'm part of it," he said, and kept climbing.

"What's your name?"

"Colt. See the one in my fist?"

She sucked in her breath and screamed at the top of her lungs. "Stop him!"

"Stand aside!" Herschel ordered. "And shut up."

A bullet crashed into the door facing beside him, and he took her down to save her from being shot. Pinning her facedown with one hand and with his gun in the other, he tried to see the fleeing men going out the open back door.

He took aim and shot at the last one. The

162

man faltered and went down.

"Who are you?" she asked through her teeth, still pressed to the floor facedown underneath him.

"Deputy U.S. Marshal Herschel Baker."

"You just ruined one helluva party we were having here."

"Lady, I could care less than you can imagine."

"What's going on up here?" a tall patrolman demanded, clambering up the stairs.

"We have a man shot up here and needs a doctor immediately."

"Who in the hell're you?"

"Deputy U.S. Marshal Baker."

The officer shook his head. Then he turned to the stairs to shout for someone down there to go find the doc. Some of the girls had the kid braced up against the wall when the two of them got back there. The front of his shirt was turning red with his blood. No telling where the bullet went in.

"August?" Herschel asked.

"Who the hell — 're you?"

"The man that's been looking high and low for you. Buffalo Malone sent you his best wishes." Herschel looked up. Three scantily dressed girls were picking up scattered gold coins off the floor. "Put 'em all on the bed. That's evidence, girls."

"Aw!"

"Watch that money they're picking up," Herschel said to the lawman. "Those other two are getting away."

"Don't you run, mister. There will be a hearing over this."

"I said I was a deputy U.S. marshal."

"Don't mean shit to me."

"I'll be here. Right now I want to catch them." Reloading his .45 Colt, he rumbled down the stairs. They must be packing and saddling in a hurry at that livery.

On the muddy street below, he crossed to the far side and edged down the side of the building. When he snuck a peek, someone clipped off chucks of red brick with a rifle.

He could hear an impatient man shouting orders. ". . . keep him pinned down, there'll be more."

Using his hat on his gun barrel, he drew their fire. Then he quickly dropped the hat and took three shots at the entrance to the livery. Picking up his hat, he knew from the sounds that they were riding out the back way.

One option he had was to run downhill, cross the bridge, and try to head them off. He took it, running as hard as he could. They tore by going south, and he decided to down a packhorse. It was not the best thought, but he shot the last paint pack-horse and it skidded down. The two outlaws looked back in shock, still beating their horses and the two big horses, still loaded, along with the two paints.

They were soon gone up the canyon. Herschel stood in the warming sunshine and reloaded. He used another bullet to put the pony down. The horse had been expend-able. He'd cut the McCaffertys' take by a third and had Malone's retirement fund.

"Why did you shoot the horse?" someone asked.

" 'Cause he couldn't hit a bull in de ass," someone else teased.

Herschel looked the crowd over. "I want to hire four stout men to carry these two trunks uphill to the Miner's Bank." He had one free chest and could barely move it.

Volunteers stepped out, and he picked four. "We have to get the dead horse off the other trunk."

"Must be valuable stuff," an onlooker said.

"Yeah, real valuable."

"Stand aside. Stand aside," two lawmen ordered, coming through the crowd. "What's the meaning of this?"

"Deputy U.S. Marshal Herschel Baker. The rest of the McCafferty gang just left. You just missed them."

Someone was pulling on his sleeve. Herschel turned to look down at a short wrinkled-faced Indian woman who motioned toward the dead horse. "You going to eat it?"

"No."

"Can I butcher it?"

"Sure," Herschel said.

"Only if you get all of it off the street, old woman," the policeman said. "I don't want no guts, bones, nothing left here."

The woman agreed, and several Indian men came forward and helped them turn the horse over. The trunks were soon undone from the packsaddle, and the men's faces took on a shocked look over the weight of them.

"What's in them anyway?" the other lawman asked Herschel.

"Spanish gold."

"Huh?"

"Take them right up the hill," Herschel said. "I'm putting them in the bank."

"Hold it. I'm writing you a summons for discharging a firearm in the city."

Herschel showed his small federal badge. "I'll be at the Miner's Bank if you want me."

The other patrolman nodded that it would be all right, and Herschel told the men bearing the trunks to proceed.

Inside the high-ceiling lobby, a teller asked from his cage what they could do for Herschel and the man.

"Have the president or the highest man here come out." He turned to the men. "Set them down."

"Er, yes, sir," said the teller.

A tall man with a thick white mustache and an expensive suit came out of an office. "What may I do for you, sir?"

"I have two trunks full of Spanish gold doubloons I wish you to hold for me until I can make arrangements to ship them back to Montana." Anger and disappointment gnawed at his conscience as he waited for the man's answer. The other two were getting away.

"Have they been inventoried?" the man finally asked, waving the four men to bring the trunks in to his office.

"Not since they came off the boat," Herschel said.

The man laughed. "My name is Bridges. Come into my office."

"U.S. Marshal Baker."

"Pleased to meet you, sir. Tell me how these trunks fell into your hands."

"I shot one of their packhorses down the hill as the outlaws were escaping from me."

"My heavens —"

"Excuse me," Herschel said, and paid the men from the street five dollars apiece and received their gratitude.

"Call on us when you need us again," the tallest one said as they left waving and talking about their generous pay.

Herschel closed the office door after them and turned back to Bridges. "This is only one third of the treasure they stole. But this will let an old man live his life out in peace."

Bridges took off his coat and began unstrapping the first trunk. When he lifted the lid, he sucked in his breath, staring at the money. "My God, man, there is a fortune in this one."

Herschel nodded his head. "That's why I'm in here and not down in that street where a half dozen Indian loafers are slaughtering that pony."

"Do you want it inventoried?"

"Is it necessary? I want Wells Fargo to deliver it to Billings, Montana."

"I don't blame you. That would be a long way to pack that much treasure. They will want it inventoried so no one can say that they lost any of it in transit, understand?"

"Fine, then inventory it."

An assistant walked in. "Mr. Bridges. There is a city policeman here wants to see Marshal Baker."

Bridges looked to Herschel for his approval. At last, he said, "Invite him in."

It was the same man that was first one upstairs after his shot.

"This is Assistant Police Chief Woodward Hogan," Bridges said.

"We met a while ago."

Hogan hefted a heavy pillowcase partially full of coins on the counter. "We got most of them." Then his eyes flickered in disbelief at the sight of the open chests. "Good God Almighty, man. Why, there's a fortune in them."

"You didn't do bad yourself," Herschel said, looking inside the pillowcase.

"Where does it all go?" Hogan asked.

"Billings, Montana, to the rightful owner. How many men on your force?"

"Ah, ten as well as me and the chief."

"Come back tomorrow and check with Mr. Bridges. I'll authorize him to pay every man on the force a hundred dollars each. You and the chief get two hundred apiece."

"That would be most generous."

"Buffalo Malone, the owner, will be even more pleased to have this much of his fortune back."

"Are you going after them?"

Herschel shook his head. "I know where

to find them. I'll get the rest of them in due time."

FIFTEEN

The gun in Wulf's fist spewed flame, gun smoke, and death. The man jerked himself upright, obviously hard hit, then tried to recover his aim. Wulf shot him again at point-blank range, and then dropped to his knee to try and see in the twilight where the man's tall partner was.

There were women screaming like murder in the house. Men cussing, and then the sounds of a horse from out front fleeing off into the night. Wulf realized, listening to the drum of hooves, that that damn Oral McKinney had gotten away.

A woman wearing a house robe and carrying a lamp came from the house. "Is he dead?"

"I don't know, ma'am." He punched the empties out in his hand and reloaded. As far as he was concerned, the dead man had caused his own demise and he'd shed no tears for him.

171

"Who did that gawdamn Kid shoot this time?" a man shouted from the house.

She rose slowly. "You know who he was?" she asked Wulf.

"A damn horse thief. I'll be getting my black horse from the pen and riding out of here."

"You've shot the Culpepper Kid."

"Who'd he shoot?" the man asked, hurrying down there to join them.

"What's your name?" she asked, looking in shock at Wulf.

"Wulf Baker."

She shook her head as if to free it of something when the half-dressed man without a shirt caught her by the arm and demanded, "Who is he?"

"His name's Wulf Baker and he just killed the Culpepper Kid."

"You come looking for me, too?" Wulf asked sharply.

The man threw his hands up and then spread them out in a defensive way. "Don't shoot me, mister. Anyone fast enough to shoot the Kid I won't mess with. Besides, I'm not armed.

"What's he want?" the man asked the woman.

"The damn black horse the Kid stole, I guess."

172

"You're the animal trainer, ain't you?" the man said at his discovery. "The one sold the Injun pony and dog to the Colonel, ain't cha?"

"My stepfather sold those to the Colonel. Not me." With that said, he holstered the .45, took a lead rope, and went in the pen to catch Kentucky. Speaking to him all the time, he soon led him out, mounted Goose, and started south. Any minute expecting hot lead or a knife in his back until he was far beyond seeing the lights of Kate Molloy's place.

He rode into the night, slept a few hours beside the road in a meadow, and then pushed on toward Mason. The only thing he couldn't solve was how to find out who'd put the thieves up to stealing the black horse. The answer to that mystery could only come from the Kid's partner, Oral McKinney, and he'd left with his tail feathers on fire.

The man at the crossroads store came out with his broom when Wulf stopped to water his horses. "See you got him back all right."

Wulf nodded. "He's fine."

"What about the rustlers?"

"The short one's dead, the other one run off."

Acting busy sweeping, the man said,

"Yeah, but you got your horse back. People who ain't been paying you respect will start from now on. You showed 'em."

"I guess so. See you." He left the man leaning on the broom that he'd soon wear out.

At midday, he arrived at the Matters place and the man came outside. "Oh, thank heavens, Wulf. You are all right. Go after a stolen horse and bring him back. That's amazing. I'm sorry that it even happened."

Wulf dropped heavily off Goose and started for the barn. "He hadn't forgot a thing I taught him."

"What about the rustlers?"

"One's dead. One ran off."

"Damn shame, Wulf, that you had to do that."

"No. It's not, Mr. Matters. I know now when people are ready to kill you, you have to do something or die."

"If I may ask, who was he?"

"Called himself the Culpepper Kid."

Matters looked taken aback by the information. Then he nodded. "I'm glad you have your horse. Tomorrow you can start back training him."

"I'll be here, sir. Tell poor Paulo thanks, too. He got us on the move in time."

"He's a good old man. I'll tell him."

Wulf put Kentucky in his stall and then took Goose back to Jerome's house. The man came outside, scratching his belly. "You get your horse back?"

"Yes, sir."

Jerome put his hand on Wulf's shoulder as he started to uncinch the rig. "I been thinking it over ever since you took him. You might need him. Two good hosses are always better than one. You're going to Montana. That's a long ways. A real long ways. You know, your daddy and I fought them Injuns around here together. I owed him that horse and I'm giving him to you."

"To train him, tell everyone. I don't want Hughes selling Goose out from under me."

Jerome scratched his thin hair on top of his head. "I savvy that. Tell me what happened up there getting him back."

Wulf squatted down, realizing for the first time in days that he was wearing his father's boots. He'd been so busy getting Kentucky back that he'd never noticed much except that a Colt needed to be shifted a lot to wear it. He even did that without thinking much about it.

"Well, I trailed them north out of here." He wound it up with the Kid dead and him headed home.

"I'm proud you have Goose. Tell Herschel

Baker when you get up there, I wish him the best. Must run in the family. When we were growing up, your cousin was the toughest bronc rider I ever knew. His brother, Tom, was just as good. Those boys could have rode a snake to town. Must be in your veins."

"I hope so."

"Send us some word how you're doing. We'd all like to hear."

"I will, sir."

"You better get along. That Dulchy'll be getting off work soon." Jerome gave him a big broad smile and a clap on the shoulder. "If you wasn't going with her, why, I might even ask her out."

Wulf suppressed his laugh and redid the cinch. Then he vaulted in the saddle, thanked him again, and rode off on his big gray to see about Dulchy. From in front of the café, he could see her going down the side of the street a half block away, headed home. He sent Goose up to within a few feet behind her, shut him down, and swung off on to the ground.

"Who —" Her arms open, she flew to him. He caught her and swung her around in the air.

"You're all right? You're all right."

"I'm fine. See my new horse? And my old

one is back in his stall."

"How wonderful. I was so worried when Myrna came and told me where you had gone. But she said for me to have faith in you. I did."

"Let's not talk about it. How is your aunt?"

"Oh, she is fine, but I bet she doesn't have any pastry made."

"Oh."

"She didn't know that her favorite suitor was coming by. How did you get this wonderful horse?"

"Jerome Kane loaned him to me. Then he said I'd need two horses to get to Montana." They walked side by side with Goose trailing them to her aunt's house. Wulf made him stay out of the yard, and closed the gate.

"Oh, you come back," her aunt said, and rushed out to hug him. Then she took him by the hand back into the house. "Come in. Come in. I am so glad you are all right. I have a hot apple pie I just made."

Wulf could smell the cinnamon and laughed. Dulchy was embarrassed by her aunt, and he tried to signal to her it was all right. Not many folks besides her aunt were that nice to him.

That night at Andy's kitchen table, he wrote a letter to Herschel Baker.

Dear Herschel,

My name is Wulf Baker. I am the son of Lonnie Baker. Lonnie died a year ago.

My mother, Jenny Baker, remarried a man named Kent Hughes. I don't expect you to remember me. I was a kid when you left this country, but my dad always spoke highly of you and your late brother, Tom. Your sister, Susie told me what you were doing. I decided I needed to see Montana, so I will be calling on you up there.

> Sincerely yours,
> Wulf Baker

He handed it to Myrna to read. "I guess that's the best I can do."

Under the lamplight she read it, then looked up. "I think he'll be glad to see you. Nice job."

He addressed the envelope, dipping the straight pen in the inkwell, to Sheriff Herschel Baker, Billings, Montana.

"I'll get this mailed and my things ready. I better head that way before Hughes figures out something else."

Myrna stood up and hugged his head to her apron front. "Oh, be careful. It is a long ways to Montana and I will worry about you. You know you are like my son."

"I know. I know."

He felt the emptiness inside as if his own mother had died. It was that damn wall that Hughes had built between them. He had no answer to how to tear it down and go back to before. No way. Lucky he had Myrna, Andy, Dulchy, and her Aunt Frieda.

He could be all alone.

SIXTEEN

Herschel wired Billings to tell Marsha that in a few days he'd be heading home. His prisoner, August McCafferty, was improving from his gunshot wound, and as soon as he could travel, Herschel would be taking him back via public transportation for trial. Since Herschel had recovered two of the six trunks, he also wired to tell Malone he was having Wells Fargo deliver the two trunks to the First Bank of Montana in Billings. Another wire to the bank to have them prepared to receive the trunks since they might beat him home.

On purpose, he neglected to say in his dispatch that according to Bridges's bank inventory, there was over thirty-three thousand dollars in each of the two trunks. That was way too much temptation for anyone that might be listening along the singing wires.

The day was sunny when he walked out

of the telegraph office and stood on the boardwalk and looked at the street. It had gone from mushy to mud. The teams coming up Main were only hock-deep fighting the grade and poor footing. Maybe spring was coming to Deadwood. He was ready for some relief.

"What are ya doing, Baker?" It was Deadwood's Assistant Chief of Police Woodward Hogan.

Herschel shrugged. "Watching the girls go by, I guess." Referring to all the brightly dressed doves coming in small flocks up the far boardwalk.

"Give me a few minutes of your time. Last night, a married woman of not too good a reputation was murdered in a hotel room. Her lover said he left her alive and I kinda believe him — but I ain't sure."

"Anyone else been in the room since they discovered her body?"

"I locked it and told them to keep the hell out."

"How was she murdered? I mean, what killed her?"

"She was stabbed in the heart, the doc thought, by a stiletto. The person stuck it between her ribs and into her heart."

"That either was lucky or done by a professional. To do that is not what you'd expect from your average killer in a rage. In a rage, he would have stabbed her two-handed in the chest."

"That knife, of course, was not up there." Hogan smiled. "I wasn't sure about anything in this case, but you just brought up something never entered my mind. It could have been a planned thing."

They strode into the lobby of the Killian Hotel. The clerk looked up.

"Oh, Hogan. Her husband came by and I let him have her small valise."

"You did what?"

"He said all he wanted were her private things. I felt sorry for him."

"How long ago?" Hogan asked.

"Oh, thirty minutes. He was on his break from the Four Deuces, where he deals."

Hogan turned to Herschel. "What do you think?"

"You look through her bag?"

"To be honest, no. I didn't see how it could help me anyway." Hogan shrugged. "I may have been wrong."

"We better go see about why her husband would have needed it."

"His name is Norman Felts. A dealer. We have no charges on him. He and her came here from Denver. His late wife, Marie, was a looker. Might have been a high-priced dove in her past. He dealt the house cards while she laid on her back with men who were, shall I say, well to do."

Things were in a midday slump when they walked in to the Four Deuces. A man with gray temples stood behind an empty table.

"Did — did you find her killer?" the man asked.

"No," Hogan said. "I'm sorry."

Herschel squatted down and lifted the felt cloth to see better underneath the table. He reached in and dragged the drawstring bag toward him.

"Some woman left her purse under there," Herschel said.

Looking a little shocked and also uncomfortable, the man spoke out sharply. "It belonged to my wife. Give it back to me."

Herschel shook his head and watched him for his reactions. "Heavy as it is, it may have a weapon inside of it."

Then he spilled the contents on the gaming table, and the last thing to fall out was a thin long-bladed knife. He'd hidden the murder weapon in her purse, of all places, and they'd have probably missed it if Felts hadn't gone back for it.

"Hogan, there is your murder weapon." Herschel looked the killer square in the eyes. "Why did you kill her?"

"That cheating bitch was holding out money on me."

"What for? To run away from you?"

"The bitch —"

Hogan stepped in with his handcuffs. "I am arresting you, Felts, for the murder of your wife, Marie. Baker, don't leave too quick. I can use your help around here more often."

Herschel laughed, picking up the contents and replacing them in the bag. "My wife would kill me if I don't get back to Montana."

Lord, he'd be glad to be back home — eating her cooking and listening to his stepdaughters. It would sure beat the tinny sound of pianos and music makers up and down Deadwood's main street.

He still had to get the other two robbers and the rest of the loot. If he let their trail cool, they might think he had given up on them and ease up on their place in Nebraska. He hoped so.

Seventeen

Dulchy stood back and watched Wulf finish shoeing Goose. When he dropped the last hoof and straightened up, he smiled at her. "I'm glad that's over," he said.

"I bet you are. In the morning you leave?" She chewed on her lower lip.

"That's right. And I'll write to you and when I can — well — when I can find us something we can live on, then I'll send you the money to come and join me, or I'll come back here and get you."

"I can wait. But I want you to hurry, too."

He agreed as he washed his arms and hands in the basin beside the water barrel. With the soap lathered on them, they looked like they were snowbound. He wondered how spring was coming up in the north country. It was warming up in the hill country of Texas. It would soon be blue-bonnet time.

"Do you think Montana is all mountains?"

she asked.

"Dulchy, I have no answer. They took lots of cattle up there and said it was great grass country. I'll write and tell you all I see."

She hugged his arm. "Oh, I'll be glad when we're back together again — you with me."

"So will I. So will I." He grabbed Goose's lead, took him out back, and put him in the pen with Kentucky.

"Aunt Frieda has made some pastries. We better go see her."

"Lead the way. I'm coming."

In a while, with a deep pain in his heart, he finally left Dulchy with a kiss, thanked her aunt, and hurried back to Andy's.

"What did Bob say about your probate case?" Andy asked as they stood around in the kitchen with Myrna hustling out supper from the oven.

"Next Wednesday, Hughes has to bring all the records to the court. Cattle sales, the sale of Ranger and Calico, where all the money is at, and all the other business about my portion of the will. The banker, Hugh Berry, will be there as well."

Andy nodded. "Good, sounds like he's getting the job done."

Wulf nodded. "He told me not to hold my breath — these things can be long and drawn out."

"If anything else needs done, I'll do it until you get back."

"Andy, I don't know what I'd do without you two."

"We love you," Myrna said, going past him with a bubbling pot roast.

"I love both of you, too."

Morning came, and the horses were saddled. He had the packs and bedroll on Goose. Kentucky needed the riding. He mounted, talking easy to his black horse. The gelding shuffled around, but made no offer to buck, and Andy handed Wulf Goose's lead.

"Good luck. I hope Montana treats you well."

"Be careful," Myrna said. "There are more mean men between here and there than you can shake a stick at."

"I'll watch for them."

Going out of town, he rode by the Matters place. They weren't up in the cool predawn. Their lights weren't on yet in the house. He jog-trotted the two horses up the road since they were settled down and he had miles to go. Later, he paused to water them at the crossroads store. The storekeeper didn't come out and sweep his porch either. It disappointed Wulf not to be able to share his plans with the pleasant man. He rode on.

He was past Brady before he camped for the first night. Avoiding towns as much as he could, he rode through the ones he couldn't avoid, drawing little attention except that he saw several men eye his horses in passing. Four days later, when he neared Fort Worth, he noticed the Colonel's red wagons parked in a field south of the city. The draft teams and other horses were hitched on a long picket line. He looked for Calico, and at last spotted him.

Head hung low, Calico stood hipshot between two teams of draft horses. The dried black blood inside Calico's hind legs shocked Wulf. Those worthless sons of bitches had castrated him. The telltale dried blood told him everything. One of the last links to the Comanche bloodlines had been neutered.

He thought he might vomit. And they called themselves animal trainers. He reined Goose back toward the road, grateful he had not seen a single person to shoot standing around the wagons. They'd not recognize the farm boy from Mason in his garb any-way, and just as well. With a weary shake of his head, he swallowed a hard knot in his throat and shifted the Colt on his hip.

He found Fort Worth, with its fancy women under parasols strolling the sidewalks, the horse-drawn streetcars, and the confusion of traffic, hardly a place for his two horses and himself. He crossed over the Trinity River and north of town, found a farmer who let him camp in his barn.

"Going far?" the gray-headed man asked, chewing on a straw.

"Montana."

"Never been there. But I hear it's a fur piece, too. Fifteen years ago, I came down from Arkansas to here. Like to never got here with oxen and a family. Buried my oldest son in Texarkana, my first wife two days later at DeKalb. Tried to farm west of here, but that ain't farming land 'cept in the creek bottoms. Met my second wife here. She was a widow and had this place." He dropped his head and shook it ruefully. "She died and I married her oldest daughter. I've sure had real bad luck with wives."

"You sure have." Wulf wasn't in a big talking mood. The picture of Calico standing straddle-legged with the dried blood inside his legs made him too upset to even eat anything.

The farmer at last left him, and Wulf curled up in a blanket in the hay. Maybe sleep would make him forget the dreadful image of his stallion's fate.

Colonel Armstrong, you bastard, you better be wearing that pearl-handled pistol next time we meet.

EIGHTEEN

Herschel and his prisoner, Auggie Mc-
Cafferty, left Deadwood by stage for Buffalo before sunup. The eighteen-year-old,
with his left arm in a sling, was recovering
from Herschel's bullet, which had pen-
etrated his left shoulder and emerged out
the front of his upper chest. He looked pale,
but Herschel figured he was tough enough
to survive. By the time they stopped at
Spearfish, the day had warmed. The road
was a muddy slurry and the driver had his
hands full, crossing several swollen creeks
and fighting the mud.

Herschel sat back and enjoyed the warmer
air coming in the coach for a change,
wondering how the man he met coming
over had done at acquiring deposits of coal.
Maybe if Herschel had Buffalo Malone's
money, he could worry about buying things
like that for future gain. Instead, he worried
about buying a couple of new shorthorn

bulls out of Dakota to improve his cattle herd.

"Guess your brother and father are in Nebraska by this time," Herschel said.

Auggie twisted and looked crossly at him. "Where you getting that from?"

"That's where you live, isn't it?" Rocked by the stage's churning, Herschel sat up straight again.

"We ain't got no place in Nebraska."

"We need to get one thing straight, Mc-Cafferty. I ain't putting up with any lies. I know for a fact your father owns a place south of the Sioux reservation in Nebraska."

Auggie became sullenly silent.

Herschel didn't give a damn. Before they got back to Billings, he'd know the exact location of that ranch and all about it.

"I never ever heard of a sheriff coming that damn many miles just to get back some old squaw man's money," Auggie finally said.

"Been ten bucks, I might not have gone quite that far, but you boys stole too much money."

"Hell, I knowed we were in big trouble when I seen six of them boxes."

"Yeah? What did you say?"

"I told Paw we should only take one or two of them. Take all six, and we'd not only have the law after us, but every frigging outlaw as well."

"Why only one or two?"

"That old buffalo hunter wouldn't have turned us in. He didn't want anyone else to know he had all that gold. So even if we'd left him two trunks, he'd not've ran to you."

"What did your paw say?"

" 'Screw the old man,' he said. So we took all six and stole three horses to pack them. Paw never rode a paint or loud-colored horse in his life. I bet you tracked us by just asking about them three ponies."

"I called them my markers."

Auggie hunched up with a grimace of pain. "I told them two that we needed to buy some bay horses —"

"Tell me about the rape of that woman at the stage stop north of Buffalo."

"I never raped anyone."

"You guarded the horses, huh, while your father and brother raped her?"

"Not my gawdamn idea."

"Guess it was your paw's."

McCafferty's blue eyes looked set on some distant object out on the brown prairie — no answer.

"I asked you a question."

"Yeah, Paw had to have her. Grayson, he was reeled in to the deal." The youth dropped his gaze to the floor. "I never minded robbing that old man. I just watched the torture, and that was hard, but her — that made me sick."

"Then you stayed at Kate Devero's above Buffalo?"

"Man, she was a pretty woman, but she's meaner than a rattler, huh?"

"Yes, and your paw knew her from the Whitten brothers days."

"They lynched them when I was little, so I'd never met her."

"He didn't rape *her,* did he?" Herschel stretched his stiff arms over his head, touching the roof of the stage.

"He was smarter than that. I don't figure Kate let anyone touch her that she didn't want them to." McCafferty laughed.

"They say you and Grayson are half brothers."

"We are. My maw was his third wife. Grayson's was his second."

"Has the old man got any more kids?"

"Not that I know about. He never said much about his first wife. I kinda figured he simply rode off and left her in Kentucky or somewhere back there where he came from."

"Your maw on his place in Nebraska?"

"No. She left when he moved in with a

Sioux squaw."

"Ever hear from her?"

"No. She's in Ogallala."

"What's her name?"

"Ezra McCafferty."

"Ezra?"

"Ezeriamorya was her full name."

"Where does she work?"

"Same place he found her. Silvia's Whore House."

"Guess your paw and Grayson are going to live it up now they have all that money."

"I damn sure won't be there to help them." He became silent again.

He must be thinking about all he was missing. Herschel went on. "Reckon they'll go to Ogallala and do it?"

"He said no, but knowing him, what he says ain't always what he does."

It was late in the evening as the stage was making a hard grade and the horses were down to a crawl when the driver shouted, "We're fixing to be held up. Be calm. All they want is the strongbox and mail."

"Don't anyone try anything," the rider with a flour sack on his face said, riding up to the coach.

Herschel made no move for his gun deep under his long coat.

"Hey," McCafferty called out. "Let me go

with you fellas. He's taking me to jail."

"Who?" the rider asked as the driver threw down the strongbox and the canvas mailbag.

"Don't do it," Herschel said under his breath. "It'll only grow harder on you."

"Get out. Who's holding you?"

"A U.S. marshal —"

"We ain't messing with no gawdamn U.S. marshal," another man shouted.

"Get out here," the first bandit said.

McCaffery started to leave the coach, and nodded smugly at Herschel.

"Get on behind me," the holdup man said as his horse fidgeted around. His prisoner was soon on behind him and the gang was leaving. Three men, now four, were leaving, leading a braying mule they must have put the strongbox on. Two of them were whipping hell out of the mule, and soon they were all out of sight.

Herschel regretted his .45 had been deep under his coat. He swung down outside and looked up in disgust at the driver.

"Who's that bunch?" he asked.

"They call them the Humbolt Gang, but I don't know none of them."

"How far do I need to ride to get a horse and go look for them?"

"Sundance."

He considered it all. Go home, get some rest, make certain his family was all right, and then come back with some help and find them. If Wyoming law couldn't get them, he would.

"What'cha going to do?"

"Ride on." Herschel shook his head in disgust. "I'm going home. Head her for Sundance."

He'd been through enough. Damn, a bunch of holdup men taking his prisoner. The West was chock full of their kind.

The law in Sundance took his information, but he felt it was like marking it on a slate board in chalk. As soon as he was gone, they'd erase it and put someone else's up there.

Finally back in Sheridan, he switched to the Billings stage line, and knew in another thirty-six to forty hours he'd be home with Marsha and his girls — where he belonged.

He needed some time with them before he left on another wild-goose chase.

NINETEEN

The Red River ferryman cranked Wulf and his horses across the tree-choked stream. A large black man with thick arms worked the reel. "Better leave you whiskey for me."

Wulf laughed loud enough to be heard back at Fort Worth.

"Dem U.S. marshals from Fort Smith will sure enough fine you for bringing it in the Indian Territory."

"I don't drink," Wulf said.

"They's might plant some on you's and then arrest you. I's never said they was all honest."

"I'll watch for that."

"Good thing not to drink the devil's brew, but you can read their threat going up de bank. You a smart man and can read. Lots of dem boys goes up there past it can't read shit. I likes to warn them — no spirits beyond this dock."

Wulf missed his friends at home a lot as

he crossed into the Indian Territory and headed northwest for Kansas.

The trip across Texas had been uneventful, aside from his discovery of what Armstrong had done to his horse — *that worthless outfit.* Again, he was glad no one had shown their faces when he rode by. What had they done to Ranger? No telling. Then, as he rode up the steep embankment onto the Indian Territory, he wished he'd've found Ranger, too. The situation with his animals grated on his conscience. As he rode by the sign, he glanced at the rules about no spirits in the territory.

He had been teaching his horses to come when he whistled sharply. Rewarding them with sugar or grain had worked well. His first night on the prairie in the Indian Territory was marked by a thunderstorm that blew up out of the west in a great curtain cloud that flashed and roared like an insane thing. He'd seen some storms, but this beat any he could recall at home. Maybe because there was so much to see of the storm coming at him — like a sea washing in.

His boots still soggy, the next day he headed north, scattering killdeer and bobwhite quail in his advance. Meadowlarks sang to him and red-tail hawks screamed at his invasion of their sanctuary. He passed scattered small farms, and the world he rode through was wide with few people. Some thickets of wild plums had already bloomed, and several wildflowers like Indian paintbrush had already broken out as he rode on north.

Wrapped in their filthy blankets, two Indians on horseback stopped him. "You got some gawdamn whiskey?" the older one asked.

The other one rode over and began looking at his panniers like he was going to take them away.

"You two want to become good Indians?" Wulf asked, his anger growing by the minute.

"We plenty damn good Indians," the one close to him said, beating his chest with his fist.

Wulf's eyes narrowed at the man. "No, I mean good Indians."

"What you mean?"

"If you don't get the hell away from me and my horses, I'm going to make real good Indians out of you. Dead ones."

When he drew his .45, they both looked shocked, turned their mounts away, and rode off beating their skinny horses to go faster. He watched them look back and talk loud in some guttural language. *Plenty crazy mad gawdamn white man.*

He didn't care what those two thought of him. His purpose was to get on north in one piece, and that required both his horses and his supplies.

Late afternoon, he was in the hills. Earlier, he'd taken the wrong turn in the road. A freighter he stopped, who was headed south, told him it made no difference which turn he took. If he kept on, he'd come out on the great western road of Captain Marcy's halfway across the territory a little more east than if he'd taken the other turn.

The hardwood trees were just beginning to leaf out. Everywhere he passed a homestead, folks were out working the ground to plant crops and start gardens.

Before he reached the next crossroads, a young Indian boy running barefooted alongside his horses informed him about some stew for sale. At the crossroads store, there were two Indian women in very colorful dresses who were busy dipping stew from a great cast-iron pot for ten cents per customer. One of them was thickset and older; the other one looked to be in her late teens — very tall. Maybe a mother and daughter. He simply turned his horses free to graze on what they could find with the reins tied over Kentucky's neck and the lead rope bunched under Goose's halter.

Wulf wiped his own spoon on his pants and stepped up to the young lady, who had to be inches taller than he was. "Ma'am, I don't have a small pail like these other folks. Do you have a bowl I might borrow?"

The tall girl blushed and dropped her gaze to the steaming stew in the pot. "I have a turtle shell is all."

"Hey, a turtle shell sounds great to me. He won't miss it, will he?"

She looked aghast at him as she wiped a shell out with the tail of her apron for him. "No, no, these all died naturally."

"Good to know." He used his finger to show her the white inside of the shell. "You pour that hot stew in there. I don't want him coming back for it."

"You are very funny. Very funny," she said, laughing easily at his words.

"My name's Wulf Baker. I didn't catch yours."

"Mary Ann Donavan. Are you Cherokee, too?"

"No, ma'am. I'm mostly German." He shrugged like he couldn't help it. "Some of our family were horse thieves and we were never sure of their nationality."

"Won't your horses run away?" she asked, chuckling at his words.

"No. When I finish my stew, I'll show you how I gather them."

The straight-backed girl with the high cheekbones and the deep black hair tied behind her neck with a leather thong shook her head in amused disbelief at him. "You are a clown."

"No, ma'am, I am a horse trainer, among the things I do well," he said between spoonfuls of the tasty stew. It had been days since he'd talked to anyone besides his horses, and he certainly enjoyed the chance to visit with her.

When he handed her back the shell, she simply refilled it. "It is all you can eat for ten cents."

"Really? You could go broke doing that."

"No, we won't. But look at all the people who are eating here. Many would eat something like old cooked rice or burned hoecakes."

"You are good people to do that," he said, starting on his second bowl.

"I want to see how well trained your horses are when you finish." She folded her arms over her bustline like she was skeptical.

Wiping his mouth on the back of his hand, he gave her back the shell.

"No, you should keep it," she said. "It

203

could bring you good luck. We have many more. Here, I will wash it for you." And she took the shell and spoon away and went to the two pails of hot water on the grate over the fire, washing the shell and spoon first, then rinsing them. Then she carried them back but refused to give them to him. "I can hold them. Let me see you bring in those horses."

By then, Kentucky was grazing upon a high bank across the road, snatching dry grass like he was starved. Goose was in the other direction, eating some grass that was under an old parked wagon.

Wulf put two fingers in his mouth and whistled loud and clear. Kentucky half reared to turn back, and then he bailed off the dirt bank on his heels and hit the road trotting. From the west, Goose came at a jog nickering. Both horses jogged up and put their faces against Wulf. Disengaging from them, he broke out some corn from canvas nose bags and fed them.

She handed him back the shell and spoon. "You are a good horse trainer. I am pleased to meet you, Wulf Baker."

"The same here, Mary Ann." He tipped his hat to her.

"May I ask where you are going?"

"Sure. Montana. Have you ever been there?"

"No. I was in Fort Smith once. It was so busy, I about got ran over."

They both laughed and he excused himself. He needed to get set up somewhere for the night. It soon would be dark. There was little twilight in this country after sundown. But he felt exhilarated over his conversation with her as he mounted Kentucky. Headed north down the dusty ruts, he wondered how Dulchy was doing.

He should stop more often and simply talk to people. They didn't have to be girls his age — just ordinary folks to talk to and connect him again with the human race. Since he'd left Mason, that was one of the longest conversations he'd had with anyone.

Around midnight, thunder woke him up coming out of the west. Flashes of lightning made the trees in the grove beyond him look like giant upside-down icicles. He could tell the shape of all the mountains between him and the incoming storm. There were no buildings around. He and his horses would have to weather it out.

He put on the canvas coat and spent a soggy night sitting up. Lightning danced all around him, and the shattering cracks of thunder made him wonder if he'd live through till dawn. One tremendous strike on the hill above him shattered a great tree and sent it crashing down. There were storms like this in the hill country, but there he knew where to go for shelter.

A dark dawn came, but the rain was lighter and he rode on. Everything was soaked through, and a cold north wind had come in by midday, and he wished for a fire to get warm by. He found a general store with smoke coming out of the stove pipe. The notion that they might have a heater to warm him made him stop.

"Hello." The deep voice of a man came from behind the counter in the dark interior.

"I just wanted to warm a little and get a few things," Wulf said.

"Traveling through?"

"Yes, sir." He unbuttoned his coat and held out his hands to the heat coming from the wood stove. It felt wonderful.

"Going north, I see."

"Yes, sir."

"If you skipped out on the law somewhere, I have to tell you Parker's men been here the whole damn week."

"Who are they?"

The man grunted. "You've never heard of the Hanging Judge Isaac Parker at Fort Smith?"

"I guess I've heard of him."

"Well, when you crossed the ole Red River down there, you came into his jurisdiction. And his marshals are working this district hard and arresting folks."

"I see."

"No, you don't see if you don't live here. There are men they've arrested whose families will starve without them to provide. President Grant appointed him, and he's part of that leftover carpetbag government that we ended up with because of the war."

"I see." Hell, he didn't know much about politics, least of all about Judge Parker.

Warm at last, he bought a sack of hard candy, thanked the grumbling man, and headed out. Dried out some, he didn't feel as squishy as before. He mounted Goose and rode on north.

Later that day, two men in suits riding horseback stopped him. They had a very haggard-looking bushy-headed Indian wearing only his filthy red underwear on foot, and they were leading him by a rope tied to his handcuffs.

"U.S. Marshal Sam Piper," the heavier man said. "That's my posse man, Billy Graig. You live around here?"

"No, sir, I live at Mason, Texas."

207

"Fur piece for a boy like you to be away from."

"My father died and I'm on my own."

"Watch yourself, boy. This country is full of horse thieves and murderers."

"I will. What did he do?" Wulf asked, motioning to their prisoner.

"Robbed a country store."

Wulf nodded to indicate that he'd heard him. "Good day, sir."

He didn't like being called a "boy." Kinda got under his skin. If those lawmen talked to everyone like that, no wonder the man back at that store hated 'em. Besides, he was hardly a *boy.*

He met an old Indian man and his wife who were making camp late in the day in a clearing. The man's face looked like polished leather and his smile seemed genuine. His hair was done in thick frosted braids.

"You looking for a place to a camp?" he asked Wulf.

"Yes, sir."

"They won't charge you nothing to camp here."

"Good. I don't have any money," he said, extending his hand. "Wulf Baker."

"Charlie Deadman. That is my wife, Judy." The woman, bent over building a fire, looked up and smiled at him. In her youth, she must have been the prettiest woman in this part of the country — her smile warmed him.

"What can I contribute to this effort?" Wulf asked.

"I have a dressed chicken to cook." She straightened up and moved her bangs aside.

"Then can I buy supper from you?"

"Not if you don't have money." She laughed.

"Oh, I have money for that."

"Good, we can start a café here, huh, Charlie?"

"I don't want to wash the dishes."

She turned her palms up. "There goes another fortune."

"Where you going?" Charlie asked, looking over Wulf's things as he unpacked them.

"Montana, to see my cousin."

"That's a long ways away, ain't it?"

"Yes, a real long ways. Where are you going?" He could see they had stuff to camp with in a single wagon pulled by a fat mare.

"To a dance. You should go with us. It will be lots of fun."

"What kind of a dance?" He knew about schoolhouse dancing.

"Indian stomp dancing."

"I'm not Indian."

Charlie laughed. "They won't know that.

The Cherokees have so many mixed bloods in them, they can't tell if you are one or not. Join us. You would like it."

"I might do that."

Charlie's narrowed brown eyes looked at him like he was peering inside him. "Why are you going to Montana?"

"Aw, I was about to kill my stepfather over some things he did to me. Thought I'd go see my cousin who's a sheriff up there."

"I should have killed three men in my life. Two are dead now. I wish I'd killed the other one that is left."

When Wulf's horses were unloaded and watered, he put on their feed bags while supper was cooking. The wind was cool, and he knew the temperature was going to drop since the storm had gone on east.

"You got some damn good horses," Charlie said, admiring them.

"Goose was a gift of my father's friend after my stepfather sold my good Comanche horse to a traveling show."

"Was he a real Comanche-bred horse?"

"Yes."

"I saw them as a boy. They walked on feathers."

Wulf nodded. The old man had seen real Comanche horses in his lifetime. The grim picture of Calico after they cut him made a lump in Wulf's throat he couldn't swallow. Charlie was right. There was a man in his life, too, that he needed to kill — Kent Hughes.

One thing led to another and he enjoyed their company so much, he went with them to the Blaine School House the next day for the dance. They chose a place in the trees outside the great circle of grass around the building, and made a picket line between two post oaks for the three horses. En route, they found lots of firewood to stack in the back of their wagon because Judy warned them that every speck was used up around the campground. It was near lunchtime when they set up. Wulf noticed several other families were setting up. He took Judy's ax and went to work chopping up her wood. Charlie sat on the wagon tongue and talked to him as he worked. It felt good to be using his muscles again.

"Some Cherokee mother may kidnap you for her son-in-law. You are a hard worker at this wood business." Charlie chuckled.

"Hey, my dad was sick for two years. I've been doing this for years. You got a stone? This ax is getting dull."

"Sure, sure." Charlie got up to go get it.

There were three riders coming across the school yard. Something about their looks made Wulf wonder. They looked tough, and the one with the darkest skin wore leather cuffs like some kind of gunfighter.

"Who are they?" Wulf asked.

Charlie looked and shrugged. "Some killers, I guess. Oh, that one's Sequoyah Hawks, the darkest one."

"He mean?"

"I guess he can be. I'll get that stone."

The three went to the wagon south of the Deadmans' Wagon and spoke to the man there. Wulf kept them in mind while he chopped some more wood. Charlie came back with the round whetstone for him, and Wulf got busy sharpening the double-bitted ax.

The three then rode up and reined in their horses. Hawks called out something to Charlie in Cherokee that Wulf did not understand. But the two skinny-looking ones with Hawks laughed. Wulf had a feeling he was the butt of the joke. He went back to sharpening the ax and they rode off. But the youngest one cast too long a look over at Wulf's horses to suit him. He'd remember him.

"What did he say?" Wulf studied their backs as they rode off across the grounds filling with people and their rigs.

"He asked if I had a new squaw cutting

wood for me."

"I see why those other two laughed."

"They are just a little drunk and it was a Cherokee joke."

Then, testing the new edges with his thumb, Wulf agreed with a short nod. "I bet they could get awfully troublesome if they really were drunk."

"You know, you're right, and probably the cause of all their trouble with the law is from too much alcohol."

Wulf sunk the ax in a block. "Think your wife has enough."

"Oh, yeah, you will spoil her with that much." Charlie stood up to his full height of five-six and laughed, looking up. "Come along, I want to introduce you to my friends. We are going walking," he said to his wife, who was busy sewing on a blue shirt.

They went to the next camp south and Wulf met Bill Pearson, the man who had spoken to Hawks.

"I see Hawks came to see you," Charlie said.

Pearson nodded. "He wanted to borrow some money for hooch."

"What did you tell him?"

"I was broke. What did he ask *you* for?"

"He saw Wulf chopping wood and asked in Cherokee if I had me a new wife."

Pearson laughed.

Wulf decided that must be a real funny joke to Cherokees. Maybe he shouldn't be affronted by it.

"He has bad taste to say that in Cherokee," Pearson said, and shook his head to show his disapproval to Wulf.

"I didn't want any trouble with drunks," Charlie said. "Besides, Wulf is a patient man. Anyone who sharpens my ax for me is a good friend."

"You can sharpen axes?" Pearson perked up.

"Sure. Do you have a stone?" Wulf asked.

"No."

Charlie shook his head. "I'll go get mine."

Next, a woman came to see Pearson's wife, Honey, and when she discovered that Wulf sharpened axes, she half ran back for hers. Wulf didn't mind. They were polite, and he could listen to tales while he put edges on butcher knives, axes, and pocketknives.

Each person wanted him to take something for his services. They were small things like a jar of jelly or honey, some hulled black walnuts, or some salve for sore muscles. Charlie told him not to eat it. A bar of homemade soap. One woman gave him two brass cavalry buckles for a bridle headstall with *U.S.* in raised letters.

"This is too much," Wulf said, considering it valuable. Did she even understand him? Then he looked around for his translator, but couldn't see Charlie anywhere.

Pearson leaned in and said, "Don't worry. She is going back for another ax."

The crowd laughed.

Finally, Judy came over and held her hands in the air. "He is my guest. You must let him rest."

The crowd began to melt away, and he completed the last jobs. He handed an ax back to a woman who had no teeth, and she thanked him.

"I have nothing to give you," she said.

"That's all right."

Then she got a funny look in her good eye. "You could come sleep with me tonight."

"No, thank you. It's fine."

"All right, but I wish I had something."

"It's fine." He couldn't reassure her fast enough that he wanted no part of that offer.

She shrugged and went hobbling off, taking her sharpened ax with a home-carved hickory handle.

"It is time to eat," Charlie announced.

"I was going to buy something for Judy to cook," Wulf said.

They each carried an armful of Wulf's "gifts." "I bet she could use some of these," Charlie said, and laughed. "Unless you need them."

"What all did you get?" Judy asked, setting what they brought her in a row on a log. "There was a man that used to come to these dances. He had a big wheel and he sharpened things for everyone. Where did you learn how to do it?" she asked Wulf.

"Andy Carter. I learned in his blacksmith shop at home."

"You would make a good husband for someone," Charlie said.

"I have a girl at home."

"That is a shame. I hoped you'd settle around here — by me."

Wulf shook his head. "No, I better get on to Montana."

Twilight set in when he sat down to eat Judy's beans and bacon. Wulf could have used some hot sauce in his, but it was tasty and he didn't have to cook it.

At the sound of a commotion, Wulf whirled and saw someone slip on to Goose's back and boot him out.

"He is stealing your horse," Charlie said, shocked.

Wulf, with two fingers in his mouth, gave a shrill whistle. In the twilight, he could see

Goose immediately begin bucking and throw that rider higher than the post oak trees.

"Catch him," Charlie shouted, and two men rushed in and caught the fallen thief.

Goose came back and put his face on Wulf's chest. "Good boy."

He fed him a piece of hard mint candy and led him back to the picket line. When Goose was hitched beside Kentucky, Wulf walked out to see who had tried to steal him.

Dressed only in a loincloth and moccasins, the skinny boy stood between the two captors.

"Why did you try to steal my guest's horse?" Charlie demanded.

"Go fuck yourself, old man," the drunk rustler said with a whiskey lisp.

Charlie's jaw quivered, he was so furious. "What should we do with him?"

Wulf shook his head with no answer. "I'm not the law here."

"If he was a Cherokee and we got the horse back, he would get ten lashes with a whip."

Someone said he was Cherokee.

"Then in the morning when he is sober enough to feel them, that will be his sentence," Charlie said, and the heads bobbed. "Tie him to a tree until then."

"Better yet, I have chains and locks," another said.

They all agreed that chains and locks were better than ropes, and dragged him off far enough that they wouldn't hear him wail.

That night, Wulf learned how to stomp. With his hands on the hips of some woman who had invited him to dance with her, he followed her moves to the drumbeat in the long serpentine lines of men and women. He met many nice girls his age. Some were very bold, and almost challenged him to meet them beyond the ring of firelight.

The stew girl, Mary Ann, found him standing by himself. "You are very talented. You teach horses tricks. I didn't know you could dance."

He laughed. "I just move with them."

"My mother has lemonade. Would you like a glass?"

"Sure."

He fell in behind her. She must be two, maybe three inches taller than he was.

"Thank you," he told her mother, drinking the cool sweet-sour liquid from a brown glass.

Her mother nodded and said, "Mary Ann told me that the horse trainer is here. I said he must need a drink. I am really surprised she brought you back here to meet me."

"She is a very kind person," he said.

Her mother laughed and tossed her head at her daughter, standing there opening and clenching her fists at her side and looking to the stars for help. "Oh, Mother, why did you say that?"

"It was the truth."

"Come, I want to dance with you," he said, taking Mary Ann's hand.

"She thinks I am taken with you," she said as he guided her through the people to where they could dance.

He went up next to the last man in line. Then he put his hands on her hips. The drumbeat was going and they followed it.

"I am not taken by you. You are a good person, I know that. There are not many good people in this world." She glanced over her shoulder at him. "You know what I mean?"

"Yes." And they danced.

Then later, they stood back in the shadows. In soft voices, they talked to each other.

"I'll have to ride on tomorrow," he said to warn her.

"I know. Is the one who waits for you at home pretty?"

"She is a nice-looking Dutch girl."

"She —" Her words were cut off by the cries of a woman.

In the shadowy light, he could see a man holding a woman by a handful of her hair and beating her with a stick. Mary Ann tried to stop Wulf, but he was already gone. He leaped over things and when he reached the man, he ripped the stick he was using from his hands. Then he went to flailing the man two-handed about the head and shoulders with the stick until he released the woman's hair and bent over crying. Holding his hands over his ears and unable to escape Wulf's beating, he screamed, "I won't do it again. I promise. I promise."

"Stop! Stop! You are killing him," Mary Ann screamed, and took Wulf's right arm in both her hands to stop him.

"What's going on here?" someone demanded.

Out of breath, Wulf glared in the night's darkness at the man who'd asked. "He was pulling out her hair and beating her with this stick," Wulf said.

"Who are you? Who invited you here?"

"I did." Charlie stepped forward. "Wulf Baker is my friend and what he says is the truth."

The big man nodded and bent over to lift the man up by his shoulder. "You all right?"

"Go ask her if she is all right," Wulf said, pointing at the woman crying on the ground. "She was the one he beat up on."

The man shot a cold glance back at Wulf. "Are you an elder here?"

"No, but I damn sure don't stand for men beating women with sticks."

"I can see that."

"Who are you?"

"I am the subchief — Leonard Swift."

"Then you do what you want. I'd tie him to a tree and do what they're going to do to a horse thief in the morning — whip him."

"You speak mighty big for a boy."

"I ain't a damn boy, that's for sure."

Swift nodded. He half turned to a woman on her knees who was cleaning the beaten woman's face with a towel. "Is she all right?"

"I think so."

Swift held his hands up. "Everyone go back to dancing. Good night, Mr. Wulf."

With a turn on his boot heels, Wulf started for camp and his things. Charlie caught up on one side and Mary Ann on the other.

"He didn't mean for you to leave," she said, pulling on his arm.

"She is right. He meant good night until I see you again," Charlie said.

Wulf stopped. "I can't stand for anyone to get beat. I took two whippings from my stepfather and no one stopped him. I won't let anyone else do that."

"I understand," Charlie said. "Go dance with her. You have friends here."

Even dancing with his tall friend and holding her hips, he still carried the fury that had aroused him. Like a bad fire, it was blazing inside his chest and he couldn't overcome it. Hard as he tried, the anger still remained inside him.

At last, she led him into the shadows and hugged him against her. "I can tell you are still upset. So much that you are trembling inside. I can feel it."

"I've tried. I've tried." His heart pounded and his breath raged through his nose.

"Let's get your bedroll and escape this place."

"People will talk. They will say bad things about you."

"What about you?"

He closed his eyes and put his forehead against hers. "I won't have to live here to listen to them."

She gave him a small push and quietly whispered, "Go get your bedroll."

TWENTY

Herschel left his saddle and things at the stage office and walked the two blocks to the courthouse. He hoped it would loosen his muscles, which were stiff from riding and bouncing around in a coach for so long. The day was cool, but rain looked imminent. Upstairs in the sheriff's department, he found Art behind his desk.

"Well, Under Sheriff, how are things going?" Herschel asked.

Art, who'd been catnapping, bolted upright. "Here, have your chair."

"No, I'm taking some time off." Herschel put both hands on his hips and strained against the soreness.

"You got one of them, didn't you?"

"I had one. Some highwaymen rescued him when they held up the stage we were on down near Sundance, Wyoming."

"Oh, no."

"Oh, yes, and they rob stages and no one

apparently cares down there at that place. They say they do it regularly."

"You got part of Buffalo's money back." Art folded his hands on top of the desk.

"Wells Fargo is shipping it up here to the bank."

"It's here. I sent word to him to come in and discuss with the First Bank of Montana on how to best secure his money or whatever it is."

"They sure didn't waste any time getting it here. Now, I'm going home and sit in a tub of hot water until my hide peels off and then sleep for a week. What else?"

"Oh, here's a letter for you. We never opened it."

Mason, Texas, was the postmark. He opened and began to read Wulf's letter.

"Good or bad news?" asked Art.

"Well, Art, a cousin of mine is coming. His name's Wulf Baker. His dad and mine were brothers. Says here his dad died a year ago."

"Say why he's coming?"

Herschel shook his head and smiled. "I reckon, for a family reunion."

"If he's anything like your dad, he'll make us a hand. My heavens, he pitched in and we cleaned up those rustlers and that bunch trying to run everyone out up here. His name's Wulf?"

"Yes. I imagine it's from Wolfgang. That's a common German name."

Art agreed. "I had some horse stealing reported, but I fear that the thieves were just passing through and they each left a pony behind that had been rode into the ground."

Herschel nodded. "I'm off to the house. Need me — holler."

When he got back to the house, he was busy between hugging his wife and kissing his stepdaughters.

"Is it all over?" Marsha asked when the air cleared.

"No. I had to come home to see you all. I arrested one of the three in Deadwood, but he escaped during a stagecoach holdup, and I imagine he's back at home in Nebraska by now with the other two."

"All that time and work — I can't tell you how much we missed you."

"Me, too. Oh, my cousin, Wulf Baker, is coming to visit us. I got his letter today."

"When will he get here?" Kate, the oldest, asked.

"Oh, sometime. It depends how fast he rides. It's a long ride up here from Texas."

Kate wrinkled her nose at his answer. "Do you remember him?"

"Just a barefoot boy when I left Mason."

"Did he send a photograph?"

"No."

"How're we going to know him when he comes?"

"I'm certain he'll introduce himself," her mother injected to conclude the conversation. "What would you like for supper?" she asked Herschel.

"Anything you have to cook and I'll be pleased as a kitten."

There was lots for Herschel to do. He arranged for the large garden to be plowed. Mr. Hansen, a truck gardener, put him on his list and smiled. "I be dere in a few days."

Herschel thanked him. Everywhere he went, the talk was all about gardening and planting. Despite the chilly swings back and forth, spring was sure in the air and the robins were early harbingers.

Back at his desk, he set in to read the reports made to his office about crimes in the area.

Someone stole two horses from Urey Alfred. He gave a description and said they were worth twenty dollars apiece.

A chicken-napper stole four hens from Mrs. Clayton's coop. She was satisfied it was not a fox since they'd opened the door to the chicken house and left it open.

Hansel Bloom reported that three un-named suspicious men offered to sell him a team of part-shire horses for fifty dollars. Bloom added he did not have the money to buy them, besides the fact that he felt they were stolen. He didn't know the men — one was a freckle-faced boy in his teens with red hair. The three and their team rode on north. No one else reported seeing them.

The body of a man was brought to town by two Double T cowboys. They thought he'd died of exposure in one of their line shacks. No one knew him and there was no identification on the body. Art had noted that since the man wore overalls, it might have been why the two brought him into town instead of simply burying him. Obviously, the big outfit wanted no reflection on them or their personnel.

Many folks set out and got caught up in wintry weather without resources and became victims. He needed to send the ranch a thank-you note for their thoughtfulness. Montana was becoming a much better place than it once was.

Art came into the office and broke Herschel's concentration. "Someone here to see you."

Herschel looked up. "Who is it?"

"Buffalo."

"Good. Show him in."

Buffalo was on crutches. His silver-streaked shoulder-length hair had been brushed and no doubt treated with bear grease. Behind him came three of his wives. The same smoky aroma his tepee held lingered with them.

Buffalo stopped before Herschel's desk and shook his hand. "You did very well, my friend. I know you went many miles for me." The sincerity in his gray eyes ran deep. "We might have starved without that money. My women and the children and me."

"Have a chair and we can talk."

The women arranged the chair and helped him into it. Then, despite Herschel's protests, the three sat cross-legged on the floor around him.

"They are fine. Now tell me about how you got those two boxes back."

"I finally found their horses, and then learned they were in some house of ill repute celebrating."

"Whorehouse?"

"Yes."

Malone translated and his wives giggled. Indian women giggle more than laugh. Even grown ones.

He told about shooting the youngest one going out the back door. Then how he ran downstairs and had to shoot the paint horse to secure those two boxes. The women laughed more when Malone translated the story about the Indian woman wanting the dead horse to eat. The women giggled, but told him through Malone that he had done the right thing giving it to her.

After he told how the holdup men took his prisoner, he leaned back in the chair, waiting for Malone to finish his translation. "Well, I guess you settled with the banker about the money?" Herschel asked.

Malone shrugged good under the buckskin-beaded coat. "I don't understand what he means — invest some. I did any-way." He motioned to the tall woman who'd shown Herschel into the tepee that day. She rose to her six-foot height and put two papers on Herschel's desk before him. They were official-looking papers, and Herschel frowned, confused, as he opened them.

One was the mortgage on their ranch for two thousand dollars, marked paid in full; the other was the mortgage on the house for one thousand dollars, also marked paid. The notion shocked him, and he knew his eyes must have widened to double their normal width.

"Why — why I can't accept this —"

Malone nodded smugly that he could, and

the women giggled at something he said in Sioux to them. "What else do you need?"

"I was just doing my job. I didn't go down there for a reward."

"That man at the bank told me that, too. But this way, you can't give it back." Malone's eyes danced with mirth. The three women all nodded. They were in on it, too.

"Oh, yes," Malone said. "I am giving your wife two shorthorn bulls when they get here."

"Why, they cost —"

"No matter. Without that money you recovered, we would have starved. Now we can live out our lives and not worry."

"I'm going back and get the rest of the trunks and the other two men, but I can't promise how much I can get back."

"It will be fine whatever you can do." Malone rose. The women scrambled to fuss over him and to get his crutches in place. He soon leaned on them and shook Herschel's hand. "Now, when is the election?"

"It'll be a day or so. But thank you."

Malone started out. "Come see me. With only women to talk to, I get lonely for a man's voice."

He waved, and then hobbled out with his entourage.

Herschel leaned back and drummed his

230

fingers on the paid-for mortgages on his desk. Get lonely for a man's voice — at a loss for words or thoughts, he slumped in his chair.

"Whoever said that old buffalo hunter was a skinflint?" Art asked from the doorway.

Herschel began to laugh. "And he didn't even vote for me in the last election."

"Hellfire, Herschel, I'd bet he never voted for anyone in his entire life."

They both laughed. Herschel, shaking his head in disbelief, went over and opened one of the office windows to ventilate it a little. Too much Injun aroma still in the room.

Don't worry, McCaffertys. I'll be knocking on your door soon.

TWENTY-ONE

Wulf never saw Fort Smith, the place where Judge Parker hung so many men. When Mary Ann told him it was such a busy place that she about got run over in the traffic, his travel plans took him west of the river city.

As he headed north by northwest, he recalled her helping him pack his horses that next morning as if it was the usual thing to do. She acted like he'd be back that evening at dark. But he'd never lied to her or promised her a thing. And when he rode off, he wondered about what he had left unsaid.

The matter of their affair bothered him. He had Dulchy to think about, too. It niggled his conscience, but like spilt milk, he couldn't undo anything he'd done. That half-crazed or drunk man beating his woman or wife had sparked it all. He'd never felt that obsessed before about anything he could recall. Maybe the man's action had turned a screw or two loose in Wulf's brain.

Could he call a night in a bedroll with a generous woman a calming presence, or was it selfish for him to have accepted her? Had he been — he shook his head to try to clear it.

Wichita was next, five days later, and after he took the ferry across the Arkansas, he avoided it. An old man near Fort Worth had told him to head north to the Platte River Road in Nebraska. He'd called them honyockers, but he meant farmers who would feed him along such a route. The farther he went west, the fewer settlers, the fewer chances to find meals, and the fewer chances to find water.

But there were places like the small crossroads store in Kansas where he bought a ten-cent ham and cheese sandwich, fresh-made mustard, and a bottle of homemade root beer for ten cents. The man who waited on him was short, with a clipped mustache, and wore a suit.

"You going far?" he asked.

"Montana."

"That's a fur piece from here."

"A man told me to take the Grand Wagon Road across Nebraska to Cheyenne."

"Or go to Fort Laramie and save some miles and then take the Bozeman Trail."

"That goes to Montana? I'm headed for Billings."

"Goes right there. Goes right past the Little Big Horn."

"That's where Custer died?"

"Yes. I was there."

"Why, I thought he and all his men were killed."

"I was with Major Benteen and Reno."

"Oh. Thanks for the food and root beer."

"Stop by any time."

"Sure." Wulf didn't reckon he'd ever be back for anything as he took the feed bags off his horses' heads and prepared to ride on.

He'd met a man that had lived through an Injun war where all the rest had died. Life sure proved strange. All kinds of challenges and few answers. Was he growing up, or growing younger? He booted Kentucky on with a wave at the Kansas storekeeper who'd outlived his commander.

He stopped one rainy day in a small village in Nebraska at a smithy that was surrounded by teams of draft horses that obviously were waiting to be shod. He found the burly owner bent over and putting plates on a big Belgium mare.

"Could you use some help shoeing them?" he asked the man.

His mouth full of nails, the man looked up and then nodded. "Do the other one," he mumbled.

Wulf hung up his hat, holster, and canvas coat on a nail, found a leather apron, and went to work. The coal smoke made a light fog in the dark building, and he was reminded of Andy's shop at home. Someone got down a reflector candle lamp and began to track him carrying the light. He went to work removing the old shoes, and soon drew as observers part of the crowd of farmers that were waiting there.

"Where you from, laddie?" one asked.

"Texas, sir."

"How old are ya?"

"Nineteen," he lied.

"What did you do in Texas?"

"Ranched and shod horses, when I wasn't training them."

"Where ya be going?"

"Montana."

The old plates off, he began trimming the horse's frog, then rasping the large hoof down to size. The man who owned the place came over and examined the first one he had shaped.

"This ain't your first horseshoeing." He

235

clapped him on the shoulder. "Damn glad to have the likes of you here, me lad. Need anything, holler."

"Wulf Baker, sir."

"I can't tell ya how much I appreciate you stopping to help."

"It was good to get off my horse."

Later, while they both took turns heating the shoes in the forge and beating them into shape, the owner said his name was Walter Coats. Late that night, they had finished all that they could shoe, and had put the rest of the horses in a large corral. His own horses were eating hay and standing hipshot as he and Coats traipsed off to Coats's house.

A big woman, rawboned, with stringy brown hair and arms like a man, met them at the doorway with a loud rusty voice. "You must be trying for a damn world's record at shoeing, Walter Coats. Your supper's about cold in the oven."

"This is Wulf Baker, Marthy. He's a lifesaving man. And he can shoe horses good as any one I know."

"Well, it's about time you hired someone. You moving here?" she asked Wulf.

"No, ma'am, just helping out. I'm going to Montana."

"What in the hell for?"

"To see my cousin."

"Hmm," she snorted. "By gawd, ain't none of my kin ever come see me."

From the looks of her poorly kept house and from the sorry food she served them that evening, Wulf knew why no one dropped in on the woman.

"I was going to offer you a partnership if you'd stay," Coats said. "I hope you can stay for a few days anyway."

"I'll give you two more," Wulf said, feeling that should help the man catch up. It didn't — instead, more people brought horses in when they learned that Coats had help. Wulf also met several of the farmers' daughters who came along to meet the new smithy from Texas.

"Now that Karney girl, Dot, she's the kind ya need for a wife. She'll make a nice big woman the likes of which would keep ya warm on a cold winter night up here."

Wulf shook his head. "I have one in Texas. She'll do fine."

Washing up for a lunch that his wife delivered them, Coats laughed. "I'm doing me best to bribe ya to stay."

Her food would not do it either. Smoked sliced cow tongue lathered in mustard on near-stale bread and with her cow-stinking milk.

Coats paid him fifteen dollars, a generous amount, and invited him back to stay on the fourth morning when Wulf saddled his horses and set out west on the Platte River Road alongside the Union Pacific tracks.

The land, they said, was rich, and farmers were planting lots of hill corn in crisscross patterns. Folks lived in dugouts and soddies to prove up on their homesteads. This and Kansas might be the best land for farmers to take up.

When he arrived in Ogallala, he saw enough cowboy hats to warm his heart. They'd thrown open the grassland north of there. Taken from the Sioux who didn't use it, the land clear to the Dakota line was open to cattlemen and farmers.

When he stopped at a mercantile, an old man came to the edge of the porch to spit tobacco in the mud. He shook his head warily at Wulf. "You better kept your pistol cocked and one eye open all the time. Them's fine horses and I bet a dozen bastards already *seed* them and aim to steal 'em."

Wulf thanked him and went on inside the store. Horse stealing must be a plague in Nebraska. Several farmers he'd spent the night with coming west had spoken about it. When he came out with his food sup-

238

plies, he stopped and asked about a place to camp. The old man told him he could find one down on the Platte River.

He made camp in the head-high box elders that were barely leafed. Since he'd grained his horses well, he put them on a hitch line close to his bedroll. Besides, the grass had not broken dormancy yet and this area had been grazed down. After a meal of jerky and water from his canteen, which he'd filled earlier out of a well in town, he spread out his roll and with his .45 close by his head, turned in.

In the night, his horses' shuffling awoke him. Pistol in his fist, he rose to his knees. The sound of Kentucky's protesting squeal and the loud crack was followed by a man's scream. "The sumbitch broke my leg."

Good.

He put two fingers in his mouth and let out a whistle. Someone else went to yelling in protest. There was no moonlight, and with only the stars shedding any light, it was difficult to see much. Kentucky came dragging his lead rope, and Wulf could hear Goose trampling down brush to get back to him.

The man on the ground was moaning.

"Get your hands in the air."

"I can't. Damn horse broke my leg."

"I said get your hands in the air or I'm shooting."

Goose was soon in Wulf's face nickering to him. "Easy, big boy. They ain't stealing you."

Where did the other one go? He wasn't long wondering.

"Where are you?" came a voice from the brush.

"Tell him over here and no tricks," Wulf whispered. Then he saw the outline of the man coming around the brush. "Get your hands in the air."

The orange blast of the man's pistol cut the night. At that close range, Wulf expected to be hit. He wasn't.

After a second of hesitation, he fired his pistol twice in that direction. The other man gave a cry.

"Get your hands up."

No reply.

Wulf about stumbled over him. Stopping short and making certain he was unarmed, he holstered his own gun and half dragged the wounded man to his partner. Both must have been Indians or breeds.

He tied them back-to-back, then jumped on Goose, leading Kentucky to ride to town. He found a deputy, who promised to come right out there and arrest the horse thieves.

The mustached deputy found two more men and armed them with lanterns and rifles. They followed Wulf back to his camp.

"You say you shot one of them?" the deputy asked, walking beside Goose.

"Yes, sir. He shot at me first."

"How old are you?"

"Nineteen," he lied, with no idea how old he had to be to shoot an outlaw.

"You ever shoot anyone before?"

"Once."

"Who was that?"

"The one that stole the black horse."

"You might get a sign to wear."

"What's that?"

"It should say, 'Two fellas done got shot trying to steal my horses. You want to be next?' "

The lantern bearers laughed at the deputy's words. Wulf didn't even smile. He was relieved when he saw two thieves back-to-back in the lantern light.

The deputy called the one with the broken leg by his name. "Fat Bear, you stealing horses again?"

The Indian, who hardly looked fat, grunted, "Sumbitch kicked me. I was only walking by him."

"This is Johnny Run," one of the light bearers said about the other one.

"I never caught your name," Wulf said to the deputy.

"Alfred Bonner. Nice to meet a real horse thief catcher."

For the first time, Wulf felt relieved. He'd worried the whole trip back they wouldn't approve of him stopping the thieves. A smile crossed his face.

"Where are you headed?" Bonner asked.

"Montana."

"You ain't seen your last horse thief then," Bonner said.

"What can I do?"

"Keep on mowing them down. These two will see three years in the penitentiary. If locals had caught them, they'd got their necks stretched on a rope."

"Thanks."

"No. Thank you for your bravery. A lesser man would have hid and let them take them the horses."

The other two shook his hand as well, telling him how brave he was to do what he did. They marched off the two thieves, and left him alone in camp to hitch his horses and try to go back to sleep. That was not a success, so before dawn, he saddled and rode on west while gnawing on jerky.

More sagebrush began to show, and he saw range cows and calves. They were chasing down anything green that showed up. Farming was reserved to the creek bottoms. After the next night's sleep, he threw frost off his cover sheet — when did spring get to Nebraska?

Past the fort at Sidney, someone told him to go up to Fort Laramie. It was a shortcut to the Bozeman Trail north. But he went to Cheyenne instead.

The railroad center was bustling and mired in mud. He boarded his horses, got a haircut and bath, plus had his clothes laundered. It was still a long way to Billings, but the washing made his shirt and pants fit better, like the old man had promised him back home.

He ate a large steak dinner in a café — his first real meal in a thousand miles or so. The entire serving tasted like honey — it was so good.

Two weeks without trouble and he should be at his cousin's — Herschel Baker's place. He felt ready for that, too. Have to remember not to talk their legs off. He'd be so full of all this. In a stationery shop he bought two sheets of stationery and two envelopes. Ink and pens were free at their writing desk.

Dear Dulchy,
I am in Cheyenne resting my horses. I seen many Indians in the territory. Lots of farms and farmers. Antelopes look like a deer-goat cross.

I should be in Billings in two weeks. I took a bath and it is not even spring here. They say it comes in May. So it must be close.

I sure miss you and your aunt's pastry.

My best,
Wulf

Dear Myrna and Andy,
It is a long ways to Montana. My horses are doing well. Captured two horse thieves at Ogallala. They did not get my horses. Helped a smithy shoe draft horses in Nebraska for a few days. Big horses. They say spring comes in May up here. I am ready for it. Miss your good cooking.

Wulf

The next morning he rode north, past lots of sheep outfits. He made notes about the wagons that were with each flock and the dogs working them. They fascinated him the most, but he took no time to stop and talk. He was grateful for the wagon yards for stopovers.

They hardly had the best eating places or the nicest beds to sleep in, but they were there and he could buy grain and hay for his horses. The teamsters cursed the railroads laying track all over and putting them out of business.

The next morning, he saw his first elk. Three cow elk and two awkward calves were trailing them. Snow remained under trees Wulf called cedars. Pines began to show, and he climbed higher on switchbacks and steeper grades.

That evening, he camped at a ranch-store that also boarded some wagons. The woman ran it was tough as a horseshoe rasp, and even wore a short-barreled pistol on her waist.

She met him with her hands on her hips.

"My name's Lacy — Lacy Moore. I run the place. I set the price. Collect the fees. Manelita cooks. Ain't neither of us whores and we don't mess around. It's twenty-five cents for each horse. Feed over one full scoop of oats, it's more. Your supper, breakfast, and bed cost twenty-five cents. So you owe me seventy-five cents."

She held out her hand for payment.

Amused, he paid and thanked her, then went to put his horses up in a pen. By dark, two more teamsters had arrived. They complained about the road conditions, worthless Indian camp robbers, and other things on their mind. Wulf listened.

At last, one of the teamsters turned to him. "You ain't talking much."

"I'm learning all about the road."

"You're lucky. Seven years ago you would have been scalped this far north."

Wulf nodded that he'd heard the man.

"Yes, sir, there's been lots of men and their horses lost on this road. You ever hear of Fetterman? He and eighty some soldiers got it in '66. Custer came back ten years later and lost again. They damn near got Crook as well at the Rosebud a few days before."

"Crazy Horse and Sitting Bull went to Canada. Mark my words, they'll be back."

Wulf had heard the same said about the Comanches in Texas. *They'll be back.* So as long as they left him alone, he didn't care.

He mentioned he was going to Billings. He told them he was visiting his cousin who was sheriff up there.

"If he's ever home. Why, Sheriff Baker runs outlaws clear down to Nebraska to arrest them. I never knew another sheriff who didn't believe in county lines and went right after them."

"Maybe we need more like him," the other

man said.

Wulf acknowledged his words — sounded like Herschel took his job real seriously.

The next evening, he made his camp along a small stream. Sticks and cow chips made the fire that heated his coffee water.

Sometime during the night, his horses' uneasy rustling woke Wulf. His fingers closed on the grips of his .45 while his eyes adjusted to the starlight. A tin pot rattled, and he could make out someone pilfering in his panniers. Easing quietly out of his blankets, he slipped up behind the figure and took hold of the buckskin shirt, jerked the short individual up, and stuck the pistol muzzle in his face.

"Who in the hell are you?"

Must be some boy. An Indian? No, it was a female.

"Who are you?"

No answer.

"I said, who are you?"

"Mona."

"What were you looking for?"

"Food."

"Why mine?"

"You have some."

"Where do you live?"

She pointed south.

She couldn't be hardly more than in her

teens. He looked across the sweeping desert. Where were the rest? A girl in her teens wasn't out robbing panniers in the night by herself.

"Where are your horses?"

She shook her head. "No horses."

"Why were you robbing me?"

She opened her mouth and pointed inside. "To eat."

"How many are in your camp?"

She showed four fingers to him. "No food."

"You have a man?"

She shook her head. "Yutta has bad foot — no walk — baby — Crazy Mary."

"Where is the father?"

"Him die."

Pitiful little thing — he felt bad for pushing her around. How was he to know? He went to the pannier, took out some jerky, and handed it to her. "We'll go find them in the morning. Here."

He tossed her an old blanket. "We'll go feed them in the daylight."

How did he ever get into these deals? He uncocked his pistol and went back to his bedroll. With the revolver back in the holster, he brushed off his socks, climbed into his bedroll, and started back to sleep

"Too cold," she said, lifting his covers to

get in with him.

Raising up, he shook his head, then surrendered with her pressed to his back.

He should have killed her when he had the chance.

TWENTY-TWO

"He did what?" Marsha's eyes flew open and her jaw dropped.

"Buffalo Malone paid off the ranch and the house mortgage." Herschel stood before her in the front entryway and beat his hat against his leg. He fished the papers out and handed them to her.

"But-but why?"

" 'Cause we saved him from starving, I guess. That was his retirement. Some folks say if McCafferty had left him enough to live on, he'd've never reported the robbery."

"But that's lots of money."

He hung his hat on the peg and then the coat beside it. "I guess we can quit worrying about paying it anyway."

His arms around her, he squeezed her tight against him. Burying his face in her soft hair, he nibbled on her ear. "I know it is crazy, and I never went to Deadwood for some reward. I went to catch the robbers."

"I know. Your friends who know you know that, too."

"Hell with the rest."

"I agree. When are you going back after them?"

He chuckled. "You've been reading my mind."

"Hey, I know lots about you and when you're getting restless.

"Someone on horseback is in our yard," she said, looking out the glass window in the front door. "Looks like Indians."

He shook his head and opened the front door.

The fresh-faced lanky youth bounded off his gray horse and took off his hat. "You must be Herschel Baker."

Herschel nodded slowly, surveying the others mounted on some thin mustangs. An Indian woman, a papoose, a girl in her teens, and another girl making faces at him.

"You must be Wulf Baker." Herschel began to grin. What in the hell was he up to?

"I am indeed. I'm sorry, but they were starving when I found them, or they found me. I had to catch some mustangs for them to ride. They were down in the desert with nothing to eat. Yutta's man was killed."

"Well, tell them to come in," Marsha said

251

to Herschel. "I can tell he's sure your cousin. He's got your big heart. No one else would break horses for them to ride."

Laughing, Herschel hugged him and then shook his head. "Welcome to Montana."

"Boy." Wulf looked back as Yutta used the crutches he made for her to hobble to the house with Marsha carrying the papoose. "It is sure a damn long ways up here. That's Mona, and they call her Crazy Mary, but she won't hurt you."

The two Indian girls were awed, but Kate took Mona and Crazy Mary by the hand to the back porch to wash up. They followed along, looking around in disbelief at the house's furniture and polished hardwood floors. Yutta sat on a kitchen chair and rocked the papoose and sang softly to it. She looked so tired and drawn, Herschel wondered how she even was alive.

"I'm sure sorry, ma'am," Wulf said to Marsha. "I been in trouble all my life with bringing in strays. Most of them were dogs, but I couldn't leave them to starve."

She hugged his shoulders and then hurried off to fix food. "I wouldn't have expected less from a Baker. You know, I married one."

"Aw, hell, let's put those horses up," Herschel said.

"I have some money left," Wulf said as they went outside in the sunshine. "To help feed them."

"Aw, we have enough food," Herschel said. "You said your father died. What happened to him?"

"He had cancer, Doc said. It wasn't a lot anyone could do. Doc said there were some springs up in Arkansas cured some folks, but not everyone. Paw said he wasn't going. It was hard to watch him die.

"I ran the place, paid off the bank — worked in the blacksmith shop in town. Trained horses and dogs. Six months after Dad died, Ma married Kent Hughes. He took over everything, even sold all the yearling heifers and steers. There was no market for them. Sold them anyway and put the money in his own bank account."

"I knew him. He wasn't worth killing years ago. His dad had a little more money than the rest of us. He raised him spoiled."

"I came close to killing him. He whipped me with a girth and the next time with reins. I've got these scars." Wulf gathered the rope reins of the mustangs and headed after Herschel, who was leading Goose and Kentucky out back of the house. "The next time he came at me, I used a singletree on him. He wouldn't quit and I busted up his

253

ear with it."

"Let's put them in the lot and the good horses in the stalls. These are sure good horses."

"Yes, I rode them up here."

"What happened next with Hughes?"

"He had me arrested for attempted murder. I had a trained dog and horse. After I beat this Colonel Armstrong with my trained dog, then Hughes sold him the dog and horse, saying I was a minor."

Herschel shook his head wearily as they unsaddled and took off the packs. "What did your mother say?"

"Nothing. Nothing. She's under his spell, I guess."

No wonder he rode to Montana. "I don't blame you for coming up here."

"I have a good lawyer working on my behalf. That ranch is supposed to be mine. Dad left it to me. But I'm still a minor, they say. But by winter, I'll be eighteen. I had to get out of Texas or kill him."

"I understand that."

"Tell me one thing. Those four have no one. Yutta broke her foot and it never healed, so she can't walk. It's her baby. Crazy Mary's loony but she's sweet, and Mona is a pack rat. That's how they ate, she was a camp robber."

Herschel nodded. "We'll find them a place."

"I about shot Mona. I've shot two horse thieves — but I guess God told me not to shoot her."

Herschel shook his head. "You been through enough. We'll settle them somewhere and get your things straightened out."

Wulf put his forehead against the barn post and he couldn't hold back the tears. "Go on to the house. I'll be fine. I don't want anyone to see me cry."

"Don't worry, we can straighten it out, Wulf. We're family."

Family. That was a word that Wulf had forgotten. He'd finally found his own.

TWENTY-THREE

Things were crowded at the Baker house with all the company. Wulf found Herschel's wife, Marsha, a strong person, and that made the intrusion of five people as strange as the five of them no big problem for her. The deaf-mute Crazy Mary soon made certain there was lots of split stove wood in her box beside the kitchen range. She and Herschel's youngest stepdaughter, Sarah, formed a bond. Sarah became her guide and the two became inseparable. Yutta and the baby became the focus of Kate, the oldest, and Nina, the saucy tomboy, fell in with Mona.

Wulf quickly learned about the jail and law enforcement work in Montana. His stay in the jail in Mason had not been forgotten — he wasn't ever going back as a prisoner. When he showed Herschel the scars on his back, his cousin shook his head.

"The man must be mad."

"If he ain't, he ain't far from it. When are you going after those robbers?" Wulf asked as they walked back to the house for lunch.

"I need to soon as I can get away. But there is always something."

"I want to go along." Wulf wondered what Herschel's answer would be as they strode the way in the warming sunshine.

"I reckon we can do that."

"Good. Thanks. You won't regret it."

"No, I know I won't do that. So you learned animal training from Sam Bellows. He was a great old man at that."

"Yes, sir. Oh, I get about half sick thinking how they cut my stallion Calico and wondering whatever they did to my collie Ranger. Wish you'd seen them two coming through the crowd that day. Ain't many dogs will ride a horse." Wulf dropped his head. "And that son of a bitch sold them."

"Tell me about Andy," Herschel said. "I knew him well enough. Great blacksmith."

"He is, and I can do most of the things he can do."

"I've been dreading shoeing my own horses."

"No problem. We can crank up your forge and I can start."

"Hey, I didn't —"

"Herschel, I am so glad to be among family, I can't tell you how happy I am to be here sponging off you. Shoeing horses is my business."

"You have some nice horses."

"Ule Matters, you know him? The sheep and goat man who gave me the black horse Kentucky, who was an outlaw and I broke him. Then the Culpepper Kid and another rustler named McKinney stole him. Jerome Kane gave me Goose, the gray, to go after them. He was broke. Said he owed my dad."

"I recall Matters had a red-brick two-story house?"

"Yes, sir. He still lives in it."

"And Kane was a cow trader with my dad."

"I heard that your dad has a big ranch in south Texas?"

"Yes, he could have used your help down there."

"Well, despite all that's happened, I'm glad that I came to Montana."

"I'm proud you came. Especially since there is someone else in my family that shoes horses."

They both laughed.

After lunch, Herschel showed him the forge, the coal, and the tools in the barn. Wulf thought the outfit was fine, and said he'd get started that afternoon.

Herschel tried to talk him into waiting until he himself could help, but Wulf waved him off. So, wearing the leather apron, Wulf started the fire in the forge and began with Goose, the easiest one to shoe.

He was tacking a plate on the gray's front foot when Kate arrived. "You have a letter today."

"Who's it from?" he asked, his mouth half full of nails.

"Stamped Mason, Texas. Dul — chy Hiestman."

He nodded and drove the rest of the nails in, anxious to read her note. He clipped the nails off while wondering just what his Dutch girlfriend had to say. Then, after taking a rasp to the edge of the hoof, he finally set it down.

"Thanks," he said, and took the envelope.

Dear Wulf,

I hope you are in Montana by now. I got your letter and I had been so worried maybe you'd been scalped or hurt. Oh, I can imagine a million things going wrong. I had lunch with Andy and Myrna. She showed me your letter to them. Is Montana pretty? You missed the bluebonnets. They were everywhere this spring.

Aunt Frieda sends you her best.

Your dear friend Dulchy

"Can I read it? Are you real serious about her?"

"Sure." He handed it to her.

"Scalped? Doesn't she know the Indian wars are over?"

"I guess not."

"Who's Aunt Frieda?"

"That's her aunt who sponsored her coming to America from Holland."

"She tell you what Holland was like?"

"They have lots of windmills and marshy land. They skate on ice in the winter."

"We do that in Montana. Can you?"

"Never tried. There isn't much ice in Texas."

"Will you marry her someday?"

"If things work out." Bent over, he trimmed the frog on Goose's other front hoof. Kind of different to have a girl in his life.

"Must be nice to have your life all planned out," Kate said. "I wish mine was that way."

"Oh, it will be someday."

"How did you get yours straightened out? I mean, how did you meet her, I guess I am trying to ask."

"The day I met her, at first, I tried to run

her off. I told her there were lots of rich German farm boys that would love to have her for their bride. Who was I?"

"What did she say to that?"

"She didn't want any rich German farm boys —" He looked kinda pained as he started out the open barn door. "She wanted some fella who shot a rabid dog in the street."

"You did that?"

"It wasn't all that special. A big brindle cur was fixing to attack a lady with a baby. I just borrowed some man's pistol and shot him."

"Why didn't the man who owned the gun shoot him?"

He paused. "I never was sure, but someone had to do it."

"I see why she thought you were special."

"Oh, she's very pretty."

"I bet she is pretty. What will you do in Montana — shoe horses?"

"Kate, I'm not certain of anything in my future. My father left me a ranch I love. But my stepfather has it right now. He and I don't get along — so I left." He straightened his back and dropped the hoof. "I left so I wouldn't kill him."

"Oh —"

"I know that's wrong, but he sold my

trained dog and horse. And kept the money. I got a lawyer working on it. It's better than me taking the law into my own hands."

"We were lucky. We got Herschel. He's the best stepfather in the whole world."

"He seems like that."

"No, Wulf, we couldn't have done any better."

"Then you're lucky." He laughed. He hadn't laughed about much of anything lately, but just being around this bunch was like being alive again. "How come you don't have a dog?"

"Ours died."

"Well, we need to get one and train 'em."

"I heard you say you trained 'em."

He shook his head and drew up the hoof again. "It's not hard."

"How's the shoeing going?" Herschel called out to him. "Toss a saddle on a horse. We need to go investigate a crime."

"Fine, I'll take the black horse. He's ready."

Herschel turned back to his oldest. "Kate, run to the house and tell your mother we may be back for a late supper."

"How late?" she asked.

"Maybe real late."

"Was someone murdered?" Kate asked.

"Maybe. We don't know yet."

She looked pained. "Is there a body?"

He nodded and she took off.

"Now you have me puzzled as to what happened," Wulf said.

"Oh. There's a body in a cabin that a man found yesterday. He thought the man had been shot, but never really looked around closely — I think it spooked him and he busted on down here to tell me."

"Anyone he knew?"

Herschel shook his head. "He said he didn't know him."

When the horses were saddled, they led them outside. Marsha and Kate brought them coats.

"It may get cold again," Marsha said, shaking her head at the two of them.

Wulf thanked Kate for his coat, and Herschel kissed his wife good-bye. Wulf had to hold Kentucky in. As he watched Herschel's roan, Cob, sidestep out to the road, he about laughed. That horse might really buck.

Their horses at last settled, they trotted them north and east, catching the main road, and headed for Miles City. Herschel assured him they didn't have to go that far before they'd turn off and go north to this shack.

"How do you solve a murder?" Wulf asked.

"It's kinda like you probably learned how to swim. You jump in and flail your arms and legs a lot."

"Meaning you have to figure things out as you go?"

"That's the main way. You get clues from the wildest things, and some you think are great aren't nothing at all."

"Well, I'm along to learn all I can."

"That makes two of us." Herschel laughed.

"You know, I've been around folks all my life, but they don't seem to have as much fun as your family has. What brings that on?"

"Aw, don't take yourself too serious. Don't mire down on the things that are wrong, and work hard on things you think are right."

"I'll do that. Try it anyhow. I brought enough trouble in your lives with those three Indian women, and I ain't a easy boarder — but it don't get you all down."

"We've had our bad times. These are the good times and we're enjoying them."

"Who brought you word about this dead man?"

"Charlie Haught. He's a rancher up on Beaver Creek. Haught ain't God's bravest son and he comes untracked easy."

"That his shack?"

"No, it's an old homesteader's place. There were several of them up here before the Little Big Horn battle down at Hardin. Many such folks took that battle as a bad omen and left their claims. All they had was a shack, and in the passage of time most are in need of repair."

"How did Haught find the body?"

"Said he was passing through and saw signs someone had been living there."

Wulf nodded to show that he understood.

They reached the cabin in the late afternoon. There were lots of tracks going and coming from the shack to the tilted outhouse. There had been a horse kept in a shed. Looked to Wulf like he'd eaten lots of old dusty hay, but he was barefoot and now he was gone. From the fresh hair that Wulf found on the corners and ends of boards, he'd guess him to be a pinto.

Wulf came outside in the late afternoon sunshine, and Herschel waved him over to the cabin doorway. "He was shot twice at close range. Powder burns on his shirt show that much. What did you find?"

"A barefoot horse's been kept out there. Probably a pinto. He's gone, too."

"So we have a murder and a horse stolen."

Wulf shrugged. "That horse probably wasn't worth much."

"The old grizzly character inside suited him, or he suited the horse. But no one's going to cry over either, I don't reckon."

"What do we do next?"

"Ride over to bum us a meal off the next rancher and borrow a horse to carry the body in on."

"Can I look at the dead man?" If he was going to be any help, he needed to learn all about this business — like it or not.

"Help yourself. He ain't saying much. I never recall seeing him around here before either."

"What was he eating?" Wulf asked, going by him and steeling himself for the sight of a dead man. Kind of an eerie feeling inside, but he knew it was something he had to do.

"Canned beans, I guess. There's some empties in there."

On the floor in the dark shack was a body lying on its back. Two black holes with powder burns. The man's beard was tangled and his greasy hair streaked in gray. Herschel must have closed the man's eyes. His lips were open and showed his yellow teeth. The old red-black checkered wool shirt was worn, and the man had on a canvas vest and wool pants that were threadbare. But

266

he wore new knee-high boots.

"He had a dollar and forty-two cents on him and no identification." Herschel was standing above him as Wulf squatted down, looking for an answer in a silent void.

"What about them boots?"

"They are the most memorable things about him."

"Can we pull one off?" Wulf asked.

"Sure. Never entered my mind."

Wulf held onto the man's leg, and Herschel removed the boot with some effort. A shower of twenty-dollar bills floated out of the first boot, and more floated out of the other.

They counted them and Herschel made a note — 380 dollars.

"Lots of money for an old bum to have, isn't it? These boots were made in Miles City by a boot maker named Tree." Wulf had read the label sewn inside the vamp.

"I bet he'd know this fella or whoever he made these boots for."

"You're thinking this fella is the second owner?"

Herschel nodded. "Let's go find a horse to haul him back to town on."

Wulf agreed, feeling better being outside even in the setting sun and with the air turning cooler. He shrugged on his jacket, grateful for Marsha thinking of them, and they rode over to Jack Nipp's place. He loaned them a packhorse and packsaddle. Jack'd seen some smoke over by the cabin, figured it was some fugitive moving through, maybe headed for Canada. Folks like Nipp learned to mind their own business about men on the move, and they only hoped such men didn't steal a horse on their way north.

Mrs. Nipp fed them some corn bread and hot brown beans from a kettle that hung in her hearth. They were tasty and well cooked, with some onion and bacon in them. It was past dark when Wulf and Herschel loaded the dead man on the horse, and they rode back by the starlight.

Marsha met them with a lantern at their house after they left the corpse with the undertaker. "Took you long enough."

"We were coming all the time, weren't we, Wulf?"

"Sure were."

"Who fed you?"

"Mrs. Nipp."

"Ah, how long were you there?"

"How long does it take to eat two bowls of brown beans?" Herschel asked.

"Well, did you learn his name? The dead man's."

"No, but we know where his boots were made."

"Oh?"

"Miles City, and my deputy Wulf Baker is going over there and learn all about those boots."

"So he's shipping you off already, huh? Well, I have some apple pie that's still hot. We better go have a piece of it."

Wulf felt good retiring to his pallet in the tack room, which smelled of oats and saddle leather. With so many women in the house, he took his place out there. Come sunup, he'd be a deputy investigating the murder over in the next county. He needed to write Dulchy and tell her all about his adventure. She'd not be interested in the dead man, but he could think of something else to tell her about.

The stage ride took eight hours to Miles City, and he felt well rocked arriving there in the late afternoon. He found the Boot Tree Store, and the bell rang overhead when he entered. He drew the boot out of his satchel and put it on the counter.

A balding man looked at it with a frown. "That's Jim Robbins' boot. Where in hell did you find it?"

"Where can I find him?"

"Ain't no one seen him in over a month.

Went off on a cow buying trip and ain't been seen since. Who're you?"

"Deputy Sheriff Yellowstone County, Wulf Baker. We found these boots on a dead man in a shack over our way."

"Land's sake, who killed him?"

"That's why I'm here. Could be there might be more than one dead man."

"Sheriff's gone, but Biff Adams, his head deputy, was in here an hour ago. Maybe he can help you. They've been looking high and low for Robbins."

"This fella was whiskered, long greasy gray-streaked black hair. Stood five-eight or nine. Wore a checkered wool shirt and canvas vest."

"Sounds like the kind of riffraff comes in on the railroad. How old are you anyway?"

"Nineteen," he lied.

"Guess 'cause you're kin to the sheriff is why you have that commission. His father was a deputy, too. He was a tough old gun-hand. Had it out with some Messicans last year who'd chased him up here from Texas."

"That was Thurman Baker, my dad's brother, I guess."

"That was his name."

"How do I find this deputy sheriff?"

"Jail down the street. Since they quit construction again on the railroad tracks, he ain't very busy."

Wulf thanked the man and hurried off to find the deputy.

Biff Adams wore a large mustache, two six-guns, and had shoulders wide as a longhorn's rack. He stood in the doorway of the jail as the daylight slipped away. "Howdy, what can I do for you?"

"I'm Herschel Baker's deputy. Looking, I guess, for a Mr. Robbins."

"I doubt he's even alive. No one's seen him in months."

"A man wearing his boots is dead, too. Killed this week in a shack in my county." Wulf went on explaining the situation.

"Let's go eat. We can eat and talk at the same time," Adams said. They went to the hotel, had a large steak and all the trimmings.

"If the killer came back here, he led back a sorry, crooked-legged mustang with a saddle. Probably a pinto," said Wulf.

"You see it?"

"No, but I looked at the tracks, seen his hair on the corners of the corral, and saw his diet. Old hay."

"How long ago did this shooting occur?" Adams asked.

"Four days ago, give or take one."

Adams clamped his mouth in his hand

and nodded. "Stovall Lane did that a few days ago. Led a pinto Injun horse, about a rack of bones, into town. Let's go look him up."

"Who's he?" Wulf asked, standing up and washing down the last of his coffee before they left.

"I got the meal," Adams said, and they hurried out in to the cooling night air. "Ah, a worthless no-account. He's always stealing things. Hard to catch at it."

"Will he talk?"

"I figure so."

Keeping up with the long-legged Adams wasn't a problem, but Wulf decided that when the deputy started somewhere, he really moved. They were soon at a junkyard and dogs were barking at them.

"Who's there?" a woman shrieked from the lighted doorway.

"Biff Adams. Tell Lane to get out here. I want to talk to him."

"Why? He ain't done nothing."

"I'll go around back," Wulf offered. "In case he goes out that way."

In a stage whisper, Adams said, "Watch the dogs. They might bite you."

"I can handle dogs." He hurried through the broken-down wagons and piles of junk. When the two black dogs came for him, he hissed them away in the moonlight. They withdrew. Neither was that vicious, he decided. Satisfied he had the back door in his sight, Wulf put his hand on his gun butt. Adams and the woman were still having a verbal battle in front.

A bare head appeared thirty feet away in the dark doorway. Wulf drew his Colt and let the man slip outside. "Hold it right there and get your hands high."

"Who the hell're you?"

For a few seconds, Wulf's finger tightened on the trigger. Then the man threw his hands up in surrender. "Don't shoot."

"He's back here," Wulf shouted, turning the man around and jerking a revolver out of his holster from behind. He stuck it in his waistband and headed his prisoner around the shack.

"Well, Lane, leaving, huh?" Adams said.

"What the hell you want me for?"

"He wants you for murder."

"Huh?"

"Murder of someone wearing Jim Robbins' boots over in Yellowstone County."

"I don't know nothing about no murder."

"Except you shot him and brought his pinto horse back here afterward," Adams said.

"I bought that horse."

Wulf holstered his own gun and walked behind the two down the boardwalk. He needed to learn all he could about quizzing a killer like this one.

"Yeah, with a bullet. Where did you plant Robbins?" Adams demanded.

"I don't know nothing about him."

"Well, that horse ties you to the murder. Who was the dead man?"

"I bought —"

"Lane, we ain't listening to lies all night."

"Oh, all right. Ernest Scranton. He was holding out on me."

"How much?"

"Five hundred bucks or so."

"Money you got off Robbins?" Adams glanced back at Wulf before they crossed the empty street. Wulf agreed with a nod of approval — it was going well so far.

"I said I never had nothing to do with him."

"But Scranton had lots of your money?"

"He owed me some."

"So you shot him and took his horse."

"There was more than that."

"You got his gun, Wulf?"

"Yes, I have."

"That gun is going to point to you shooting him. The hair off the corral belongs to that pinto you stole, and your tracks all say you killed Scranton."

"Sumbitch had it coming."

"Who shot Robbins?"

"I don't know nothing about that." Lane stopped talking.

With Lane locked in a jail cell, Wulf and Adams sat in the sheriff's office, figuring out what to do next. Wulf was letting the more experienced man take the lead.

"I'd sure like to find out what those bastards did with Robbins' body. His wife would like to put him to rest. Besides, we've looked the country over. Reckon he's at the place where Lane shot Scranton?"

"I can go back up there and look. We didn't see any fresh grave, but it was getting late."

"Hell, if you hadn't figured out he took a pinto horse, we'd still been looking. That was good work."

"How we going to find out where he stashed Robbins' body?"

Adams looked grim. "Cut him a deal. I'll tell him I'll let you take him back to Yellowstone County on the next stage if he tells me where the body is. Otherwise, he can wait for the local mob to come down here and lynch him for doing it."

"Will that work?"

"I'm thinking it will. He won't want a

lynch mob to drag him out of here and hang him."

"Sounds sensible."

They sauntered back to the cell where Lane lay all stretched out in the iron bunk.

"What do you bastards want?" Lane grumbled.

Adams hissed at him, "Come over here."

"What for?" Lane threw his legs off the bunk, ran his fingers through his long hair, and came over.

"You got two choices. Tell me where Robbins' body is at." Adams's voice dropped to a whisper. "If you do, I'll let you go stand trial at Yellowstone County for Scranton's murder. You don't, then you can count on Robbins' friends breaking in here and lynching you."

"You don't give a man much of a choice, do you?"

"Baker is leaving on the morning stage with or without you."

"I could get five for manslaughter —" Lane was thinking out loud. "All right, but this ain't no confession. He's buried up on Myrtle Creek — well, we dumped him in an outhouse on an old place up there."

Adams about melted as if he knew the very spot. "What happened to his horse?"

"Shipped him to Alberta with a fella

needed one. We got a deal?"

Adams nodded. He started back out of the cell area, shaking his head.

"You know that place he's talking about?" Wulf asked as they went back in to the office.

"Exactly. I was there. Now I know why that old outhouse stunk so bad. Damn bastards. I'll get his remains back for his wife. She's a good woman. I owe you one."

"Supper was enough. I'm kinda enjoying this law business. I came up here to see my cousin and what Montana was like. Like Texas, there's tough people in it, but I might not mind living up here."

"You're young, Wulf. So I want to warn you. Lane is an old hand at jails and incarcerations. Just remember, he tries something, kill him. He ain't worth anyone getting hurt over."

Wulf agreed. He better get some sleep. It would be a long stage ride back to Billings in the morning. With his prisoner — *kill him, he ain't worth anyone getting hurt over.*

TWENTY-FOUR

"How long do you think Wulf'll be up there?" Marsha asked. "He's mighty young to be going looking for a killer."

"Folks are old at different ages." Herschel held the warm cup of coffee in his hands and blew on the steam. "That boy's been pulling a load since his daddy took sick. He's not a kid. Life cheated him out of that."

"How old is he?"

"In age or experience?"

Marsha frowned at him and rinsed off the dish in her hands. "I mean, how old?"

"He'll be old enough in December to take over his father's estate."

"Is that why this Hughes made it so tough on him?"

"I think so. Hughes has been averse to work all his life. His daddy must have brought a little money to Texas, and they always had help to do everything for them.

'Course the war got everyone's money, and folks had to start doing for themselves. No slaves and they couldn't afford help. Hughes still had some Mexicans doing their work when I left. But he never made any cattle drives or done a lick of anything, so I think he saw a chance to get some money by marrying Wulf's mother."

"And Wulf said she defends him."

"I know it don't sound right, but it's a mess obviously. And ain't a thing I can do about it."

"I know. But you can usually figure out answers I can't." She winked at him. "Now, you two men need to stabilize Yutta's foot so she can walk on it. Some kinda brace for it."

"Yes, ma'am, I'll start work on that."

"If only that poor woman could walk without sticks. You know that Wulf made her those crutches and taught her how to use them. Before then, she crawled around."

"He also broke three mustangs for them to ride."

"I know. He's mature for his age. And that Hughes is probably lucky he is still alive. Why, I might have sent him to hell myself for what he did to that boy."

"Why Marsha Baker, you sound halfway mean tonight."

She laughed. "You know how mean I am."

"I'm going down to the jail and see if he mailed me a letter from Miles City today."

"I hope you don't stay down there all night."

"No way. I'll be right back."

He finished his coffee, handed her his cup. Kate was playing songs on her piano and the girls were singing along. They waved at him when he went out. A warm night for a change — spring was coming, but slowly.

He went inside the courthouse. He could hear Billy Short laughing and Wulf's voice — Wulf back already?

"Well, that was a short trip," Herschel said.

"He brung back the killer, too," Billy said, beaming like a cat with a new mouse in his mouth.

"Well, who is he?"

"Some fella named Lane," Wulf said. "He was partners with the dead man, Scranton, who he shot. Earlier, they both killed a cattle buyer named Robbins and threw him in an old outhouse on a deserted farmstead. Lane said Scranton was holding out money on him — from the robbery, I guess."

"Money he never got, right?" Herschel asked.

"Yes, that's the money that we found in

Robbins' boots. The deputy sheriff made a deal with Lane. He wanted to know where they planted Robbins' body so his widow could have him reburied in a cemetery. The deal was Lane could come down here and face murder charges in Yellowstone County. Up there, he faced being lynched by Robbins' friends."

"So that's settled?" asked Herschel.

"He's in the jail cell, Boss," Billy said.

"Sounds good to me. Good night, Billy. We better get home. I bet there's a fresh pie waiting on our return."

"You about ready to go after those robbers in Nebraska?" Wulf asked, going out the front door of the courthouse into the gathering darkness.

"Marsha wants us to invent something to make Yutta's foot stiff so she can walk on it. She thinks we're inventors."

Wulf scratched his ear. "Dang if I can think of anything. Straps that tie or buckle?"

"Well, we need to do that if we can find the time before we go after the robbers."

"I'll get up first thing in the morning and work on it, while I'm back to shoeing our horses."

They both laughed. Wulf was plumb taken up with how to make her ankle stiff enough for her to use it. There had to be a way.

After apple pie, Wulf was in his bedroll looking at the dark ceiling of the tack room as some starlight came in the cobweb-coated window. He hoped he was carrying his part of the load around there. Suddenly, the door creaked open.

"Don't shoot me." It was Mona.

"What's wrong?" He sat up and tried to figure out why she was there.

"Plenty is wrong." She wrapped the robe around herself and squatted down beside him.

"What?"

"You ever see I am a woman?"

"Yes."

"No. You think I am an Indian."

"Why, Mona, you're — ah, a nice woman. But I have one in Texas. Her name is Dulchy and she's waiting for me."

"See, you don't even look at me."

"Hey, they only allow white men one wife." He was sitting on his butt in the bedroll holding up a single finger.

"Dumb law."

"But those are the rules."

"Other white men have wife and mistress."

"That's not my way."

"I can see that. I am not a pretty girl."

"Who said that?"

"If I was pretty, you would look at me. I

see men's eyes go after pretty women. Yours never go after me."

"What are you going to do?"

"I will take a horse if you let me and go find a man who will look at me."

"Just 'cause a man will look at you is not the answer," he said. "It is what you see in his heart. Look in his heart, Mona."

"I will look in his heart. In the morning, I will be gone if I can take one of those horses you caught."

"Why not steal him?"

"I will —" And she leaped upon him and forced him on his back. She began kissing him until, at last out of breath, she raised up and looked him in the eye. "You have no heart for me."

He clutched her shoulders and drew her to him. Then he kissed her and took her breath away. "There, my sister, ride with the wind. I have ten dollars to help you travel. May God ride with you."

Stunned, she rose. The money he gave her she clutched in one hand, the back of the other hand held to her mouth as if to save his kiss. She turned and rushed out of the tack room. A few minutes later, he heard her ride off, and he soon fell asleep.

"Mona left last night," Marsha said to him

when he came inside for breakfast.

"Yes. She told me she was leaving."

"Why? We tried to make her feel at home."

"It was me. Yes, me. She said last night that she wanted me. I told her I had Dulchy in Texas. I guess I didn't ever take her serious as a woman in my life."

"She had no right to expect that of you. You took on her burdens."

"But not her."

"You are very wise for your age."

He shrugged. "About women I am still learning."

"Where is Mona at?" Sarah asked. "She's not in her bed."

"Darling, she had to go help her own people," Marsha said, and shared a nod with Wulf. "And as for women, Wulf, you will keep on learning the rest of your life."

He gathered his things for the trip. Herschel issued him a .44/40 Winchester for their odyssey. Art came by and went over things he had to do while they were gone after the McCaffertys. The prosecution of Lane would be left up to Art and the county prosecutor unless Herschel and Wulf made a fast trip back. Herschel doubted they could do that. It was a long ride up from Ogallala to the reservation, and another long ride back. Plus the train to and from

Cheyenne and the stage ride to and from Billings. Art would have to handle the Lane affair. Herschel was satisfied that it would be all right. They left the next day at noon for Sheridan by coach. Saddles, rifles, bedrolls all on board.

The next day, Herschel pointed out where his brother, Tom, was buried beside a small church on the Crow reservation. "A stampede got him. Came all this way and I lost him. We were going to build a great ranch up here. I think we would have if he'd lived."

The clouds threatened rain and like all Western people, they hoped it fell softly and there was lots of it. In Sheridan they were in the rain, and in Buffalo it was muddy. The Bighorns reared high above them as they rode on south past Fetterman's Massacre and rocked on toward Cheyenne.

The soft spring rains were still sweeping through the country when they reached Cheyenne. There was perfume in the showers that Herschel could scent. A new smell and a promise riding it that grazing for livestock would soon burst out.

"That should really bring up the grass." Herschel smiled.

"Maybe we ought to celebrate and buy a sarsaparilla," Wulf said.

So they had one apiece and went to find a

diner. The train wasn't coming for six hours. Not enough time to take a room, so they put off getting a room until Ogallala. Herschel was convinced they'd sleep twenty-four hours before heading out.

But Wulf wasn't satisfied they'd have that long. His cousin would be itching to arrest those robbers and get this business over with. Made no matter to Wulf. He was enjoying the company of a man. His father's long illness had made Wulf a lone rider for the past three years, and getting back into the swing of things traveling with a real man was sure a good feeling. Funny how he'd never realized the things he'd missed — like the way Herschel treated him, as his equal. None of this *boy* business. He'd made him a deputy. Sent him off to find and bring in a killer. Wasn't some big surprise that he'd got the killer either. Herschel had expected him to. It was the way he'd wanted things. Damn, why did his father have to die? Life didn't deal out the best hands all the time.

He posted Dulchy a letter from a stationery shop in Cheyenne.

Dear Dulchy,
I am headed with my cousin for Ogallala, Nebraska. I arrested a killer in Miles City, Montana, this week for him. I am now a

deputy sheriff. We are going after some men who robbed an old buffalo hunter of his treasure chests. It is going to be spring one day soon up here. I can't hardly wait. I about beat the robins coming north. Tell your aunt hi and I miss you.

My best,
Wulf

"I guess this Dulchy is important in your life," Herschel said.

"She's a mighty fine young lady. She could have anyone she wanted." He shrugged. "I feel lucky she wants me."

"She don't have bad taste." Herschel laughed and clapped him on the shoulder. "Well, you've seen part of my job. You sticking around or going back to Texas?"

"Herschel, I'd love to have the Three-Crosses Ranch back. I get it back, I'd have to go home. If I don't, reckon I'd carve me a ranch out up here."

"What did you tell Dulchy?"

"I told her the same thing. Texas or Montana. I'd decide after the court case."

Herschel nodded. "I hope you win it back."

They went inside the depot building and settled on a pewlike bench to wait for the eastbound. Wulf sat with his elbows on his legs. He was hoping he'd win it back, too. Only time would tell.

They arrived in Ogallala the next morning, and left the train with saddles and gear. Herschel hired a taxi to haul them to the Grand Hotel, and inside the two-story lobby, a young man waited on them.

Herschel took the rooms for two nights, and they sent their gear up with the bellman. Then the two of them went down the street to a café that Herschel knew. The streets were crowded with wagons and people on horseback and even on bicycles. There were folks in leather, Indians in colorful blankets, squaws carrying heavy packs that looked like they belonged on a mule.

And perfumed hussies in low-cut dresses, walking the boardwalk, were busy hustling customers. Their bold face-to-face approaches and the rank simplicity of their language about what they wanted made Wulf's face burn with embarrassment.

"I hate them," Wulf said after disengaging from one.

"Aw, they've got to work, too, I reckon." Herschel shrugged and changed the subject.

The café was crowded. The folks inside had their own horsey odor, and the smell of food over that was even stronger. A waitress waved them over to a table where three men were leaving. In her large arms, the ample-bodied woman was gathering up all the plates and cups when they arrived.

"I'll mop it off when I come back. Better put your order in."

"What's the best?" Herschel asked.

"I think the beef roast, mashed taters, gravy, and some kind of vegetable are all right."

"Bring that and coffee, too," Herschel said, and she gave him a girlish grin.

Wulf was glad Herschel had the attention of this female. That business was not for him.

"We going to sleep a few hours?" Wulf asked.

Herschel nodded. "Maybe a month."

No way Wulf could contain himself from laughing. "Why, you'll be up in a few hours ready to ride north."

"I'm trying to be relaxed this trip."

"I know."

"Did Mona say where she was going when she left this past week?"

"No, sir. She said, if I won't take her, she was going to find a man who would."

"Must have been hard — for you."

Wulf shook his head. "Women are the hardest part for me. I liked Mona. She fed them other three — they weren't her kin.

They were outcasts. She could have survived by herself, but she chose to stay and take care of them. None of them were her own people. Mona was Shoshone. Who knows what Crazy Mary is? Yutta is probably Cheyenne."

"It was bad?"

"Oh, their camp was nothing but a small willow lodge covered in rotten hides. They ate what she could steal or beg off folks on the road. She must have sold her body at times to men on the road for food. I didn't hold that against her — it was for the others she did it."

"You caught those mustangs?"

"They were unbranded and bore saddle scars, so they weren't hard to break. They'd been broke before and my horses could outrun them, they were so winter poor."

"And you made Yutta her crutches?"

"Yes. I wanted her to have some pride. She drug herself all over camp on her butt. I got her up on crutches and walking."

Herschel closed his eyes. "You did all that for three ragged Indians."

"No, I did that for four human beings. You forgot the baby."

Herschel shook his head in weary disbelief. "Most folks would have rode off and turned their backs on them."

Wulf shrugged his shoulders. "I couldn't. Not when I saw how bad their situation was. But have you ever slept in a pile with three women and a baby?"

"No."

"Trust me, it is unnerving."

Their food arrived and they set in to eat.

Herschel pointed a fork at him. "Knowing what you know now, would you do it again?"

"Yes, sir, if I thought anyone was that bad off, I'd stop and try to help them."

That boy had a way about him that Herschel really liked. No matter the consequences or his own life, he'd stop and help those who were downtrodden. It took a helluva big heart to do that — must be a Baker heart.

TWENTY-FIVE

When they stepped out of the Ogallala café into the midday sunshine, Herschel put his arm out to stop him. "Hold up. See that fella in the red plaid jacket on that mule?"

"Yes. Who is he?"

"Audrey Scopes. He's wanted in Montana for stage robbery."

Wulf looked hard at the man with the white sideburns and the stovepipe hat. "Who's with him?"

"Looks like that breed and those three others coming behind him are part of his gang."

"What do we do next?" Wulf dried his sweaty palms on the sides of his pants.

"Keep them in mind and we'll move along on the boardwalk to see where they go to."

Wulf nodded. There goes all that extra sleep that Herschel had promised him. It was already compromised by five wanted men on horseback leading two packhorses.

They looked like a tough enough outfit, the kind that bristled with weapons. Everything from tomahawks and knives to pistols. They'd never be taken without a fight. This was going to be tough going — five outlaws against two lawmen.

The five soon rode into Fracker's Wagon Yard. Herschel nodded. "We know now where they'll keep their horses."

"They know you?" Wulf asked.

"They might."

"Then seeing you might make them nervous."

"What are you getting at?"

"I could go down there and snoop around and learn all I can about them. They damn sure don't know me."

"These fellas are lots tougher than Lane, who you brought in."

"I saw all those weapons on them."

"Let's go borrow two shotguns and get the local constable to help us."

"You know him?"

"No telling. They change them regularly."

"Fine with me. Do it now?"

"I like to get things over with like this."

"Let's go find him then."

After asking around where the town law was, they found Constable William Easton in a bar drinking beer with a half-dressed doxie. He narrowed his black eyebrows at them and excused her. She left.

"You gents need me?"

"Easton, my name's Baker, this is my deputy Wulf. We're down here from Montana looking for some robbers. A few minutes ago, we saw Audrey Scopes and his gang ride into Fracker's Wagon Yard. They are wanted in Montana for shooting a mail guard and robbing several stages. We need to borrow two shotguns, and you may come along and share in the reward."

"Why, he ain't nothing but a boy," Easton said, scoffing at Wulf.

"When the smoke settles, we'll see who's got the sand in their craw."

"I don't like —"

"Easton, loan me two scatterguns and we'll go take them ourselves."

"All right. All right. But these sound like tough customers."

"Where are the guns?"

"We can get three out of Joe Harper's stock. He's across the street. I'm ready." Easton reset the flat-brimmed black hat on his head.

Wulf noticed Easton wore his pants tucked in his high-top boots and carried a revolver in a shoulder holster. The ivory grip showed at the edge of his lapel. A big man, well over two hundred pounds, he looked a little soft for any kind of hard work, and a bronc might dump him mighty fast. His remarks about Wulf being a boy had not endeared the man to Wulf either. In fact, Wulf would have been happy leaving Easton with his girlfriend in the bar.

When Easton asked for the guns, Harper never hesitated. He drew down three spanking-new double-barrel shotguns and handed one each to Herschel and Wulf, then spilled out an open box of high brass shells on the counter. Wulf and Herschel filled their vest pockets with ammo. Easton did the same with his coat. They moved out of the store drawing some murmurs from the crowd on the sidewalk, and many curious eyes followed them down the boardwalk.

When they drew closer to Fracker's Yard, Easton began waving people off the street and boardwalks. The three lawmen crossed the street with the traffic stopped, and went toward the big open gates.

"You know these men," Easton said to Herschel. "You take the lead."

Wulf was trying to see everything around them, the loaded twelve-gauge in his hands. He cocked the hammers back when he was halfway across the street, fearful that his thumb might slip and accidentally fire the gun off in the dirt and warn the outlaws in the yard. It didn't.

"Easy, men," Herschel said when they reached the open breach in the twelve-foot-high wooden fence walls.

Wulf saw Scopes's stovepipe hat on the far side of his dun horses. When Scopes discovered the lawmen coming, a wide-eyed look spread over his face.

"Drop your gun or die!" Herschel ordered with the shotgun stock in his shoulder.

Scopes sprawled on his belly under the horses with his gun drawn, and met a load of buckshot face-on. The duns whirled, and about ran over Easton going out the gate.

One of the outlaws had his pistol aimed at Easton from a side door. Wulf took him out with the left barrel of his shotgun, and glanced up in time to see the breed had a knife ready to throw at them from the loft door overhead. The shotgun against his hip, he fired, and the knife fell to the ground. The hard-hit breed began screaming that he was dying and thrashing on the loft floor.

"Over there," Wulf said, seeing a third outlaw with his gun drawn coming through the corral. Both Herschel and Easton shot him while Wulf reloaded his own scatter-gun. The breech snapped shut, Wulf indicated to Herschel he would go left. Herschel agreed, and motioned he'd take the barn. Easton, who'd lost his aloof composure, was looking everywhere for another gang member and following Herschel.

Once Wulf was around the building, he could see where the ground dropped off into a creek bed and someone hatless was running hell-bent through the brush to get away.

"Halt!" he shouted, and the man only glanced over his shoulder. Wulf knew he'd have no chance of ever catching him on foot once he got away. He aimed high, shot, and then decided he must have hit him because the man went facedown.

On his boot heels, he slid down the steep bank and jumped the small stream. The man was groaning when he reached him. Wulf had the shotgun ready. When he told the outlaw to roll over, he did, with a six-gun in his hand. But with the smoking muzzle of the shotgun shoved in his face, he dropped the pistol immediately.

Looking around, Wulf saw an easier way to get up on the bluff and ordered his prisoner to go over there. "You try something, I've got another barrel of shot ready for you."

Cursing like a sea captain, the outlaw

finally said, "You ain't nothing but a damn kid."

"Get off the kid shit. I shot your buddy in the yellow shirt and got you. Now tell me I'm a kid and I might send you to hell right here."

Seated on a wooden toolbox, Easton was mopping his sweaty face with his white kerchief when Wulf and his prisoner came in the back of the barn through the walk-through doorway.

"You get him, too, huh?"

"He's got some shot in his back."

"Doc can dig it out. These fellas were tough. I never saw the likes of them," Easton said. "Whew, I thought we were all dead."

One of the outlaws sat on the ground with a bloody shoulder, his chin dropped, and shaking his head. "All I wanted was a couple of drinks."

"I don't think we need to move the breed," Herschel said, coming down from the loft on the ladder. "He's close to dying."

"That'll make three dead and two wounded," Easton said. "Been a damn bloody afternoon. How much is the reward on them?"

"Four at two-fifty and five on Scopes," Herschel said.

"How much is my part?"

"Five hundred. That's a three-way split."

"You know that's damn near a year's pay for being constable in this town."

"It's lots of money. What're you going to do with it?" Herschel squatted in the loose hay beside the man.

Easton squared his shoulders and stood up at the sight of the curious townsfolk coming closer in the street outside. "I may marry that gal you saw in the bar today. I'll need someone when I get old to care for me." He turned back. "Wulf's your name?"

"Yes."

"What you doing with yours?"

"I'll ask a gal back in Texas what she wants us to do with it."

Easton dropped his gaze to his dust-floured black boots. "You two ever need me, you call. You are two of the coldest, toughest lawmen I ever worked with." Then he straightened, facing all the curious onlookers pouring in to the yard. "Everyone out of this barn. Couple you boys go upstairs and get that breed. Toss Scopes's body out there in a wheelbarrow, and take him and that other dead man down to the Black Brothers Funeral Home. Do the same with the breed. Harry, you run tell Doc to meet us at the jail. I got two needs his attention. You two get up and head for the jail." He looked in the outlaws' direction.

"We'll fill out the papers later," Herschel said. "Wulf and me are going to sleep for a few days."

Wulf smiled, unloading his shotgun. They were finally going to get that rest Herschel had promised — he'd have to see how long it really lasted before he went to bragging too much.

Twenty-Six

They slept into the next day, woke, and dragged themselves out of bed. On the street thirty minutes later, a newsboy was hawking the daily paper on the boardwalk, shouting, "Montana lawmen shoot it out with Scopes Gang."

Herschel gave the boy a dime and looked at the front page. "We didn't need this kind of story."

"Here's the restaurant." Wulf opened the door and Herschel went by him, still trying to read the front-page story.

"What's wrong?" Wulf asked when they finally sat down at a side table.

"The McCaffertys get hold of this, they'll know we're coming. That youngest one, August, knows me well. He's the one who escaped in the stage robbery."

"What can we do?"

"I'm not certain, but it forces our hand to get on up there."

They ordered breakfast, though the waiter must have thought it odd so late in the day. When he left with their order, Herschel handed Wulf the paper.

"They can't spell my name right," Wulf said, amused. "They have an *o* in it."

"We better get those papers filled out on those outlaws and get some horses to ride up there."

"How far away are they?"

"Two days, maybe two and a half."

"You been there before?"

"I've been up there in that country."

Wulf nodded. They were headed for some new territory he'd never seen. When breakfast arrived shortly after the coffee came, he was ready to eat. *Last night we had a shootout with five outlaws, Dulchy — no, he better write her something milder than that.*

After breakfast, they went by Easton's office and found him with his boots on his old scarred desk.

"Morning," he said, throwing his feet down. "I got their names and the posters and everything we need to collect those rewards ready to sign."

Herschel read the reward papers and handed them back. "We can sign that and get on our way. We're going after the Mc-Caffertys and I didn't want all the news to leak out we were even here. They know who I am. I had dealings with them in Deadwood about six weeks ago."

"Sorry. The mayor wanted you to come to supper."

"We'll pass, and you thank him for us. We're on our way right now to get some horses and ride up there."

The papers were signed and they were on their way. They found Ira Hansen at Swan's Livery, and he showed them several horses he had for sale. All were common as grass. Most in thin early spring condition.

"I got a few that are kinda tough. One's a big roan. He threw the last fella off in the street twice. I got him back, but if —"

"Where are they at?"

Ira grinned. "Right back here."

The dusty-looking red roan had small pig eyes, and Wulf grinned at the sight of him.

"The other two, the sorrel and the bay, are all for sale. Fifty bucks apiece."

Herschel was in the pen as the three circled away from him. He flushed them, waving his arms, and they took off running. Wulf nodded his approval. They looked sound enough, but they'd sure be "haints."

"A hundred bucks for the pen," Herschel said.

"Can't take a dime less than a hundred

and a quarter."

"A hundred and ten."

"Make it a hundred and twenty and you got them. No refunds, though, at that price."

"Deal. Our saddles are at the hotel. We'll be right back."

Ira nodded. "I want to see this."

"It won't be the show you expect," Herschel said, and they hurried after their things. In less than thirty minutes, they'd snubbed the horses down and saddled them. First, they put the packsaddle they bought from Ira on the bay, and hung the horse's left rear hoof off the ground, tied to the cross bucks, so all he could do was hobble around. Next, they roped the sorrel, who had a head-slinging fit. Wulf soon had him eared down and slipped his bits in his mouth. The red horse still had lots of white showing around his eyes when Wulf tossed his saddle blankets on him. More scared than anything else, he dropped down like he intended to spring high as the moon when Wulf applied the saddle, talking all the while. When he'd cinched up, Wulf stepped aboard him before the horse realized that was his intention.

They circled the pen twice in a long hard walk. Wulf never let him have enough rein to get his head down, and he set down good when Wulf stopped him. Then Wulf booted the sorrel in close to the roan and took a neck rope from Herschel. He wrapped it on his saddle horn and Herschel mounted the roan.

They went around and around the pen with the roan squealing like a pig caught under a gate. But he soon learned that on such a short rope, all he could do was dance. After fifteen minutes of warming them up, the riders dismounted and loaded the packhorse.

Ira shook his head. "You fellas make it look easy. Those are tough horses."

"That's what we needed." Herschel gave him a salute, and they were off toward the northern portion of Nebraska.

Riding the hell out of them would sure improve the horses' disposition. But Wulf was proud that they never bucked in the street. They rode through the midday traffic with all three horses walking on eggs, but they made it and soon were at the ferry. It was another experience that shocked the horses, but the men had them in close tow, and soon they were riding north again.

"We handled these old ponies like we did the gang — short and tough," Herschel said.

"Only thing, these three spoiled ponies ain't through with us yet," Wulf said.

"They sure ain't deadheads anyway." Both men agreed about that.

A gray-headed woman at a crossroads store fed Herschel and Wulf supper about sundown. She served them chicken stew, and it had a great flavor. Both men were impressed and thanked her.

"Be careful, young men. You have some fine-looking horses out there. There are so many horse thieves up here, you can't keep a horse."

"Thank you, ma'am, we'll watch out for them," Herschel told her. They rode on, finding a place to camp beside a moon lake, a body of water with no outlet. The horses were hobbled and there were two dragging ropes. The idea was to have them close by in the morning.

It took no coaxing to put either man to sleep. Wulf woke in the predawn and with no wood around, decided they'd gnaw on jerky with canteen water to wash it down. His head hurt, and most of the muscles in his body, but he promised himself he'd harden up in a few days. Herschel joined him, and they made their way north asking questions about the McCaffertys here and there.

Most people wouldn't say much about them. That was the way to live in such a wide-open country where there was no protection from men like the McCaffertys. Anyone talked too much might end up with a knock on the door and a bullet in their guts for their troubles.

They found a freighter named Thompson in Alliance who knew the McCaffertys. The false-front buildings and saloons in big tents in the boom city going up were alive with opportunists. The lawmen met Thompson at the wagon yard, which smelled of fresh pine, where they boarded their horses and decided to go find some food.

"Hold up, fellars," the big burly man said. "You going to eat supper?"

"Yes. Where is the best place?" Herschel asked him.

"There's a fat Mexican gal named Dora slings real hash down here a block. A little spicy, but you fellows look like you know spicy food."

He cut a big hocker out of his throat and spit it ten feet away. "This place up here is sure on fire, ain't it?"

"Booming, I'd say. Wulf and I are looking for some gents named McCafferty who have a place up north of here."

"Yeah, way north. They're up above Chadron outside of Fort Robinson. They owe you money?"

Herschel shook his head.

"Well, watch yourself. They ain't got a bad reputation 'cause they're churchgoers."

"How hard will they be to find?"

"They've got a place right off this road north of Chadron. Maybe two miles or so."

Herschel thanked the man, and the three of them ate the fat woman's spicy Mexican food, seated on the ground beside the yellow canvas wall tent she used for her house. The food made Wulf homesick, and he wondered until he fell asleep that night how Dulchy was doing. Visions of Ranger and Calico only made his stomach turn over and over.

A damn tough night. On the road, he was grateful for the meadowlarks and plovers running up the road ahead of them, a screaming red-tail hawk above, and a wall-eyed red horse underneath him that danced the first two miles on his toes.

They camped that night at a wagon yard ranch run by two old bachelors. Wulf missed Dora's tasty food from the night before. The bachelors' boiled beef was tasteless and the potatoes could have been cooked an hour longer. Breakfast was oatmeal, stiff as it could be, with no sugar or milk. Their coffee was made from scorched barley and bitter as anything.

Riding out from their place, Herschel laughed. "That fat Mexican gal could have cooked circles around them two."

Wulf agreed. "But you could look at them two and see what they cooked. Sideways, neither made a good shadow."

The roan must have thought laughing was a good time to buck. He put his head down between his knees, and Herschel had his work cut out for him getting the horse back down. He must have bucked for a quarter mile before Herschel jerked his head up.

"Things sure got Western around here," Wulf teased.

"Sure ain't any dull moments."

Chadron was made up of some log buildings with sod roofs. Corrals to hold cattle for the Indians on commodity day. Several loafing Indians wrapped in colorful blankets looked blank-eyed at their passing. The crowd was dressed in buckskin with wide-brimmed hats, and many had .50-caliber buffalo guns to lean on. They were sure tough-looking. Including the black buffalo soldiers who were stationed out at Fort Robinson and frequented the village, too.

Several stringy-headed women in wash-worn rags that barely covered their bodies made shouts inviting the lawmen over for business. Several onlookers thought it funny, but Wulf and Herschel rode on by, ignoring them.

"Watch for the ox yoke. Thompson said that'll be their place," Herschel reminded him.

"Whew." Wulf turned back in the saddle. "That was the worse town we've been so far."

"Tough place, all right."

"What if they ain't home?" Wulf asked.

"We'll wait for them if it looks like they're coming back. Remember, we may be riding right into a trap."

"I've had that feeling for three days."

They found the ox yoke on a crossbar overhead, sat their horses, and looked at a tall grassy hill with two wagon ruts that went around it to some unseen ranch. Wulf hoped they'd soon be done there. The shoot-out in the wagon yard had shown him how tough these lawbreakers could be. When backed into a corner, these men would fight like badgers.

And he wanted this encounter over — something gripped his gut — this would be the real test for him and Herschel.

"Better unlimber your rifle," Herschel said.

Wulf nodded and reached down to jerk his .44/40 out of the scabbard. He levered a cartridge into the chamber and set the hammer on safety.

"What do you reckon these horses will do when the shooting starts?"

"Good question. Maybe break in two." Herschel was looking around to be certain there wasn't an ambusher on either side of them.

They rode through a cut, and the McCaffertys' home place squatted down before them a quarter mile away in a large basin. The sun danced on the moon lake beyond the homestead, and the strong south wind rippled it. Water and grass — what made this land so valuable to cattlemen, and the cattlemen were moving in quickly to take advantage.

"Ride about thirty feet apart from me. Remember, there may be women here when you have to shoot."

Wulf nodded that he understood, and moved Red out in the knee-high brown stems. A slender woman in a dark dress came out on the porch, threw a bucket of water away, and then peered at them in shock.

"Calvin, get your ass out here! We've got us some real company."

Herschel nodded at Wulf, who'd also heard her voice carry on the wind. The next thing, a man appeared in his underwear with a rifle. Herschel took aim with his and fired the first round. Roan began to dance under him, but he checked the animal.

"McCafferty, you're under arrest."

The rifle in the man's hand must have jammed. For a second, he fought with it. Then he and the woman fled inside.

"Head to the corral for cover," Herschel shouted. "He's going to fight. I should have shot him."

The crack of pistol shots and gun smoke came from a window near the front door. Bent low in the saddle, Wulf made the corral and dismounted. He was pleased Herschel was right with him.

Rifle in Wulf's hand, he bellied down behind the rails, found a place to shoot it through, and took aim at the window. His first shot shattered glass and caused a scream. Herschel was running low to the left to get a shot from a different angle.

Only the wind made a rushing sound. No sounds came from the house but the flap of some clothes on a line. Wolf was a good distance from the front door and the single window. If his rifle didn't work — McCafferty wouldn't hurt them with a pistol except by luck.

"McCafferty, I'm a deputy U.S. marshal.

Get your hands up and surrender," Herschel ordered.

"He can't," the woman shouted back. "He's been hit."

"Then you drag him outside."

"I can't. He's too big."

"If this is a trick, you're liable to be cut down in the cross fire."

"It's no trick. No trick."

Wulf realized how hard his heart was pumping when he rose to his knees. His mind and sight concentrated on the low-roofed cabin and what happened next. He dried his right hand on his pants. Rifle cocked and ready, he advanced on the cabin with Herschel coming in from the left. This could be a trick or trap despite her denial. He didn't trust her, making step after step across the bare ground with little or no cover.

"You come outside," Herschel ordered.

Hair in her red face, swollen from crying, she shied away from Herschel. She wore a new dress. The garment looked awful fancy for housework — in her late twenties or early thirties, she had a hard look about her.

"Stay right there," Herschel ordered her, and left unsaid that Wulf should watch her.

His pistol held by his face, he stepped inside.

For a long moment after Herschel went in, Wulf held his breath — expecting shots. Looking at the anxious woman chewing on her knuckles, he wondered where the sons were at. "What's your name?" he asked.

"Lucille," she replied.

"Where are the others?"

She shook her head. "I have no idea. He's going to die." Then she went back to sobbing and sniffling.

"How is he?" Wulf asked from the doorway, watching her close.

"He'll live," Herschel said.

After looking around for the sight of anyone, Wulf said, "We're coming in." Then he turned to her. "You first."

The scent of her perfume made his empty stomach roil. No doubt McCafferty had found her in some whorehouse. Inside, the light was shadowy. He could see the man half propped up at the end of the bed, holding his bloody shoulder.

"You have a buckboard?" Herschel asked her.

She nodded.

"Wulf, gather our horses and find the team. Lady, where are the trunks at?"

"What trunks?"

"Listen, you want him alive, you better show us where they are, 'cause we aren't leaving here without them. No matter how bad he's bleeding."

She shook her head in disgust. "I told him. I told him. They'd never give up trying to get them back. It was too much money. No, he wouldn't listen."

Then she peeled back a worn hook rug and exposed the trapdoor in the floor. Then she used the back of her hand against her running nose. "It's down there. The damn bloody stuff."

Herschel opened the door and peered down into the cellar. Satisfied, he gave Wulf a nod that the trunks were down there.

"Where are his two sons?" Herschel asked her.

"You took Auggie to jail —"

Wulf stopped in the doorway to listen. Obviously, the youngest one had not returned. Strange. Had he died? Maybe he'd stayed with those stage robbers that Herschel told him about who'd helped him escape.

"Grayson?"

She curled her lip. "Whoring it up in Deadwood, I guess."

Wulf left on the run to get the horses lined up. That would require some time. But they'd be headed home soon. Or to Montana anyway. Busy catching their horses in the balmy spring weather, he wondered what Dulchy was doing. In her heavy starched blue and white dress, she'd be walking back to her aunt's house. He could imagine the cloth rustling as she strolled home after work.

When the treasure was loaded at last on the hitched buckboard, Herschel called Wulf aside for a two-man conference.

"That bunch of loafers at Chadron ever caught wind of how much gold we have, we'd never make it back. Secondly, I don't trust Lucille. With this money gone, this homestead is going to be tough living again."

"What do you suggest?"

"That we keep our eyes and ears wide open till we can get to Alliance. We can bank it there and let Wells Fargo worry about it from there on."

"How long will it take?"

"Three, four days."

"You think Auggie stayed with the stage robbers?"

"Either that or took off for parts unknown. He wasn't the most willing outlaw."

Wulf squatted on his heels and glanced over at his cousin. "Grayson?"

"He's probably where she said he was, or some other location until he runs out of money."

"What do we need to do about him?"

"There's a stage out of Cheyenne for Deadwood. We're probably three days' hard ride from there."

"But you need me now."

"I will need you. We'll get him. We've got the largest share of the gold back. This bunch didn't make a dent in Buffalo's money. What's on your mind?"

"Whatever is going on in Texas about my life, I guess."

"I bet it is. Let's get started south. There may be some news when we get back."

Wulf shook his head, feeling empty inside. "I sure hope so."

TWENTY-SEVEN

Halfway to Chadron, Herschel had a brainstorm. *Fort Robinson.* Why hadn't he thought about that sooner? They had security, a doctor, and no doubt prison holding facilities for McCafferty. His deputy marshal badge would come in handy. He short-loped his roan horse up to the buckboard that Wulf was driving, sitting beside "Mrs. McCafferty" on the spring seat. Herschel also led the packhorse and sorrel.

"Change in plans. We're going to Fort Robinson. They've got a doctor there and security."

"Sounds good," Wulf said, and smiled back at him.

It was past midnight when Herschel walked in to speak to the officer in charge in the red brick building in the fort.

"What can I do for you, sir?"

"Deputy U.S. Marshal Herschel Baker

with a prisoner and also much robbery loot."

"What will you be needing, sir?"

"A doc for the prisoner. A room for his wife, and a safe place to put the money he stole. We have — my deputy and I will have several horses to put up."

"How much money?"

"More money than I can count. It is in four heavy trunks."

"Our safe is not that large." The lieutenant shook his head.

"Lock it up in a jail cell then."

"Good idea. What will you do with it?"

"Wells Fargo can haul it to Billings, Montana."

"We can have that taken care of. Where is the man needs the medical attention?"

"Out in the buckboard."

"Sergeant Tatum, get a detail to take the man to the brig. Lock those —" He looked to Herschel for a description.

"There are four very heavy trunks on the buckboard," Herschel said.

"They need to be placed in a cell and put under armed guard."

"Yes, sah." The large black noncom nodded to Herschel. "You's going along, sah?"

"Right behind you."

"Sergeant, these men probably have not

eaten in some time."

"I'll see that they are fed, sir, and their horses put up. There are rooms ready at the visitor quarters for them and the missus."

"I hope your stay at Fort Robinson is a good one, sir," the lieutenant said to Herschel.

Later, after a breakfast assembled by a sleepy but congenial black cook, they were shown to individual guest rooms when Sergeant Tatum learned that the lady was not Herschel's wife.

The last thing Herschel told Wulf was they'd head for Deadwood from there. Under the covers with the moonlight filtering in the window, he wondered what Deadwood would be like.

He frowned when someone tried the door. Sitting up in bed with his six-gun in his fist, he faced Lucille McCafferty in a white gown. She held a finger to her mouth.

"I'm sorry to bother you — Wulf. But you must know that fortune belongs to an old buffalo hunter. He doesn't need it. If you and I and Herschel could make a fair division of it, who would know?" She stood beside the bed. The silk gown was open down the middle.

"Well, I'm sorry, ma'am, but I don't think Herschel's interested in splitting it."

She started to put her knee on the edge of the mattress.

"That's far enough. I'm not interested in you or splitting the loot." He came off the bed and began to herd her out of the room.

"How do you know?" she asked in a smoky voice.

He pointed at the open door. "Get out! Get out!"

"You don't have to be so loud and hateful."

"Yes, I do." He bolted the door shut behind her and sagged against the wall. *Dulchy, you'll never know the hell I've been through for you.* It took him several minutes to get composed and back to bed.

In the morning, they took their meal with some officers. Herschel told them Buffalo Malone's treasure story and about chasing after the McCaffertys.

"All I ever got out of that Kansas sand was gritty teeth," a captain said.

"Two arrows in my back," another said.

"Can we go look at this booty?" a lieutenant asked.

"Fine with me if it won't cause a gold rush," Herschel said.

They laughed around the table. "It might," one warned.

So, after breakfast, they went to the brig

and had the door unlocked by the armed guard. Wulf undid one of the trunks and when he set the lid back, the sight made them all suck in their breath.

"How much are they worth?" one man asked.

"Sixty to seventy thousand is my best guess in all of them."

"What will he do with them?"

"I have no idea," Herschel said.

"My, my, you and this young man are very courageous to take this on. Where will you go next?"

"Deadwood. We're leaving shortly."

Their horses saddled and the packhorse loaded, Herschel turned to Wolf. "This law business going to suit you?"

"Life sure ain't real slow up here." Wulf swung into the saddle. "No, sirree, it ain't slow."

"You done any more thinking about where you're going to settle?" Herschel asked.

"I hope when I get back, I've heard from my lawyer — Bob is a good man. I planned hard all my life to take over the Three Crosses. I grew up thinking it would be mine someday and I could ranch and train animals. I haven't done much of that lately, but I think I could go back and pick it up. Haven't had the chance lately."

"I savvy that with all that you lost. Let me tell you, I hate this country north to the Black Hills. Don't know why. It's just vacant land, but we can be in Deadwood in three days or so. I know the police in Deadwood. Grayson is there, we'll round him up easily."

"Lead the way."

"One more thing. I've enjoyed every day we've been on this trip. You're the least complaining person I ever met. But tell me one thing. Did Lucille really try to hoodwink you into helping her get part of that loot?"

Wulf looked at the azure sky for help. His face felt burning red. "She about crawled in bed with me."

Herschel laughed. "I heard part of that row and figured that was her plan."

Wulf simply shook his head. "I'd take gunslinging outlaws any day to some of these women."

"We won't see much of either between here and Deadwood. Let's ride."

The Black Hills looked majestic to Wulf from his first sight of them as a mountain range in the distance. From the magpies and blue jays to the soaring bald eagles, he felt he was in a new paradise of sparkling streams and towering mountains. Despite all the mining activity, he watched the silver trout darting for cover at the invading shadow of horse and rider going by. The turpentine aroma of the ponderosa pines filled the air. As he rode off into the canyons that housed Deadwood, he was surprised at all the fallen trees that choked the forests.

"Some place," he said, following Herschel's roan single file around a freight wagon and eighteen oxen with a bull whacker headed up the canyon.

"You are about to see the other side of the coin."

"Down there is where you shot the paint packhorse?"

"Yes. And starving Indians butchered him in the street and ate him in short order."

They rode into the bustling boomtown.

"What do all these people do for a living?" Wulf asked.

"Everything imaginable from prostitution to pickpockets. There's gamblers, craftsmen, bartenders, musicians, construction workers, lawyers, and bankers."

"But you said lots of them pan for gold in the creeks."

"The prospectors eke out a living doing that. Rich one day, broke the next."

"Where are we going to find Grayson?"

"If he has any money left, he'll be in one of those fancy whorehouses playing the big shot. If not, then he'll be down with the riffraff in the heart of town in a flophouse."

"Where are you betting he's at?"

"I'm not certain. Let's put our horses up at this livery."

"Fine."

Their horses boarded, they hiked uphill to the police station, courthouse, and jail. Assistant Chief Hogan was not in, and wouldn't be back on duty until eight o'clock that evening. But the man behind the desk stood up and extended his hand. "You got any more gold needs tending, Marshal?"

"No, but we'll get a room and be back. I'm looking for a man involved in that crime."

"Hogan will be pleased to hear you're back in town, I am certain, sir."

Outside, Herschel laughed. "I paid them well out of Buffalo Malone's money for helping me get the first two chests."

"Sounds to me like you've got their attention."

Herschel agreed, looking around. A wild and woolly place. He could hardly wait until the railroad tracks got to Billings — his once-quiet small town would be like this mad hatter's party.

They ate with a Chinese cook in a small shop that reeked of Oriental spices, and then found two hotel beds with the desk clerk promising to wake them up at nine that evening. Wulf fell instantly asleep and when Herschel woke him, he thought he'd only slept for a few minutes.

The sun was set when they climbed the hill to the courthouse. Loud barkers were hawking their base wares up and down Main Street. Flirty women in lowcut gowns were trying to intercept trade. And drunks staggered out of bars and fell facedown, to be walked around or over by the boardwalk traffic. Others, rolling their tongues around words that made little sense, took swaying walks downhill through the oncoming foot traffic.

Filthy women, sitting on their butts or knees, begged with tin cups, telling hideous stories to try and pry money out of the purses of the upright passersby. Some of the male tramps even sought discarded stogie butts and relit them for their own use.

Hogan came out and greeted them. Then, when they were introduced, he shook Wulf's hand like he was an equal. Made him feel very good from the start.

"You are back so soon?" Hogan laughed and pushed the bowler back on his head, appraising them.

"That wounded boy I started home with was liberated by some stagecoach robbers in Wyoming. He ain't been heard of since. His father took a bullet in the arm when we tried to arrest him and is in jail in Fort Robinson. But we have all the old man's treasure recovered for him, and Wells Fargo should have it up there shortly. The middle son, Grayson, is supposedly here in Deadwood living the good life."

"Any idea where?" Hogan looked from one to the other for an answer. "I wouldn't know him."

"No, but I bet if he has any money left, he's loud."

"Let's ask around the saloons. He may be using another name."

"He might. Sounds great. Let's check them out. You have time?"

"I've got all the time you need, my friend. Let's go look for him."

The night life had come alive. Wulf soon found the boardwalk crowded shoulder to shoulder, and the reek of unbathed humanity filled his nose. Most of the time, he had to go sideways through the foot traffic to keep up with Herschel and Hogan.

Inside the saloons, the faro wheels were spinning, and Hogan would find a man or woman in charge and ask them about a Grayson McCafferty. Even when Wulf couldn't hear the person's reply for all the noise and music, he could tell by their faces that they didn't know him. Then on to the next joint spilling over with hell-raisers, screaming women, and loud music. Beer sloshing out of wildly swung mugs, cigar smoke thick enough to cut and sell in cubes. It was in the House of Cards that the buxom woman nodded at Hogan's question. She had more of her large breasts exposed in the low-cut dress than was covered. Wulf could tell by how she talked to Hogan that she knew Grayson.

Herschel turned back and said to Wulf, "She says he's rooming at the Palace Hotel with a female named Sugar Doll."

That would be sweet. Wulf kept his comments to himself as they moved through the tight crowd for the door again.

Outside in the night's cooler and clearer air, Hogan said that he thought Grayson might be dealing cards at the Whiskey Barrel. That was close to the Palace, and this Sugar Doll had been a dealer there. The mud was dry, and crossing the street proved no problem.

"Will you recognize him?" Hogan asked Herschel before they went inside.

Herschel said yes.

But after a review of all the dealers around the room, he saw no one who looked like his man. Hogan talked to the boss, and came back to where the two of them stood out of the way.

"The table boss says he's off tonight."

"Should we check the hotel?" Herschel asked him.

"Sure, we can do that."

The Palace was only two doors south, so they were soon in the lobby. The clerk told them Room 212, and gave Hogan the key. Wulf felt more relaxed in the quieter lobby, and followed the two men up the stairs.

Hogan rapped on the door. "This is the police chief. Open the door."

A woman finally shouted, "I'm coming."

She opened the door, wearing next to nothing, and held it halfway shut. "What do you need, Chief Hogan?"

"Grayson McCafferty."

"He's not here —"

Hogan had enough of her. He shoved the door open and charged into the room. There was an open window that went out on the porch, and the wind was blowing the curtains back. Herschel rushed over in time to see someone jump off.

"Landed on a tarp over a wagon and went through it." Herschel pointed him out to Wulf as he disappeared into a crowd in the night, then ran into a side alley.

"He won't get far," Hogan promised.

Herschel agreed, and he and Hogan thanked the woman going out. Wulf couldn't figure out why they did that. Just sarcasm, he finally figured. They went down the stairs two at a time, crossed the street, then drew their pistols to march down the alley. No sign of Grayson.

"Daylight, we'll get my patrols out and find him for you," said Hogan.

Herschel thanked him, and he and Wulf went back to the hotel to sleep. One night down in Deadwood and their man had already escaped them. Which meant he also knew they were after him.

"You reckon Grayson'll take a powder tonight?" Wulf asked when they were in bed.

"I've been thinking that. If he realizes we're here after him, he might run. What do you think we ought to do?"

"Hey, I work for you."

"Let's check some livery stables." So they dressed and separated on the street. Herschel went left and Wulf went right. The night was howling in the saloons and bars.

It was beyond Wulf what all that was about. Men staggering around drunk, messing with brassy women — it all made him about nauseated.

"Grayson McCafferty? Nope, I don't keep his horse." That was the answer the hostler in charge at each place gave him. They were to meet back at the lobby when they felt they'd been at every place they could find. Wulf, wondering if McCafferty even had a horse, made it back to the hotel lobby yawning his jaws off.

Herschel got up from the chair. "He ain't ran yet. His horse is still at Sturdivan's."

"Good, maybe he figures he can hide from us here."

"It wasn't such a bad idea to go check on him."

Wulf shook his head. "Wish I'd known it two hours ago."

They both laughed and stomped up to their room.

The sun was up when they dressed again. Someone knocked on their door. It was a town policeman. He introduced himself as Mike Darby.

"Hogan wanted you to know he has a man at the livery where your man keeps his horse watching out for him."

331

Wulf laughed and pointed at Herschel. "He was thinking last night about him running, too."

"Thanks," Herschel said, shaking his head in disgust as he strapped on his gun belt.

"We need a description of him, too," Darby said.

"I'll write it out while we eat breakfast." Herschel looked at Wulf, who quickly agreed that eating would be necessary.

"One officer is checking the banks to see who is taking his gold coins. Hogan said he didn't feel everyone would accept them. That's O'Brian doing that. And Mel Thornton is watching the hotel. The hotel clerk is supposed to tip him off if Grayson comes in."

"Ain't much Hogan hasn't thought about."

"He's a great policeman. Knows the business," Darby said.

"Yes, he is," Herschel agreed as they pushed inside a crowded diner around the corner from their hotel.

With a table at last, Herschel wrote out some things about Grayson. Age midtwenties. Six feet or so tall, broad shoulders, brown hair, not wearing a hat last time he saw him, and dressed in a red suit coat and pants, white shirt.

"Bright red?"

"It was rust color anyway."

"That should help," Darby said.

Herschel paid for the meal and they went back to the courthouse. Hogan introduced them to O'Brian. "He's got some information."

"The Franklin Bank has been cashing the coins for him," O'Brian said. "He is supposed to come by this morning and cash some more in with the head cashier."

"Reckon he'll show up?" Wulf asked.

"Yes, he'll need money to get anywhere," Hogan said. "He might send the woman, but he's not leaving here without it. Erskine, the president of the bank, thinks he has it in a safe-deposit box for safekeeping."

"We need to get over there?" Herschel asked.

"Yes, but go in the rear door and you can sit in the president's office out of sight," O'Brian said.

"Rear door?" Herschel asked.

"Yes, knock three times and they'll let you in," O'Brian explained.

"I'm sending Darby along," Hogan said. "Good luck."

Herschel thanked them and shook Hogan's and O'Brian's hands. Wulf did the same, then hurried to catch up with Herschel and Darby.

A bank employee answered their knock, led them in to the room with the fancy lamp overhead. They took the chairs set up in the president's plush office and waited.

A straight-backed woman served them hot coffee and pastries. She also told them in a low voice, as if someone might hear her, that here was no sign of McCafferty yet.

Wulf's stomach told him it was lunchtime when a man opened the door and whispered, "He and she are both here. They're getting their gold out of the lockbox."

Darby thanked him. Then the president, Mr. Erskine, came in to the room. "They will soon be in the room next door. That door is unlocked." He indicated the one with the frosted glass.

They thanked him.

Wulf heard a man's gruff voice saying, "Put it down." They drew their sidearms, and Wulf put his hand on the doorknob.

When he opened it, Darby went in to the room with his gun cocked, followed by Herschel.

"Hands up. Don't try anything. You are under arrest."

"Huh?"

Grayson looked like a cornered wolf. But he raised his hands. Darby swept the woman's purse away without a word. Wulf noted that, and knew he had to do the same in such circumstances — she easily could have a gun in it. Both were lined up against the wall. Herschel frisked Grayson and found a derringer in his coat pocket.

The woman fussed about Darby frisking her. But he ignored her complaints.

Then, with each in hand irons, they were made to sit down.

"Is this all the gold money you have?" Herschel indicated the coins on the table.

Grayson didn't answer. Herschel turned to the woman. "I am sure we have a room for an accomplice in Montana Prison for you, too."

"That's all that's in the lockbox. I don't know anything about this damn gold," she snarled.

"That's it." Grayson looked disgusted, and clanged his cuffed wrists together on the tabletop folding his hands.

"Your father is in the Fort Robinson jail mending from a gunshot wound. Where's Auggie?"

"You ought to know. You took him."

"No, some stagecoach bandits took him away from me over by Sundance."

Grayson shook his head in disgust.

"Oh, Wells Fargo is returning those four

trunks to Buffalo Malone," Herschel said.

"That old bastard —"

"I'm sure he has the same to say about you. Darby, lock them up for me," Herschel said. "We need to go to the telegraph office and send word home that we're still alive."

"What about me?"

"Why, Sugar, prison won't be so bad in the springtime in Montana," Herschel said. Let her think about it a while in jail. She might remember more gold that he or she had stashed somewhere.

"Damn you!" she swore.

"Get moving," Darby said. "They'll be waiting for you, Marshal."

When they were gone, the straight-backed woman brought them steaming coffee. Herschel had the clerk count the coins and convert them to actual cash.

"You really taking her back to Montana?" Wulf asked.

"No, but it might sharpen her memory of where more gold is at."

"I'd not thought of that."

"I don't owe her anything. She's only with him 'cause he has this loot. He was broke, she'd've dropped him like a hot potato."

The clerk came up with 1830 dollars.

"Check that safe-deposit box and write me a receipt for that much money."

"Lots of money," Wulf said, thinking out loud when they left the bank.

"Lots. I can't figure what it was doing out in a sand pile in Kansas."

"Guess that answer we won't ever know." Wulf shook his head. If folks knew the exact place where Buffalo found it, why, there would be a bunch there overnight to dig up the whole western half of the state.

They entered the telegraph office and went up to the desk.

"I'm Deputy U.S. Marshal Herschel Baker —"

The man under the visor looked wide-eyed and shocked. "I've got some wires for you."

He handed them to Herschel, and both he and Wulf exchanged serious frowns. The wires must not contain good news.

Wulf looked out the glass front window. A yellow and white collie sat up on a farm wagon going down the street. Damn, he looked a lot like Ranger.

"Wulf — I've got some real bad news for you. This one is from Andy. Marsha forwarded it here to me."

"What is it? Have I lost the ranch in court?"

"No, there's been a diphtheria epidemic

in Mason. And — Dulchy died over a week ago."

A sour knot rushed up his throat and, not seeing, he ran outside to puke. Holding the hitch rail, he gagged and gagged. His vision was blurred by the tears. Was there nothing in his life worth having that he could keep? First he'd lost his father. Then his mother to Hughes. Then Calico and Ranger. Now diphtheria had taken Dulchy away from him. All his plans. All the things he'd hoped for had become like the vomit on the ground — a damn sour mess.

Then he realized that Herschel was standing beside him, saying, "I know how you planned on one day having her for your wife. I know how much you loved her. If anything took Marsha away from me, I'd go crazy. You tell me what I need to do for you."

"I can't think of a thing. I better go back to Texas and settle things. All living there would do was remind me too much of her every day, I figure. Damn, have I been that bad to deserve this?"

"God don't pass out punishment here."

"Man, I can't figure that."

"Maybe you're being tried for greater things."

Herschel's words struck a chord. What were they? Where did he start? But thoughts of the Three Crosses had turned out to be for him like the clabbered milk he dumped out for the hogs. He couldn't ever stand to go back to Mason and recall those walks to her aunt's or the porch swing. Crushing her starched dress against him in his tight arms and kissing her. He'd known an angel — maybe God needed her more than *he* did.

His chest hurt worse than if a Comanche had stuck a spear in it.

TWENTY-EIGHT

"Keep my horses. I may come back after them. I'll let you know." Wulf went over his plans while pacing the Deadwood hotel room.

Herschel agreed to do that. "Take the Cheyenne stage and a train from there. You can get back a lot faster."

"That sounds awful expensive."

"Never mind that. There's a train I know to Fort Worth. And another to San Antonio, but they have ticket agents know how to get you there. I'm going to pay you seven hundred dollars. Five is the reward on Scopes and two is for helping me."

"That's way too much."

"Don't be surprised if Buffalo Malone doesn't send you more. Be careful. Don't get in any fights with your judgment shaken like it is."

"I never thought about that — but I remember a man beating his wife and I was there to stop him. I overdid it that day. Not that he didn't need it."

"You get strong emotions mixed in your brain and get all upset over something, you can overdo things like that."

"Good. I'll watch that."

"Any way that I can help you in Texas or wherever you land, let me know. I can write you a good letter of recommendation for a job in law enforcement if you want one."

"Thanks. I'm glad I came to Montana. Sorry I saddled you with Yutta, the baby, and Mary."

"They won't be any problem for Marsha. She took in a stray like me. You'd never believe how dead set I was against trying to take on a wife when she set her bonnet for me."

Wulf laughed. "You were dead set against her?"

"I was having some problems trying to build up a small ranch. Why, I couldn't afford a wife with three lovely girls that I love. I was eating oatmeal three times a day and wondering where my next nickel would come from.

"I liked to died from a beating these hired thugs gave me. Somehow, I made it to her place, and she nursed me back to health and ran my campaign while I was down on my back."

"I'll remember that."

"You're going to need a money belt. Let's go get that and a good meal before you climb on that stage this evening for Cheyenne."

"I hope your life keeps working," Wulf said, "I won't ever regret coming up here. Maybe in the future we'll get together again."

"I'm ready to go find that steak before we both get teary-eyed."

They shared a great meal in the plush Capitol Hotel, and with his gear they walked to the stage stop in the setting sun. It had been raining, some light showers, and a rainbow appeared over Deadwood's canyon like a bridge in the setting sun.

"That a good omen?" Wulf asked.

Herschel smiled. "Always to a cowman."

Wulf shook his cousin's hand after they loaded his gear. Hershel clapped him on the shoulder. "Good luck."

Wulf nodded, afraid to talk, and climbed in to the coach. It was hard parting with Herschel. Damn hard. The man had become not only a brother like he'd never had before, but also his "dad" reincarnated. Herschel never complained about much of anything, and Wulf simply knew what he expected most of the time.

In minutes, the coach left, rocking south for Cheyenne. Seated facing the back, he wished for something to occupy his time as he watched the tangled steep mountainsides of dead timber while the road wound through them. Besides some short conversation with a mining engineer who sat beside him, he made the trip thinking and wondering about his future. A solemn, sobering experience. Even later, on the train chugging eastward, with the bitter coal smoke of the engine in his nose, he found few people to connect with.

Stiff, sore from all the hard seats and the lack of sleep, he arrived in San Antonio. There he took a hotel room, had a bath, haircut, shave, and slept ten hours. After breakfast, he found the mail contractor that went to Mason and bought himself a passage.

They left at mid-morning with canvas sacks and his gear tarped in back behind a spirited team. Wulf saw no chance of rain in the sky, but helped the driver tie the canvas down. The driver was a young man he didn't know by the name of Stef Schworts. He had a German accent and talked openly about his experiences since leaving the family farm near Fredericksburg.

"De one thing I don't understand is women," Stef said, clucking to his well-matched team. His *w*'s were more like vee's. He had the same accent that had gone to school with him in a one-room schoolhouse with various sessions when a teacher was available and aided by his mother's home schooling who had taken education seriously.

Wulf shook his head. "I don't score well in that class either."

"Vot do they want? I offer her a ring and she says no to me."

"It ain't easy figuring them out." He wished he'd given Dulchy a ring. Some part of him to take with her on that trip to the unknown. She'd be in heaven. He had that settled in his mind.

Past midnight, he went behind Andy's shop, spread his bedroll on the ground, and slept until the ringing of the hammer on the anvil woke him with a start. He combed back his short hair with his fingers, pulled on his boots, and stuck the hat on his head, carrying his gun belt over his shoulder as he sauntered into the building.

"My God, when did you get home?" Andy shouted, and rushed to bear-hug him. "Oh, Wulf, I'm so sorry. The doctor did all he could for her. Children were dying like flies.

It was horrible."

His friend looked close to crying when Wulf clapped him on the back. "I never doubted that one minute. I knew she had the best of care."

"Bob has some news for you."

"Good?"

"Yes. I'll let him explain."

"Fine. I'm starved. You've no doubt had breakfast already. I got here in the middle of the night with the mail from San Antonio."

"Where are your great horses?"

"In Montana with my cousin Herschel, who sent his best to you two."

"Let's go get you some breakfast and you can tell me all about that country."

Wulf laughed. "That might take a month, and I'd have to tell Myrna all over again."

"That's right. So go to talking."

As he started telling Andy about his experiences in law enforcement, they walked into the half-empty café. The rich smell of cooking about made him sick to his stomach. This was where he'd met Dulchy.

"Just bring me some coffee," Wulf managed to tell the waiter.

"What's wrong? I thought you were hungry," Andy said.

Wulf shook his head. "No more —"

"Oh, damn, Wulf, I forgot she worked here."

He reached over and clasped Andy's arm. "It's all right. I have to get used to things without her all over again."

After the coffee, they walked back to the shop and parted. Wulf went to see Bob in his upstairs office. A young man swallowed in a too-large store-bought suit introduced himself as Mark Gray, Bob's assistant.

"Oh, yes, Mr. Baker. I'll tell Bob you are here."

"Thanks." So now he had an office and a reception area and help.

"Wulf, I wasn't expecting you so soon. Come in."

After shaking hands and exchanging news about his wife and baby, Bob produced a file. "We about have this climaxed. Hughes still needs to pay the estate some monies for those cattle he sold and deposited in his own account. And the money for the horse and dog. His lawyer requested ninety days and since you weren't here, I felt the time didn't matter. Hughes has to pay it or face jail. The judge already warned him. So in three months, the ranch will be yours, with a court-appointed guardian as your counsel until you turn eighteen. Good enough?"

"What will they do about Mom?"

"She's relinquished all her rights to the estate to save Hughes's neck, so to speak."

That would be like her, she was so stuck on that bastard. "I'll see that she is taken care of."

"Well, what do you plan to do now?" Then Bob shook his head and dropped his chin. "I am so sorry. I know how sad you must be losing that pert young lady Dulchy."

"I'll be fine."

"No, you'll never be fine after a loss like that, but even if you'd been here, there was nothing any of us could do but pray the plague did not spread further."

Wulf rubbed his palms on his well-worn pants. He'd need a new pair of something to wear. "I savvy that very well."

"What're you going to do today?"

"Borrow a horse and look around. How much do I owe you?"

"Nothing. This is partial repayment for saving my wife, remember?"

"That only took sixty seconds."

"But it was worth a lifetime of work to me."

Wulf found a grin of discovery. "I guess the rest of these folks around here are paying you."

"Business has been rather busy."

He left Bob's office and went to the livery

that belonged to Jim Backus.

"I need to buy a horse or rent one," he told Jim, who stood there before him wearing stained overalls and using the suspenders for handholds.

"I'd loan ya one."

"I'd buy or rent him."

"Naw, you can put a handle on him. You're the best at that of anyone I ever knew, so I'm going to loan him to you."

"How bad is he?"

"Well, let's say he ain't no ladies' hoss." Jim hee-hawed like a donkey at that.

"You have a deal. I'll get my kac and be right back."

"No rush. Ain't no one else going to ride him off."

"Show him to me before I go get it."

They strolled out back in the warm sunshine. "He's that blood bay."

Wulf nodded. He had a good eye for appraising horseflesh. A handsome long-legged horse with lots of muscle and a quick eye — he must be a handful. Jim was not that run-away generous.

"I'll be back."

"Oh, he'll be here."

"I know he will be." And they both laughed. They would soon find out who had bested who in this deal.

He went by and stopped to see Myrna. He knocked on the open back door, and saw the surprise on her face as she ran to hug him. "You're home. You're home. When did you get here?"

He explained, and she immediately set in making him lunch. She sat him down, and in minutes brought him a huge sourdough sandwich with a glass of sweet lemonade to wash it down. Then he went over some of the details of his great adventure to Montana and back.

"Bob says the Three Crosses will be yours in a short while and Hughes will have to repay the estate all he stole from you."

"You knew she gave up her portion to save him from doing jail time?"

"Sometimes, we can't understand people we thought we knew so well."

He put down his half-eaten sandwich. "I grew up respecting her. She's left a terrible void inside of me."

"You eat. Breaking Backus's crazy horse will take your mind off things."

"Or pile me off in a patch of prickly pear."

"How long ago has it been since you were bucked off a horse?"

"When I was twelve —"

She tousled his hair and hugged him to her. "It's wonderful to have you home full of tales of all of your adventures. I can recall that bashful Herschel and Tom Baker riding horses around here that no one else could even mount. It must run in your bloodlines."

"I wouldn't say Herschel is bashful now. What was Tom like?"

"He was the ladies' man. Danced the soles off his boots at the schoolhouse dances back then. Why, he broke more hearts than any man living in the county."

"You'd really like Herschel's wife, Marsha. You and her would get along great."

"I doubted Herschel would ever get married."

"No, he's got a good woman, a nice home, and folks up there respect him as sheriff."

"Well, now you've seen the other edge of the world, what will you do?"

"I'm trying to clear my mind. Would it be disrespectful of me toward my dad if I sold the Three Crosses and went to a new land without all the scars of this place?"

"Scars?"

"Yes, not you and Andy or my friends, but her grave is here, and the way that things have turned out between Mother and me. The beatings I stood and took. It would be hard to swallow all that on a daily basis."

"Oh, Wulf. He would understand. Do

what you have to, though I'd hate to lose you."

"I want to try out this snorty horse Jim Backus is loaning me before dark. I know he must be some bronc. Jim wants me to get a handle on him."

"You just be careful."

"And I'll need to go by and pay my respects to her aunt, too. That will be the hardest."

"Oh, yes, that always is the toughest part. But she adored you."

"I'll go by and see her."

"I have some pie cooling. It may be too hot to eat. You want some?"

"Yes, ma'am."

After the delightful piece of pecan pie, he hurried to the shop, retrieved his saddle, bridle, and pads, and told Andy he'd try to be back by supper.

He discovered Jim's stout horse was frisky when he went to catch him in the pen. Walking him down didn't work, so he snatched up a coiled reata from the top of the fence post. Snaking out the stiff rawhide loop, he whirled the rope over his head when the bay went by him in an anxious run. Then he sent the oval out and when it settled over the pony's head, he jerked up his slack with his right hand and set his heels in the deep dirt. That swung the bay around in a half circle, but he ran one more pass before Wulf reeled him in.

The shaking horse acted undecided about the whole episode. Wulf talked to him all the time in a soft voice, attempting to calm his excitement. Inch by inch, the bay began to relax. Still, it was a tense truce between man and horse. But without any scent of fear coming from the conqueror, the horse's hide quit quivering at Wulf's touch. Wulf touched and patted him all over.

At last, Wulf formed a halter with the reata on his head and led the horse out of the pen. Going to his saddle and gear, he held his lead with one hand and worked the blanket first on the horse's nose so he could smell it, then rubbed the tight muscles in his neck with it, and at last settled it on the horse's back.

Bay — his new name — cow-kicked at him over the placement and let out a squeal. The horse missed kicking him and Wulf ignored him. Then he caught the saddle by the fork, and the horse shied from it. Holding the lead in his left hand, he followed him, and when the horse's butt collided with the corral fence, he eased the saddle on Bay's back. It took a few minutes to settle Bay down, but Wulf gathered the front cinch first and then the other.

Bay shied away, but Wulf managed to lead him back to where the bridle was on the ground. By then, several dozen pairs of curious eyes were viewing their every move though corral rails and from the loft of the livery. More joined in, their talk in whispers as Wulf checked the girths. Bay stomped his left hind foot with impatience.

After Wulf got the bridle on without much struggle, he sat on the ground and put on his batwing chaps. Then he strapped on his light spurs. At this point, Bay had begun to act interested in him, like who was this insistent man who'd roped and saddled him?

Wulf held the bridle's headstall in his left hand when he went to mount Bay, forcing the horse in a tight circle while he swung in the saddle and threw his left leg over him. Bay moved sideways under him until the horse slammed into the board fence.

By then, Wulf sat deep in the saddle and kept his head up. He urged Bay forward, and the horse began taking steps on eggs. Wulf kept him in check with tight reins, and the uneasy truce lasted until Bay reached the street. Then, despite Wulf's strong-arm efforts, Bay bogged his head down between his front knees and left out in a series of sky-walking jumps.

He wasn't the toughest horse Wulf ever tried to ride, but this was no pup between his knees. People ran for cover, and there was lots of hat-waving and whooping Wulf could have done without. Then, some cur dogs joined in chasing Bay, who they must have thought was running away from them. When Wulf reached the west side of town, he let Bay run, and the horse soon eased into a short lope.

But aside from some sweat on his shoulders, the horse seemed still full of fire and certainly not winded. Better broke, Bay would suit Wulf's needs. He headed him for the Three Crosses. Over the months he'd been gone, he'd thought lots about the home place.

Maybe ride up on Stoner Creek, a quiet place where he and his dad had shot a mountain lion that was getting their colts. He arrived in the great swale of grass lined by hills clad with red cedar and live oak. There were a few cows and calves who lifted their faces up when he headed for the sycamores and cottonwoods along the creek.

A good drink of that clear water would suit him fine. Wulf was on his belly, and Bay was slurping up his share as well, when the horse threw his head up and bolted backward. Wulf scrambled to his feet, looking up at the barrel of Kent Hughes's Winchester.

How had this happened? Was he so intent on his new horse and the homecoming that he hadn't seen Hughes slip up? It damn sure made for a tight place to be — him and his stepfather and Hughes in charge with his .44/40.

Hughes undid his lariat. "Here, put this around you."

Wulf had no idea of Hughes's plans, but he wanted no part of a lariat around his body. He hadn't worn his six-gun on purpose, figuring that he might lose it in the struggle with Bay. He could damn sure regret that mistake.

"You have only a few seconds or I'll shoot that bay horse." Hughes had the rifle aimed at Bay.

Whatever Hughes's plans were for him, he'd eventually find a way out. No need to get Bay killed. He picked up the lariat and settled the rope around his chest.

The pleased look on Hughes's face told him things were going to get rough for him. He'd seen that manic look before in the barn when Hughes had used that girth on him.

Hughes slid the rifle in the scabbard. "You want this gawdamn ranch so bad, I'm going to feed it to you."

Wulf barely managed to grasp the rope in both hands before he was jerked off his feet.

"Folks are going to think your crazy horse there drug you to death." Hughes, spurring his horse, headed out, dragging Wulf through the rocks, grass, and stiff brambles.

Wulf's entire life went before his hard-shut eyes. Life as a boy before his dad took sick. Brush rushed by, tearing at him; cactus pads slapped him. His vest was torn open, and he could be grateful that his chaps were protecting his legs, though until he was flipped over, they had plowed up lots of dirt.

"How do you like it? Your ranch, huh? Well, eat some more. Hee-yah, horse."

Wulf's world was filled with pain and even with his mouth shut, he still must have eaten a ton of dirt. And the dragging continued, with Hughes's lathered horse beginning to show the wear and tear as well. Then Hughes's horse stopped and balked to empty his bowels. None of Hughes's efforts or cursing untracked him.

Numb, dumb, and blinded by the grit, Wulf scrambled to his feet, shed the lariat, and swinging it like a jump rope, made three quick hitches around Hughes's horse's high tail. Then Wulf set back on it and the horse screamed.

The horse dove into the sky, and in three jumps had shot Hughes out of the saddle and into a bed of prickly pear. When the man did not move or come out of the cactus ring, Wulf hoped he'd broken his neck, and staggered to find Bay. He could hardly see anything, but in the dying light found his horse grazing.

It was not easy to convince Bay that this two-legged being with clothes shredded and dirt clinging was himself, but at last he managed, and rode for Mason.

No telling about Hughes. Wulf hadn't even heard a moan from him after he'd landed in the prickly pear garden.

Damn, what a day. He clung to the saddle horn and made Bay lope, hoping that he didn't fall out of the saddle.

TWENTY-NINE

"What in the hell got hold of you, boy?" It was Jim Backus's voice running alongside him. Four men were bearing him on a stretcher and they were in a hurry.

"I had a run-in . . ." The lights went out again.

When he came to again, he was looking up into the eyes of Andy, Myrna, Bob, Aunt Frieda, and Doc. It was daylight, and he hurt so many places he couldn't have listed them in two hours.

"How you doing?" Doc asked.

His own rusty voice shocked him when he began to speak. "I reckon I'm alive."

"Who did this to you?" Bob asked, looking as angry as Wulf had ever seen him.

Wolf tried to laugh. "Who else? Kent Hughes said I loved the place so bad, he'd show it to me facedown, then make it look like Bay, my new horse, had drug me to death."

"You kill him?"

"Not with my bare hands. His horse got lathered up, and I took the chance to shed the lariat, and then like a jump rope, I wound the rope around that horse's tail three times. He left out walking on the clouds, threw Hughes into a pear patch. He never got up. I couldn't of cared less — I got on Bay and guess I rode into town."

"I seen men been in fights with bobcats before that didn't look this torn up," Doc said, shaking his head, "but I reckon you'll heal. You're damn sure tough enough to."

"I'm filing attempted murder charges against Hughes," Bob said. "This was the final straw."

Andy and Myrna agreed. Then Aunt Frieda stepped forward and smiled at Wulf.

"She wanted you to have this for good luck."

It was a gold cross on a gold chain. He accepted it in his bandaged hands. "Thanks."

"I know how much you miss her, but she is at peace."

"I understand, Frieda."

"Good. I am so sorry about this. But you will be well soon. I will pray for you. Come by and have pastries and tea with me." Unable to hold back her tears, she backed out clutching a handkerchief. Myrna went to comfort her.

"I will . . ." And his world went black again.

Two days of laudanum to stop his pain, and Wulf emerged into the bright world of sun streaming into his room at Doc's office. His head hurt and he felt like shit. Maybe he had died and gone to hell and they'd rejected him. Whew, this was bad.

"How are you today, Mr. Baker?"

She must have been six feet tall, square-shouldered, and looked long in the tooth. Her gray hair was bound in a white scarf, and in her starched white dress she looked very official.

"My name is Gladys Morningstar. I am Dr. Martin's nurse and I have been taking caring of you."

Holy cow, that woman had been — whew. Good thing he was coming around. His face felt beet red.

"No need to be concerned. I take care of all his patients. If you like and if you feel strong enough, I can bring you a sponge and some warm water to bathe with."

"I can handle that now."

"Very good. You are really improving. They tell me that your assailant is behind bars."

"Oh, he's alive?"

"Yes. Doc went and saw about him. He has a broken collarbone, a concussion, and, they say, numerous prickly pear spines in him."

"He should have picked a better place to land."

"I suppose so."

After he bathed in his large gown, he looked around for his clothes. They were nowhere in sight. Not in the small closet or anywhere. A loud throat-clearing behind him made him turn from his search to see Miss Morningstar in the doorway.

"My clothes?" he asked her. "I can't find them."

"Mrs. Carter took them home to wash and repair them. There is a woman here to see you."

He frowned at her. What woman was coming to see him? He quickly got back in bed and pulled up the sheet.

"A Mrs. Hughes, I believe."

His mother? "Send her in."

There were dark rings under her eyes. She looked very tired and very pregnant. She stood before him, chewing her lip. "I want to strike a deal, Wulf. Drop the charges against my husband and we'll give you the Three Crosses and all the money."

"I understood the judge was ordering that

done anyway."

"Wulf," she said, louder than she intended to, wringing her hands. "Wulf, my baby needs a father and a place to live. He or she'll be your half brother or sister."

That was why she hadn't dared go against Hughes when he'd whipped him. It was the baby inside her. But still, she'd never trusted Wulf enough to take care of her. He would have. He'd've done anything for her. They'd made it without Hughes before. Damn, this was tough.

"All right. I'll tell Bob to drop the charges when the deal is completed."

"Oh, thank you. Oh, thank you. I knew you would help me — son."

"I'm not your son anymore, Jenny Hughes. You're Kent Hughes's wife. Now, I want to sleep." He fluffed the pillow and rolled over like he was going to do that. He squeezed his eyes shut hard and choked down his tears.

Damn, life was sure a bitch.

THIRTY

The Texas summer sun blazed down on Wulf in the corral. He was working the matching gray pair of mares in the corral. Prettiest set of matched ponies he'd ever seen. He'd paid a good price for them, but they were fast learning his commands and were sound as a silver dollar. In the morning, he'd hitch them up to his buckboard and drive them into Mason.

"I think, Senõr, that they are the best *caballos* in the Texas," said the short Mexican Raul, whom he had hired to look after things around the ranch. Dressed in leather despite the day's heat and wearing a great straw sombrero, Raul was a good cowman and horse trainer himself. Raul and his wife, plus four children, had come from Chihuahua to work for him.

Wulf gave a whistle, and the red and white collie shot into the corral and on a nod, ran over and leaped on the near horse's back to ride around the pen.

"All right, off, Red Man." The collie bailed to the ground and came to sit beside him.

"Where did you find a red one?" Raul asked. "It is such a rare color."

Wulf agreed with a grin. "He cost too much *dinero.*"

"Ah, but he is one in a thousand, no?"

"Yes. And they say the red ones are the smartest ones."

"Where are you going with him and these horses?"

"I have challenged a man called the Colonel, who says he has the best dogs in the world, to a match in Fort Worth."

Raul laughed. "There is no better dog that I ever see in my life than Red Man."

"We will see. Last time, the Colonel conceded the match and my stepfather sold him that dog."

"Oh, my. Does he still have your dog?"

"I don't know, but he can't get the work I got out of him."

"When is this match?"

"In three weeks."

"Then you plan to make a trip?"

"Sí. I want to find a new ranch — somewhere. I want you and your family to come with me."

"Where will it be?"

"In a place where the grass grows tall and the water is sweet."

Raul smiled. "I will go where you go, Señor."

"Good. Someday we will have a *rancho grande.*"

"Ah, *sí,* a grand place."

"Put the horses up. I need to write a letter to my cousin and mail it when I go to town tomorrow."

"No problema." Raul took over the grays.

With pen and ink, he began his letter.

Dear Marsha, Herschel, and all the fine ladies of Montana,

I am going to Fort Worth next week to compete against the man who bought my horse and dog after the competition that he conceded. Things are fine at the ranch, but win or lose, after the event I am going looking for a new ranch. This one holds too many sad memories. I hope all is going well in Montana. Thanks for the money for the horses. I wasn't seeing when I could get back up there to get them.

I'll write you after the competition and if I find anything.

Your cousin,
Wulf Baker

A wall tent, cots, blankets, cooking gear, food — his buckboard was loaded down when he left a week later. With Bay trotting along behind, he headed for Fort Worth.

The summer heat had the corn leaves rustling. If the corn crop hadn't made ears by then, it would only be poor cattle fodder. He saw fewer freighters on the road. Railroads crisscrossed the country everywhere.

He found a small rancher on the outskirts of Fort Worth who let him camp on his place. When the tent was set up and all the things were ready, he rode into the stockyards the next day to see if the Colonel was going to show up. He left Red Man and Bay at a hitch rack and studied the large poster.

"The Greatest Stock Dog Competition in the world," the sign said, and signs just like it were plastered all over. "Admission one quarter." His price had gone up.

Wulf found a Jewish tailor whom Robert Fiest had told him to go to, and had a brown business suit made. Next, he found a boot maker, and then located a haberdashery where he bought a silver belly Boss of the Plains Stetson with a silk rim. Satisfied he'd be dressed to the nines, he rode back to camp without a soul recognizing him.

He cooked himself supper and the rancher

came by. "Yesterday, you said your name was Baker. You the Wulf Baker they're all talking about going against Colonel Armstrong in that stock dog competition?"

"I am, sir. Get down. I have coffee made."

"I will, and you can tell me how that red and white dog of yours can beat him. He's got some real smart dogs. I've been to several of his shows."

"Red Man, go lay over there. No, farther. You watch that sun go down. Turn right. Good, you stay there." Wulf went over and poured the man some coffee.

"How long will he stay there?"

"Long as I tell him to, I guess."

Wulf gave a short whistle and Red Man busted to get back and sit by him. "I'm going to send him after Apple, the oldest of the gray mares.

"Red Man. Go get Apple."

They stood up in the twilight to watch the dog start out head-high, looking for the mare. Then, in a bound, he was off on a tear to bring her in. When she got close, Wulf raised his hand. "Up, Red Man."

When the collie flew up on the back of the gray and stayed there, the old man shouted, "I'll be damned."

"They make a helluva good team. I hope. I'm betting five hundred bucks on it."

"That's a lot of money to bet on a dog."

"I know, but the last time, the Colonel bowed out. I bet if he makes a big gate, he'll do the same this time. His fancy dogs are too valuable to match up against those wild range billies."

"Were the folks there that day mad?"

"No, they were so glad that we beat him, they all applauded."

"I bet this crowd out of Fort Worth would tar and feather him if he don't try."

"We'll see."

"Thanks for the coffee. Where you headed next?"

"I'm going looking for a ranch of my own."

"Well, good luck, young man. I hope you beat the pants off ole Armstrong."

He'd need lots of good luck to ever beat the Colonel at anything, but he was out to try.

He drove up to the farm where the competition was supposed to take place late in the afternoon on the day before. Red Man sat on the seat with him.

"My name's Wulf Baker. The Colonel is expecting me."

The tough-looking gate man scoffed at him. "So you're the hayseed going take on the Colonel, huh?"

"That's me," he said, determined that the man wouldn't be able to raise his ire.

"Camp anywhere you want." The man laughed out loud. "You should have stayed on the farm, sonny boy. Colonel's going to whip your ass tomorrow."

"He might." Then he clucked to the grays, and they swung into the opening and set out for the ridge where some tall trees were silhouetted against the sky. His tent was soon up and the fire started, and then folks began to drop by when they realized that he was Wulf Baker.

He shook lots of hands. Most wished him luck and urged him to beat that snooty Colonel.

Early the next morning, he had his horses back on the picket line. Things in his camp had been shut down, and he was now dressed in the new suit and boots. Wearing a white shirt with his dad's neckerchief and the new Stetson, he headed for the main area where folks could sit on the hillside and watch the competition unfold.

Armstrong's circus wagons were lined up on the east side of the field at the base of the hill. Wulf set down his folding chair, and then took Bay aside to hobble him. He hiked over to the lemonade stand and bought himself a tall glass of the ice-cold drink. The woman in charge was in her thirties. With hard lines around her mouth and eyes, she nodded when he paid her.

"You must be the man from Mason."

"Yes, ma'am." He doffed his hat to her.

"I seed you win at that goat contest. He still ain't got a dog can beat you on wild goats."

"He has my old dog."

She shook her head. "Naw, he died months ago. Got so he wouldn't eat. Him and the Colonel never hit it off. Oh, he worked, but not like he did for you. Made them mad, too. They used medicine on him even, but he wasn't never like the dog when you had him."

"Is he going to use one of his fancy dogs today?"

She glanced around. "Don't you tell no one I said it, but he's got a bad black-mouth cur that I figure is going to jump on and kill your dog before it all starts."

"I owe you, ma'am. Thanks."

He took a refill on his lemonade in the glass full of ice spears. Then, shifting his gun holster, he went back to his chair with Red Man at his side. Wagons and riders were streaming in the gate. If that dog tried one run at Red Man, he was a dead sumbitch.

Seated in the chair, Wulf checked the loads in his pistol, then reholstered it. One wrong move was all it would take, and that dog would be in the ground pushing up bluebonnets come next spring.

The Colonel rode up on a white horse and handed the reins to a groom who had run alongside it. "Ah, sir, you must be the agent for this Wulf Baker."

Armstrong looked around the grassy knoll as if searching for the real Wulf Baker. His man arrived and set up a folding chair and umbrella for him.

"No, Colonel. I'm Wulf Baker."

"Well, my, my. You have dressed up. A marker, huh, at Mason dressed like a farm boy?"

"No, that was me then. This is me today."

"I must say, you've come a long ways in your clothing. Is that your dog?"

"That's him."

Red Man began to growl, and Wulf turned in his chair to see the large brindle dog on a chain lunging forward on his handler's leash as the handler brought him over from the wagons. The dog must weigh over a hundred pounds.

"I see you can see Jolie Blank. He's my wild goat-tending dog." Armstrong smiled and touched his hat brim in a salute.

Wulf stood beside his chair, watching the dog, who had his mouth gaping open while slinging saliva and growling like a freight train. Then, when they were seventy or so feet away, the handler spilled facedown and the chain slipped from his grasp. Black Mouth came at a dead run for Red Man.

The Colt in Wulf's hand blasted and the big dog whined, but he kept coming. Round two between his hard-set eyes drove him face-first in the grass and he flipped over.

"Why? Why did you kill my good dog?" Armstong screamed.

Wulf leveled the Colt at him. "I overheard your plan to kill Red Man with that sumbitch and call it a no-show on my part. Well, your plan didn't work, Colonel. Better send for your stock dog. We're competing, or you can forfeit. You're good at that."

"I ought to —"

"You better shut your mouth and get on with this competition. They tell me they tar and feather welshers in Fort Worth."

"Was that cur coming for you?" a curious onlooker asked.

"He got loose. Handler couldn't handle him," Wulf said.

"You ain't bad with a gun."

"No. I'm a deputy U.S. marshal." Who in the hell could tell any different? It might shore up the way things were run from there on out. He also might need to kiss the lemonade woman when it was all over.

"You are what?" Armstrong asked.

"You heard me. Now get on with this competition."

Things at once took on a new tenseness. The Colonel gave orders, and the wild goats were delivered to the holding pens and unloaded one at a time. The goats were alternated between the two pens. Four hundred feet to the south stood the tall wooden panels forming the two enclosures that the dogs had to put the goats in.

"Do we flip for first or second start?" Wulf asked the selected official, a justice of the peace who wore a top hat and was dressed very fancy.

"I shall ask the field judges." He called over the other two men, who looked like ranchers in business suits. They conferred and the decision was to toss a coin.

Armstrong won the toss and chose to go first. His white-eared Border collie was the dog, and he took him to the side of the field that would be used. On the Colonel's nod, the goats were eased outside. The collie left in a crouch headed for his "bunch."

Range-bred hair goats are fierce enough to fight a coyote. These billies were some that obviously would. A big gray one caught sight of White Ear and charged. Head and horns down, he still hooked White Ear in his desperate attempt to slip away from his attack.

The crowd groaned as, next, a white and black billy joined the fray, and they caught the collie between them and gave him a good whacking.

"They're killing that dog!" Wulf pointed to the poor stock dog.

"Let him die." The Colonel folded his arms, ready to let them.

"You're worthless. Red Man, get those damn goats in the pen. Hee-yah."

"That is interfering —"

A judge, holding his hat, ran over. "What's happening?"

"That Border collie is hurt. Those billies would kill him in one more charge."

"What about *your* dog?"

"We'll see."

Red Man bit an ear on the white goat till he quit his charge. Then he nipped the shoulder of the gray one, spinning the rest into a mass of high-headed concerned animals. As he worked his way down the field, Wulf encouraged the young dog to keep the goats in a tight bunch and to punish any of them that didn't mind.

The crowd was cheering by the time they were halfway to the pen. With the goats finally inside, Wulf said to the man on the megaphone, "Since the other dog was hurt, I'll take the second bunch down and pen them, too."

He shouted for Red Man, and the second pen was released. Wulf and his dog showed them how to really move bad goats. These may have even been the tougher bunch, but Red Man took no chances, and he snapped at any that even acted like they might challenge him.

When the goats were in the pen at last, the judges declared him the winner. The crowd went wild. On the ridge, he could see the red wagons were already leaving.

"Wait," he said to the JP. "They owe me —"

"I've got it right here. Five hundred dollars." He handed him the envelope.

It was all there.

"Thanks."

"First you shot his cur dog, then you saved his other one. Mister, you are something. Folks going to talk for a long time about the man from Mason beating Colonel Armstrong, the world's greatest animal trainer." The JP gave a deep throaty chuckle.

"Beats all I ever know. Hey, where are you going?"

"To kiss the lemonade lady and give her fifty bucks."

"What for?"

"Because she deserves it."

THIRTY-ONE

Wulf studied the snag-filled Red River. It was like his own life. Lots of water had flowed downstream over the past three months. He'd sold his father's ranch — he couldn't live anywhere near his stepfather. The only reason he'd let the worthless Hughes off the hook with the law was because of his mother. Regretfully for Wulf, his mother wouldn't leave Hughes. New baby and all.

Wulf's loss of Dulchy had left a big hole in his heart, and staying around Mason only knifed him harder. The letter in his pocket from his cousin, Herschel Baker in Montana, offered him a full-time position as deputy sheriff. Tempted to accept the job, he still wanted a place of his own. Herschel had told him before he left Montana that a man had to find his own spot in this world and be happy — life was too short not to be happy. Wulf had the money from his ranch sale to buy a place. But where? He'd seen lots of great cow country going north and coming back. Maybe he could figure it out — where to settle down.

There was one more thing he couldn't forget. A willowy Indian girl named Mary Ann who he'd met going north. She'd served him food at a crossroads, and he recalled the night they'd shared his bedroll. But by this time, she'd probably found herself a real man. Still, there was something about her kindness and soothing ways that he found worthwhile enough to try and find her again. Even if he couldn't have her, perhaps simply seeing and talking with her would ease her out of his mind.

"Did you leave all your whiskey behind?" the man reeling the ferry over the Red River asked. "Them damn marshals from Fort Smith'll sure fine your ass if you ain't."

"I left mine."

"Good-looking grays you've got there."

"Thanks. They aren't for sale."

"Where are you headed?"

"Oh up the road a ways."

"Well, the territory is a tough place to be. Folks get robbed and kilt every night up there."

"I'll remember that."

"What's the matter with that black and

white stock dog you've got in the wagon?"

"Oh, he got ran over. But he's going to heal all right. It was touch and go for a while, but he's getting better."

"Them two dogs of yours any good at herding stock?"

"The best two stock dogs in the world."

"Where did you get them?"

"Texas."

"Oh."

Two evenings later he pulled up at a crossroad store. He unhitched the grays and went to search in the back of the wagon until he found his turtle-shell bowl. With it and a big spoon in his hand, he got in line behind some Indian women.

"You don't have ten cents?" the voice he recognized at the head of the line asked. "Go on, Shelly. Pay me next week."

"Ten cents —" She looked at the turtle-shell bowl and then at him in growing shock. "I almost did not recognize you. Why — why are you back?"

"I am hungry." He met the gaze in her large brown eyes.

"No — I mean —"

"You better fill my bowl. There are people behind me. They're hungry, too."

She caught his arm. "Why are you back?"

"The turtle brought me back here." He

held up his steaming bowl.

Her frown sent him on. "I will talk to you later."

"I'll be here," he said, with no plans to run off.

"Rentsloe, where have you been?" she asked the next man in line.

The old man laughed. "Waiting for you to get over the shock of seeing that fella again."

"You saw all that, old man?" she asked, sounding in shock.

Wulf smiled to himself. Good, his appearance had her shaken. He saw no suitors lounging around. Maybe he wasn't too late after all.

From the serving table, Wulf used one of their cracked cups for his coffee, and also floated some squares of sweet corn bread in his stew. He took a place on the ground with his back against a post oak tree to watch her feeding the line of people. Slowly, he savored each spoonful of the flavorful food, and observed her movements, which were like a willow tree in a soft wind. She looked every bit as pretty as he recalled her. His heart was thumping hard, but he was in fact more pleased with her than he'd even expected to be.

The people in line were finally fed, and she hurried over to join him, sitting on the ground with her many-colored skirt over her knees, which she hugged.

"I thought you had a woman."

"Diptheria stole her from me while I was in Montana."

"I'm sorry. Did you like it up there?"

"It's fine. But I want a new ranch where there's grass and clear water."

"Where will you find it?"

He glanced at the ground. "I'm not sure. But I came to ask if you would go with me and search for it."

She blinked and looked ready to cry. She wet her lips. The tears spilled down her high cheeks. "Why would a rich man like you want a poor Indian woman like me?"

"Oh, I'm not rich, but someday we will be, and I want to share my life wherever I find this new ranch with you."

"You better tell him yes before he changes his mind, girl." Her mother, standing above them, winked wickedly at him.

"Mother! Go on."

The woman sauntered back to refill their empty bowls. Wulf smiled at her words. Obviously, her daughter was embarrassed by her mother's directness. All the same, he had one ally in this camp anyway.

Mary Ann raised up on her knees, put her arms around his neck, and kissed him.

Excited, he reached out, gathering her onto his lap.

Then she cupped her hand and whispered in his ear, "Go find your bedroll. We will need it again."